THE SECOND CHRONICLE OF DANIEL WELSH

RISE OF THE MORTOKAI

D.G. PALMER

THE RISE OF THE MORTOKAI

First edition. January 26, 2020.

Copyright © 2020 D G Palmer.

ISBN: 979-8607080747

Written by D G Palmer.

To my Muse

Ambition and love are the wings of great deeds - Goethe

You give me both, now I will do great things

RISE OF THE MORTOKAI - THE SECOND CHRONICLE OF DANIEL WELSH

By

D G Palmer

Also by D G Palmer

The Chronicles of Daniel Welsh

Birth of The Mortokai
Rise of The Mortokai

Standalone

The Choices of Man

A Call To Action

Thank you for taking the time to read this book from the mind of
D.G. Palmer!
If you enjoyed it, please take a moment to leave a review at Amazon, Bookbub or Goodreads to help spread the word, increase its visibility and help it reach more readers.
Leave a note even if you didn't, after all, one person's trash is another person's bestseller!
And finally, don't forget to sign up to <u>The World of D.G. Palmer</u> to stay up to date with new releases and get exclusive short stories and extra prologues and epilogues for the Daniel Welsh series!

Chapter One

Forests and glades are usually thought of as being benevolent mystical places. Places that you would go to reconnect with nature or for quiet reflection. The forest Trinity Evergreen now found herself in wasn't so idyllic. Far from it.

She walked along its woodland path surrounded by dark trees; elms, oaks, firs, and many more, their spindly branches, stripped bare of leaves, looked like the elongated fingers of an old crone as they stretched up into the sky, allowing only a few of the sun's rays to penetrate the darkness below.

Trinity didn't know where she was much less how she got there and as the druid with the teenaged appearance looked around and saw no one else, the realisation that she was all alone struck her.

Like any master-level spell caster, she had some control over her negative emotions, the ones that would impede magic use. Fear was counted among them meaning that not much could scare her but this place certainly made her anxious. A sense of foreboding was definitely in the air, the hairs on her arms standing on edge were testament to that fact. But it wasn't the trepidation of death that she felt, it was more like the feeling you would get in the presence of something divine.

'This is the darkness the Mortokai brings,' a voice in the shaded woods suddenly announced, but it wasn't just one voice, it was many; different tones, different pitches, different accents, all saying the same words. 'This is the future you see before you. This is the future the Mortokai will bring about. This is the future Daniel Welsh will unleash on this world.'

'Daniel?' Hearing her friend's name along with this Mortokai again caused Trinity to recall the conversation she had with the hazel dryad back on Earth, when it had tried to convince her that Daniel was a danger; but she had defended him then, and she would do the same again now. 'I've heard all this before.'

'And you did not heed the warnings of the hazel dryad, now the Mortokai has been born.'

'Daniel isn't this Mortokai.'

'He is a faerie with a soul. He is the trophy of the dark fae. He will herald their return.'

'I was told that there were other human/fae offspring, perhaps one of them is the one you speak of.'

'Gydion was right, there are others. Not all the kidnapped children were left at Almedia. Some were kept by the dark fey and, when the time was right, they would be "used" for experimentation. But the offspring those unions bore were either wholly human, with no essence, or wholly fey, but all were monstrous deformed creatures.'

All of a sudden Trinity could see several figures shuffling out of the shadows towards her. The few rays of light that had pierced the darkness illuminated random features of the grotesque misshapen beings. Their unexpected appearance compelled the youngster to take a few steps back until, without warning, she was grabbed from behind.

The malformed entities surrounded Trinity and, no matter how much she struggled, she couldn't break free as they lifted her into the air and carried her towards a large trunked ancient tree.

'You must forsake Daniel and fulfil your destiny; only then will you be able to stand against the Mortokai.'

'You're wrong! I won't do it!'

'You have no choice. A darkness is coming. You must accept your destiny. Forsake Daniel. Accept your destiny.'

The words resonated deeply throughout the forest, and try as she might, Trinity, couldn't block it out. She wouldn't abandon her friend; she couldn't do that to the person she cared so much about.

The roots of the ancient tree suddenly burst from the ground and wrapped around her arms and legs. Her scream was cut short as they forced their way down her throat until they erupted from her nose, eyes and ears. Trinity was no more.

SHE SHOT UP IN HER bed. Strands of her red hair clung to her sweat-drenched face. It was the first time that Trinity could ever remember having a nightmare and one thing was certain, she didn't much care for them.

After gathering her thoughts for a moment, she slipped out of bed and padded across her room to the wash basin. She splashed some refreshing water onto her face and as she dried herself with a towel, her mind flitted back to the nightmarish events of her slumber.

Forsake Daniel. Accept your destiny. She didn't know what destiny it could be, but if it involved the rejection of Daniel from her life, then she would just forge a new destiny for herself. But even as she said it, something was troubling her. This was the second time Daniel's name had been mentioned along with this Mortokai; first by the hazel dryad and now in her sleep. Sheer coincidence, or could there actually be something to it? Before he returned from within the Shade she would have vehemently said no, but the way he seemed so distant before he collapsed made her question her judgement, if only for a moment.

She knew Daniel, the real Daniel, the shy and reserved Daniel who loved history and gaining knowledge, the Daniel she was developing feelings for.

Trinity's mind drifted back to when she had first arrived at the college and seen him. She had been intrinsically drawn to Daniel. Throughout that day she had found herself stealing glances at him and, on occasion, their eyes would lock momentarily. She had put it down to her sensing his Essence, but now she knew it was something more. Especially after they had had that moment when he had been released by the Council of Three. When she had felt his breath on her lips. If either one of them had the courage to take that final step, it would have been *her* kissing him and not Finn.

Fungal had been right; it was difficult seeing them embrace like that, and she promised herself that if she was ever given the opportunity again, she would grab it.

Chapter Two

Daniel opened his eyes, looked around and realised that it hadn't been a dream. None of it. Not the magical journey on the London Underground, not the fact that he is the son of a fae hero and not the fact that he was in a bedroom in a palace on another realm. It was all real. Everything! Daniel Welsh was a mage! A mage in training, but a mage all the same. Just saying it put a broad smile on his face. 'I am a mage!'

Suddenly a groan from beside him and an arm coming to rest on his chest shocked him out of his reverie. Perhaps this *was* a dream after all.

Daniel looked sideways and saw the distinctive violet hair of Finn Jesson.

He was more than a little shocked to find the free-spirited girl sleeping next to him and he slowly slipped out of his bed, trying desperately not to wake his unexpected companion. He found himself dressed in rather comfortable dark blue silk pyjamas and racked his brains as to how he got into them and then about the previous night's events as a whole.

Bits and pieces came slowly back to him, like a fog dissipating in the wind. The Beltane fire festival had culminated with the crowning of its goddess and her consort, namely Finn and Daniel. This had been followed by a closing ceremony in which all the households took a firebrand from the fate chosen pair, which was taken from the bonfire they had all contributed to, in the hope of receiving luck for the coming year. After the ceremony, the celebration began, and Daniel's memory about that got a little fuzzy.

There was drinking, lots of drinking. In fact, he remembered being amazed at just how much ale Finn was able to put away and still have enough presence of mind to win more hands than she lost at Assault and Conquer. He also remembered the way that whenever he had a moment alone with Trinity it wasn't long before Finn would find her way over to them.

At that moment, a deep loud yawn signalled to Daniel that Finn had roused from her slumber. She scratched her stomach and looked around in confusion with her blurry eyes, then she saw Daniel and smiled broadly. 'I hope I didn't snore too loudly,' she said slightly embarrassed.

'To be honest, I have no idea. Most of last night is still a blur.'

'That's the sign of a great night!'

'I don't even know how I got into these,' Daniel said indicating the pyjamas.

'Probably the same way I got into this,' replied Finn as she pulled her matching blue silk nightdress over her head and threw it at Daniel. 'As if I wear that kind of stuff to bed.'

Luckily for Daniel, the offending item of clothing landed on his head obscuring his view as Finn strode pass him towards the armoire. 'Jeez, Finn! A little warning next time.'

'Where's the fun in that?' She smiled, 'I would have missed out on seeing you squirm.' Finn grimaced at her reflection in the mirror and as she desperately tried to tame her wild bed hair, she stole a glance at Daniel. She might have worried if her not-so-flattering morning-after image might change his opinion of her, if she were some other girl. But she was Finnoula Jesson, she was who she was and people could either take it or shove it! 'Now, let's see what we have here.' She threw the doors open wide and was greeted by dress upon dress upon dress. 'You have got to be kidding me,' she groaned.

Just then, there was a knock at the door, and after throwing the nightdress back at Finn and pleading with her to cover up, Daniel bid them enter. It was a servant come to tell them that a bath had been drawn for Finn in the adjoining bathroom. Daniel's own bath was next to his room... down the hall.

Finn broke out into laughter hearing this and teased Daniel about him sneaking into her bedroom to be close to her, no matter how much he professed his innocence.

With mounting embarrassment and even more confused questions about his antics the previous night, Daniel followed a servant back to his room and to his scented bath, he also swore off touching another drop of that ale.

ALTHOUGH IT MAY NOT have been palace etiquette, Daniel refused the helpers offer to attend him; much to his chagrin, he had been hoping to spend as much time as possible in the presence of the consort hero. The servant had laid out suitable court attire for Daniel consisting of a dark grey jerkin, loose fit cotton shirt and dark brown pants. There was also a note from Bertram, the major-domo, laying out the itinerary for the day. Breakfast would be served in Finn's room (as her balcony afforded better views of the gardens), followed by a guided tour of the palace and grounds by the major-domo himself. This would take them to lunch where they would dine with the Council of Three and their distinguished guests.

As he finished reading the note the servant returned to escort him to breakfast. Whilst walking down the corridor Daniel's mind reeled with images of Finn fighting off her attendees as they tried to wrestle her into yet another dress. He chuckled as he imagined the inevitable sight that was about to be revealed with the opening of the doors to Finn's chambers.

But the scene that greeted him was one he was not expecting at all.

Not only was Finn not battling with the servants, but she was also actually directing them! Making sure her boned, off-the-shoulder bodice was accentuating all it needed to and that the drapes of her skirt were hanging perfectly. At several moments, she was actually acting like a petulant princess, much to Daniel's amusement.

'And what are you gawping at?' Finn said when she saw Daniel at the door. 'I thought you'd done enough of that yesterday.' She shooed the servants away so they could bring the breakfast and once they were alone, she struck a pose, 'So, how do I look?'

'You look great!'

'I do, don't I?' she enthused. 'And no blast goggles this time. And no guns,

either.' Finn began pulling the hem of her skirt up to prove the point.

'Finn!' Daniel's shriek stopped the hems advance just as it reached her knees.

'Daniel!' she mockingly imitated. 'When are you going to stop being so bashful?'

'When *you* stop being so brazen.'

There was a moment of silence, then they both burst out laughing. After they had calmed down and got a hold of themselves, Finn led the way out onto the balcony and into the warming rays of the twin sunrise above the city of Almedia.

'You look like you're getting used to this dress-wearing thing.'

'Well, after being attended to in a bath and then being pampered, you kind of start feeling like a princess, so I thought I'd go with the flow,' she said with a giggle. They were quiet once more as they took in the beautifully landscaped gardens.

'You know something, Daniel,' Finn finally said after mulling things over in her mind. 'Usually I don't have any problem sharing my feelings with somebody. But things are different with you and I don't know why. Ever since I first saw you arrive here it's like something has come over me. Made me less sure of myself when I'm around you. Made me do things I wouldn't normally do. I don't usually give a vekt what other people say or think about me, but I had to make sure I got you alone to give me the strength to tell you. Love or lust? I don't know, but I do know that Trinity is my rival for you and that she may have the advantage of knowing you longer, but I have the advantage of being with you... now.'

Finn closed the space between them and wrapped her arms around Daniel's neck before passionately kissing him.

It was the kind of kiss that you never forget. The kind of kiss that all subsequent kisses would be measured against. It was the first time Daniel had experienced a "real" kiss so, not knowing what to do, he just held her tight around the waist and mimicked her actions.

It wasn't until the servants arrived with breakfast that they separated. Finn's cheeks were slightly flushed and Daniel was taken by how a woman so feisty and fiery, as Finn was, could suddenly look so demure, like Trinity.

Chapter Three

Bertram led Daniel and Finn down a passageway, at the end of which were a pair of huge gilded doors. A page stood at the handle of each door and as the procession approached, with drilled-in precision, the doors were opened.

The major domo entered first. Curiosity pushed Daniel and he poked his head in and looked around in awe. Before them were four rows of tables each seating twenty-five dignitaries from all around Ariest. Colourful crested flags and banners, representing one of the houses of the region, hung down from the vaulted ceiling.

'Finnu—' began the announcer before correcting himself after feeling the look Finn gave him. 'Finn Jesson, Beltane goddess and Daniel Welsh, consort of the goddess!'

There was a resounding round of applause.

'Are you ready for this?' Finn asked Daniel.

'Not in the least.' He glanced at her and slowly shook his head in disbelief. 'Aren't you nervous at all?'

'Nope. I've been waiting for this day. For too long I've been told that I won't amount to anything, that I need to change my ways and now I get to shove it right back up their noses that they looked down at me with. Come on, take my hand.'

Daniel was glad to and with their fingers interlocked together they crossed the threshold into the banquet hall. They followed

Bertram down the central aisle and the youngster could see that something was troubling the major domo.

'Is something wrong?' Daniel asked.

'What? No, no, no, nothing at all. Everything is just fine,' Bertram replied, waving off Daniels inquiry.

Daniel didn't believe that for a second. He could see how flustered Bertram was, no matter what he said. And at least one over person noticed the major domo agitated state, a rather plump man in a rather garish green and yellow outfit.

Applause accompanied them all the way to the top table, where the council of three and only the most important of guests would sit. Since the council always sat together it meant that Daniel and Finn would be seated apart. But Finn, ever the opportunist, saw this as the perfect moment to pull Daniel towards her and kiss him before they were separated, which garnered several hip-hoorays from the gathered crowd.

'Just so you don't forget me, while you're sitting all the way over here,' she whispered.

Once the goddess and her consort had assumed their seating, a fanfare rang out signalling the arrival of the council of three at which point everyone stood up. From a door Daniel hadn't noticed, until now, behind the top table, the three ruling royals of Almedia filed in and took their seats. The royal luncheon for the goddess and her consort could now begin.

This celebration was a complete contrast to the one Daniel and Finn had attended the previous night; that one had been loud and rambunctious this one was far more sedate as you would expect in the presence of royalty.

Daniel knew a little about the pomp and pageantry surrounding state visits from watching the news about the British royal family. And although this was more akin to what he would expect in a medieval kingdom as opposed to that of Elizabeth II, that knowledge still helped a little. Basically, he knew enough not to make a complete fool of himself.

As he sat at the top table, he wished Finn were sitting next to him. Her confidence in herself and attitude of not giving a damn what people thought about her would be perfect for him right now. He felt a little self-conscious being the centre of attention but if he was with her then he could deflect some of that her way.

He glanced down the table; Empress Xu ping was to his immediate left followed by King Ewynn then Chief Seydou and finally Finn, stuffing her face whilst cracking a joke with the chief.

Daniel chuckled to himself. He had to admire her for being so ballsy. Secretly he wished he could be like her. In the few days he had been in Ariest he had become somewhat of an overnight sensation; rescuing the boy you were accused of killing and becoming the consort of the goddess would do that, but he didn't crave the limelight. *That's for the Finn's, Tristan's of the world*, he thought, and probably his dad back in the day. For Daniel however, it wasn't that long ago that he would have been hiding and avoiding contact with people, being the centre of unwanted attention. He still was, to some extent, but the looks he got here were of admiration not the stares of curiosity he got back home.

It may just have to be something I need to get used to, Daniel mulled over in his mind as he listened to the empress tell him stories about Gydion battling a Wyvern singlehanded and others about his dad, Eric Mondragon, saving her daughter, Princess Sun Siu Ping from a varg, the description of which sounded much like that of the Fenris wolf from Norse mythology to Daniel.

'So, tell me, what great adventures has your father had in your world?'

'Adventures? Well, he got married and they had me,' chuckled Daniel, who instantly got embarrassed after seeing his joke drop like a lead balloon. He cleared his throat and began again. 'Earth is a very different place to Ariest. Sure, some things might look familiar to you but they are things from our history. There are no quests to be had, no vargs, no princesses needing rescuing. No magic.'

'And what of war?' King Ewynn asked. 'Surely a great warrior such as your father must be leading an army in some campaign.'

'He's a builder now. He builds houses, but he has seen the news reports about war. In my realm there is no glory in war. War is waged because of greed. They kill people because of commodities. Or they interfere with other countries politics. But there have been a few times the world has united to battle a common enemy, much like Ariest has done in the past, but every time it's the innocents who suffer.'

'And that's where the glory can be had. It's not by killing ten gnolls by yourself, it's by defending a building full of the very young and the very old from ten gnolls. That's where you show traits of your father, Daniel, and your mother. Both try to help those that can't help themselves. And you have done the same. You are a credit to them. I'm sure they will be proud of you.'

He hadn't thought about his parents for some time, but the king was right, saving people is what they did. And when Daniel was put in a similar situation, he instinctively did exactly what they would have done, even if it meant saving someone that apparently hated him like Jimbo.

As a child, you always hold your parents in high regard, put them on a pedestal. But to hear other people, people of such high standing, do the same, gave Daniel a huge sense of pride, but also trepidation. People would expect him to carry on building the legacy his dad left behind. Eric Mondragon may have retired but his presence would live on.

The weight of expectation rested heavily on Daniel's shoulders.

Chapter Four

'I can safely say, that without a doubt, that meal was fit for a goddess,' Finn announced as she and Daniel, arm in arm, were led back to their rooms by Bertram and two guards. 'Namely me!' She concluded with a cheeky grin.

Even though Daniel agreed with her, in that the whole experience was amazing, he could tell that something was still not right with Bertram. The way he creased his brow and slightly shook his head from time to time was a giveaway.

'Come on, Bertram, I can see something's on your mind.'

'As the major-domo,' Bertram relented, 'I take pride in performing my duties well. It may be a small thing to others but to have a dignitary seated in the wrong place could be seen as a slight by the council.'

'Do you mean that man in the brightly coloured clothes?'

'Yes. That man is Prince Gillygon of Mionechinko.'

'Really? Isn't he supposed to be a handsome man?'

'The most handsome of his people!'

'I see.'

'Anyway, a man such as he should be seated near the top table, as is the custom, to reflect his standing.'

'So why was he sitting near the door?'

'I have no idea.'

'Surely, being a prince, he should know the proper protocol?'

'Well, yes. And when I offered to have him moved to where he was supposed to be seated, he declined. He even left the luncheon early.'

'That's a bit odd,' Daniel thought aloud.

'And that's even odder,' Finn added as they rounded the corner and into the corridor their domiciles were located. 'Isn't that your room the prince is coming out of?'

'And where is his escort?'

'Oi!' Daniel shouted.

The prince stood stock still for a moment before he turned away from them and walked down the corridor in the opposite direction.

'Oi!' shouted Daniel again, louder this time.

'Perhaps he's lost,' Bertram offered as an alternative, but when the prince seemed to pick up speed after Daniel tried to get his attention again, the major-domo had to conclude that Prince Gillygon was indeed up to some funny business and sent Daniel and Finn's escorts after him.

'Woohoo!' There was no way Finn was going to miss out on the opportunity to see a royal get a beat down like a common criminal and she set off after them.

'Finn! No, wait!' An exasperated Daniel called as he reluctantly gave chase. He had the funny feeling that he might end up having to rein her in and to temper her exuberance which she, in the short time he had known her, tended to allow to run wild.

She was fast, and the chubby Prince Gillygon was surprisingly just as fast. The group quickly pulled away from Daniel. They rounded corner after corner. Several times they disappeared from his view.

Then her heard the scuffle of a fight getting louder as he neared another corridor, but the scene that revealed itself wasn't what he was expecting. One of the guards was out cold slumped on the floor and the other was being flipped this way and that by Prince Gillygon.

With the second guard unconscious, the prince turned his attention to the two youngsters.

Daniel flashed a nervous smile as he eyed the unpredictable prince. Finn, however, had a wide grin on her face as she loosened her shoulders, settled into a stance and prepared to fight.

'Give me the book,' the prince demanded. 'Give me the book and I won't have to hurt you.'

Daniel was a little taken aback by the prince's voice; it was a lot higher than he was expecting. 'What did you say?' He asked after he had gathered himself

'Give me the book King Noi of Murias City gave to you.'

'You're not getting anything, tubby,' explained Finn, 'except a beating from me!'

Again, someone was after the Book of Azul, thought Daniel. First that Shadow Dancer and now this hooky prince. There had to be something about it. Something he had missed. He hadn't believed it when King Noi had told him but maybe it really had been written by a god.

And then a realisation came to him - he didn't actually have the book!

Everything had happened so quickly after he had been arrested and brought before the council of three; he'd been released, drafted into the Beltane games, fought and destroyed a Shade and become consort of the goddess.

He hadn't been back to his room at The Dirty Dog. And that's where he had last seen the book, unguarded. He knew he had to get back as soon as possible he had been more than a little careless with someone else's property and he had to be responsible now.

Finn and Prince Gillygon circled each other. Every now and again they would throw a feint jab. It was the prince that made the first meaningful attack as he suddenly shot forward with a knee strike which caught Finn in the sternum.

As the fight progressed, it was plain to see that the prince surprisingly had the upper hand in the speed and agility stakes whereas Finn won out when it came to tenacity and ferocity.

Although Finn connected with several heavy blows, a headbutt to the bridge of the princes nose a particular highlight, on more than one occasion Daniel observed that the prince had his friend in a position where he could have seriously injured Finn thus ended the fight and made his escape. But each time he wouldn't make the blow. He tried to but his arm would shake and strain, it was like something was holding him back.

Daniel didn't have the time to dwell on that however, as he watched Finn get slammed against the wall. He had to do something and although he was loath to do so, desperate times called for desperate measures.

Daniel quickly searched his database-like memory for a suitable spell he'd read from the Book of Azul, then using what he'd learnt from Trinity, combined with that from Aradia, he began to cast the spell.

To Daniel the whole process was like rubbing your stomach and patting your head whilst reading Dr Seuss. It took him several attempts to get the combination of hand gestures, magical incantation along with concentrating on the right Essence pool but finally Daniel cast the spell.

A light blue bolt of frost shot from his hand in the direction of Prince Gillygon who amazingly evaded bolt after bolt with flips and somersaults. The prince however couldn't dodge Daniel's frost attacks *and* Finn's shoulder charge at the same time blasted him against the opposite wall.

With the prince momentarily stunned, and at his mercy, Daniel had no trouble hitting true with his spell this time. Several rings of ice clasped around the rotund prince, pinning his arms to his body and imprisoning him.

'Now that's what I call teamwork!' A sweaty, slightly bruised and dishevelled Finn enthused. She threw her arms around Daniel. 'That's our first victory as a couple!'

They held each other and bounced around, his enthusiasm at their win matched Finn's. It was the first time that Daniel had intentionally used magic on his own and he was elated, he was sure that Trinity would be proud. A part of him couldn't wait to tell her.

At that moment, Bertram, no longer hearing the sound of battle, popped his head around the corner. He asked 'is it over?' Then he surveyed the damage that had been caused by the fight. His jaw dropped in disbelief.

'Yeah, it's over,' Finn answered as she tried to make the most of what was left of her dress, and failing in the attempt. 'Your prince put up quite a fight but he couldn't take on the both of us.'

Bertram was still stunned by the devastation before him as he looked over the torn drapes, broken pottery and patches of jagged ice everywhere. Once he'd taken a moment to make a painful mental inventory of the cost, he let them know what he'd discovered. 'That is not the prince. We found him tied up and gagged in his room. He was not best pleased, as you could imagine, and there will no doubt be some recompense by the council to avoid an incident.'

'So, if this isn't the prince, who is it?' Daniel was just as puzzled as the others.

'Do not worry, we will find out in time. Guards, take him to the gaol.'

The four armed palace guards who had arrived with Bertram advanced on the prisoner. All of a sudden, they came to a halt, as right before everyone's eyes, the flesh of the imposter prince began to bubble and he started to groan in agony. His girth shrank as did his height, accompanied by the sound of bones snapping and cracking, which made Daniel cringe. The hair of the imposter grew longer and changed from brown to golden-blonde. Ears became pointed and ear-ringed. The painful groans of the peculiar male voice transformed into a distinctively feminine one. A red line tattoo appeared across her eye, down the left side of her small heart-shaped face.

When the transformation ended, the same elven female Shadow Dancer that had tried to steal the Book of Azul at the Dirty Dog, stood before them, perspiring and breathing heavy from the exertions of her radical change.

'Oh, oh!' Exclaimed Daniel. The ice rings that he had been so proud about magicking up, were made for the much larger body of Prince Gillygon. With the Shadow Dancer returned to her true form, the rings simply fell to the floor.

She smiled and stepped over them. Then all hell broke out.

In one swift motion she pulled off the garish coloured clothes she wore as part of her disguise and threw them at the guards, which concealed her movements momentarily, more than enough time for her. With lightning fast kicks, in a matter of seconds, she had knocked out two guards, grabbed the spear shaft of a third and dragged him towards her before knocking him out with an open palm strike under the chin. The final guard thrusted with his spear, and immediately regretted it, as she easily parried it before battering him around the head.

Then she turned her attention to the others, took the stance of a javelin thrower and aimed at Daniel. But again, she hesitated. She grimaced and clenched her teeth then her throwing arm began to shake. Her left hand was balled in a fist so tight her knuckles were white and Daniel could see the veins standing out along her arm. A tattoo of knotted thorn-vines swirled around it and the leather bodice she wore suggested the design covered the entire left side of her body.

The Shadow Dancer assassin suddenly relaxed and after taking a couple deep breaths snapped the spear over her knee. She glared at Bertram, Daniel and finally Finn with her yellow-green catlike eyes.

The major-domo shivered under her gaze. Then without warning she jumped through the window and was gone.

Chapter Five

It was a beautiful afternoon in Almedia. The suns shone high overhead and there was barely a cloud in the pink sky as the city was bustle with energy. The repairing of the buildings damaged in the conflict with the Shade had already begun, and life continued unabated.

The work was being undertaken by the Ganygu Conglomerate, the rich family company that made its doubloons from mining. Bad publicity a few decades ago, when several men turned up dead in one of their mines couldn't stop their growth, and in recent years they had expanded into construction, winning contracts from long established constructors.

Daniel looked on as he and Finn rode past, and saw all manner of beings at the worksite; Dwarfs, goblins, gremlins, ogres, pixies, leprechauns all working together with corporate banners that had a picture of a winking goblin with toothy grin that read "Ganygu, sounds like poo but we smell better than a Caribou!" all over the place.

He turned to his left to point out the signs to Finn but she was too preoccupied with waving out of the carriage to her new fans to notice.

When Daniel had told Bertram that this was the Shadow Dancer's second attempt to steal the book and the fact that it was back at the Dirty Dog unattended, the major-domo had made a request to the council of three and they had granted Daniel and Finn permission to use one of their carriages to take them to the Dog and then deliver Finn's new dresses to her home.

Now making their way to the notorious tavern Having the goddess and the consort parading through the streets in an ostentatious horse drawn carriage was too much for some and they began to line the streets, first a few at a time and then more as the word spread.

'This is awesome!' Enthused Finn as she waved and lapped up the adulation. Some brave souls ran alongside the carriage and threw her paper and a quill wanting her signature, which she duly did, signing it "The Goddess". Every now and then someone would call out for Eric Mondragon's son or the Shade slayer but when Finn tried to get Daniel to "give the people what they want" he was reluctant to get involved.

'Come on Daniel loosen up and enjoy the ride. It's only going to be like this for a year. After the next Beltane festival, we'll be back to being plain old Finn and Daniel; no more goddess or consort.'

'But I'll always be Eric Mondragon's son. Things will always be expected of me, especially now everyone knows who I am.'

Finn was silent for a moment. 'Nothing's ever been expected of me. Sure, uncle Quinn is known throughout Ariest for his inventions and engineering, but no one's ever really expected me to follow in his footsteps. I'm a damn good engineer mind you! What I'm trying to say is that just because your dad is who he is it doesn't mean you have to follow in his footsteps. You can be who you want and do what you want.'

'Maybe you're right. Maybe I'm putting pressure on myself. Maybe it's me that is expecting things because it's only since I learnt about his past that I felt like I had a mantle to carry.'

The carriage pulled up; they'd reached their destination.

'Come on,' Finn said, as she took Daniels hand and led him into the tavern, 'the first drinks on me.'

AS THEY ENTERED, DANIEL couldn't help but feel like they had gone back in time, that they were having a case of deja vu. So much had happened to him since he had first arrived in Almedia and yet it seemed like nothing had changed at the Dirty Dog. The patrons were still loud, people still played Assault & Conquer, Tristan was still all over Eveline as she brought her delicious foods to tables and Mavis still admonished him for interfering with her staff.

The only difference from Daniel's first day at The Dirty Dog to this, was the fact that Trinity was there.

She slowly stood and smiled widely as the two friends made eye contact across the tavern. She waved and Daniel was about to make his way over to her when there was suddenly an increase in volume from the crowded tavern and the next thing he knew, he was dragged by Finn and kissed ferociously.

The feisty Finn released him and revelled in the cheers from the crowd whilst Daniel, however, could see that Trinity's smile had vanished and she looked more forlorn as she retook her seat.

'Och, looks t'me like ye may 'ave missed the boat wid the wee lad, lassie,' Fungal said as he puffed on his cigar and blew rings in the air. 'You can trust old Fungal when it comes to matters of love. Beltane always strikes!'

'When it comes to you, Fungal,' Trinity responded, 'the only thing that I can trust with any certainty is that Fungal will only do what's good for Fungal.'

The crafty boggart laird gave a hearty laugh. He loved nothing more than causing mischief through trickery and deceit. Her words didn't hurt him, they let him know that he was doing something right.

'Hi, Trinity,' Daniel said as he came over to join them. He found it strange that whenever he was around his school friend, he always got a fluttery sensation in his stomach and his hands tended to get hot.

'Hey,' she replied. 'Are you ok? You look a little agitated.'

If only you knew. 'Yeah, I'm fine,' Daniel said, 'just a little hot.'

She offered a bemused smile, as if she could read his mind.

'It must 'ave been that kiss Finn gave ye,' Fungal nonchalantly added. A comment which prompted both Daniel and Trinity to give him stares that could kill. 'Don't shoot the messenger! I'm just saying that it was one hell of a kiss that's all.'

Trinity turned and was about to punch the boggart into next week but he had anticipated possible retaliation and already tele-ported to the bar. Now, the two friends were alone without Fungal's interference.

'You can sit down, you know,' Trinity said to Daniel. 'We need to talk about some stuff.'

'Oh, right, sure,' he replied as he pulled a chair out. Daniel had barely sat down when Tristan, Eveline and Finn joined the pair, much to Trinity's despair.

'Is this a private party or can anyone join in?' Tristan said, a flagon of mead at his lips.

'Why would it be a private party? Where the consort goes the goddess goes. Isn't that how it's supposed to be?' Interjected Finn.

'If the Beltane winners were meant to stick together for the year do you think this happy go lucky guy could stomach that?' Eveline remarked as she squeezed her man's cheeks.

All of a sudden, Trinity said, 'Daniel, I've got your book upstairs,' and stood up. 'Mavis gave it to Tristan. Perhaps I should give it to you now before I forget.'

'Phew! I was hoping someone would say that,' Daniel breathed with relief. 'I've got something to tell you about that book.' He took a step to follow Trinity and Finn made to go with him. 'Why don't you wait here?' he said to her, 'I won't be long,' then went to catch up with his school friend.

'Hmmmm,' Tristan began as he rubbed his chin. 'Perhaps it was a private party after all.'

Eveline hit him across the back of the head and glanced at Finn who was watching Daniel and Trinity intently as they made their way upstairs.

THE SPARSELY-DECORATED room was a far cry from the one Daniel had slept in last night. These rooms at The Dirty Dog were only really there for people that had imbibed rather too much to find their way home, and the decorations, or lack thereof, were testament to that. They didn't care what they looked at when they wore beer goggles.

Trinity and Daniel sat next to each other on the edge of her bed. 'I had a dream about you last night,' she suddenly blurted out.

'What?'

'Well, you weren't in it—'

'Oh'

'But it was about you. I was in a forest, a dead forest. And there was this voice. It said you had destroyed the forest. That you would bring destruction. That you were something called The Mortokai.'

'Really?'

'I've heard the name before. When I was looking for you, the hazel dryad said the same thing.'

'I've heard it before too, from Aradia.'

'The Tolgarr you met inside The Shade?'

'Yeah, it was When I told her about my photographic memory. That I could recall all the spells from the Book of Azul, but she said people would try to use me or kill me, not that I would destroy stuff. She basically said I had two choices; either train hard to become a mage and defend myself or hide and hope I'm not found.'

'Maybe we should release her and ask her some questions about it.'

'We can't. I promised that I would take her back to her people. Besides I don't know what kind of physical condition she'll be in when she's freed.'

'So, what are you going to do? Hide or train?'

'I have to train,' he said with a shrug. 'I don't have any real choice. Do you remember what I told you when I was in the Shade? When I was boosting my Essence and I got that euphoric feeling and how that was the last thing I remembered? You don't think that has anything to do with this Mortokai thing, do you?'

'I don't think so. I mean, it is possible to overdose on Essence, to boost beyond your capacities. And if you don't release it, you can become addicted to it; some become catatonic, lose all sense of reality. But that's not you.'

'Too much of a good thing and all that I suppose.'

'We'll find out what this Mortokai is together.' There was a moment of silence as Trinity gathered her courage and decided what she would say next. 'The dream also said I should forsake you,' Trinity began. she looked down at her hands, reluctant to make eye contact. It wasn't that long ago that she had been smiling at Daniel's awkwardness when she was showing him the locations of the Essence reservoirs. Now the shoe was on the other foot. 'It said I should forsake you... but I can't do that. These feelings I have for you, I can't deny them, not any more. Seeing you kissing Finn at the crowning was hard to deal with and again downstairs—' she suddenly stood up and walked over to the window. 'I'm sorry. I shouldn't have said anything.

I've put you in an awkward position. You two are obviously in a relationship now.'

'I don't really know what we are,' Daniel replied. 'She just kind of took charge of everything.'

'She is a force of nature,' Trinity admitted. 'So, uh, do you - do you have feelings for her?'

'Sure, I do! I like being with her, she's fun and kind of crazy. I've never met a girl like her.'

'I see.' Trinity was rather despondent hearing that news. A moment later, however, and things had changed.

'But I could say the same about you, well maybe not the crazy part,' he corrected, 'but I do have feelings for you too, different, stronger. I have ever since the first time I saw you. But you were out of my league, you still are.'

'Don't be silly,' she said as she came back to sit next to him. She took his hand in hers and they both gained some comfort and pleasure from the contact.

'If I didn't have the social skills of a prehistoric frog turd, we might have been together.'

There was a moment of silence then they both burst out laughing, the brevity cutting the tension that had been building.

Daniel wanted more than anything to take that moment to sneak a kiss, when she least expected it, but his courage failed him.

'Prehistoric frog turd? Are you kidding me?' She said between laughs. 'Where did that come from?'

'I don't know. It just kind of popped into my head. I stick by the sentiment though.'

'I know the way you have been treated has made you reluctant to open up to people, but surely not with me, not now.'

'You're right, speaking to you is easy, but speaking like this, about feelings, is a little different.'

'I'll admit sometimes it does seem to all come easy for me. People tend to flock to me.'

'They love you, love being around you.'

'But did you know that the only person whose love I really wanted was yours?'

Daniel turned to face Trinity and they gazed deeply into each other's eyes for the first time. She moistened her lips, he parted his, expectantly, and at the same time they leaned in.

If the kiss Daniel had with Finn that morning was indeed the standard bearer of kisses, this one surpassed it with room to spare. Some kisses are described as being electric, this one literally was. As they parted lips there was a crackle of lightning which left their lips tingling.

Trinity touched her lips. 'Did you feel that?'

'Wow! That was... wow!' Daniel seemed to be in a daze for a moment, then he abruptly stood up. 'I have to go.'

'What?'

'I need to go back home and say a proper goodbye to my parents. Let them know that I'm staying in Ariest to become a mage.'

She gave him a big hug. 'Are you sure? I'm a hard taskmaster, you know.'

'I'll take my chances. When I come back, I'll have to set things straight with Finn.'

'That's not going to be easy.'

'WELL, THEY TOOK THEIR wee time, didn't they?' Fungal being Fungal had been entertaining himself by planting thoughts in Finn's mind, telling her stories of unrequited love and betrayal. 'Is it me,' he started before he took a puff on his cigar, 'or are they looking a little... flustered?'

Finn watched them over the rim of her mead glass. Something was off. Maybe Fungal had been right all along. Trinity was her rival. Letting her be alone with Daniel had been a mistake. She should have insisted on going with them.

'Ah, Fungal, just the person I wanted to see,' Daniel said making a beeline for the boggart laird. 'Now that the Beltane Festival has finished, I suppose your FTN is back in service.'

'Sure is. What of it?'

'I need to get back to Earth.'

Finn couldn't what she was hearing. 'What did you say?'

'I need to go home and—'

'This is all her idea isn't it?' Finn interrupted pointing at Trinity. 'She couldn't stand seeing you with me!'

'This has nothing to do with me!' Trinity fired back. 'Daniel made the decision himself and I think it's right he should go back—'

'See! I told you she was behind it!' By now Finn was right in Trinity's face but the young Druid wasn't intimidated or taking a step back. Things were about to boil over.

Then Daniel jumped in to separate them. 'I'm going back to see my parents because I didn't get to say goodbye before, and then I'll be back before you know it.'

Finn however wouldn't be pacified and she shrugged off Daniels hands. 'We're not finished, Trinity, not by a long shot.' After that declaration she stormed out of the tavern.

'What got into her?' a bemused Daniel asked.

'A couple flagons of honey mead and Fungal in her ear,' Tristan replied after a big gulp from his own flagon.

'Why am I not surprised?' Trinity stated as she made Fungal nervous with her glare.

'I KNEW THIS WOULD HAPPEN,' Finn muttered under her breath as she stomped down the road. 'I should have just punched that little princess right in the face,' she slammed her fist into her palm for emphasis.

'You seem agitated, young Finn,' Hyasda said as stepped out of a back alley. 'Is something the matter?'

'Daniel is going back to Earth realm, that's what the matter is,' Finn spat.

'And? Surely you're going with him.'

'No.'

'Then I insist that you do.'

'I don't think—'

'Do I have to remind you how you won the festival? How you came to my shop begging to be alone with Daniel? How I gave you a potion to sprinkle on your garland so that he would be drawn to it no matter what? How you didn't have enough money for my services and I told you that you would owe me? Well, now it is time to pay your debt.'

'Fine, I'll do as you ask,' Finn reluctantly replied.

'Yes, you will,' she replied in an ominous tone. 'Now, go home, pack some clothes and come back quickly before he goes, that's a good girl.'

'What is it you want me to do?'

'I want you to get me the location of Eric Mondragon, to see him with your own eyes. That's all. Nothing too difficult is it? You get to visit a new world and just think of all the time you will be spending with your dear beloved Daniel, away from everyone else.'

'You're right! I'd better hurry up! He was already talking to Fungal, probably sorting out a ticket back to Earth.'

Hyasda smiled as she watched Finn run off home. She had a feeling that the rage and jealousy that the girl harboured would come in handy one day. And now she was being proved right.

'ARE YE SURE ABOUT THIS, lassie?' Fungal was flabbergasted.

'Yes, Fungal, I'm sending you back to your beloved station. You were supposed to help me find Daniel and I guess you kind of did,' Trinity explained. 'Besides, it'll get you out of my hair and you won't be able to cause any more trouble if you're back on your FTN.'

'True on both counts,' grinned the troublesome boggart. 'And just to show there are no hard feelings—'

'Excuse me?'

'—I'm going to give yer wee man here a little gift. Jes make sure ye dinnae give it to that blasted Rustin.' Fungal licked his hairy-knuckled finger, wrote a signature in the air which suddenly disappeared in a shower of faerie dust and in its place appeared a platinum train ticket. 'This ticket will give ye unlimited travel on the FTN. T'enter a station all ye need do is hold the ticket when ye open the door. Simple.'

'Wow! That's pretty cool,' Daniel exclaimed. 'So, where's the nearest pickup point?'

'Turn the ticket over. It has a wee map. The blue dot is you and the red one is the nearest station.'

'It's not far. So, I'm ready when you are, Fungal.'

'Me too!' Finn burst through the door of The Dirty Dog. 'I've decided to tag along. I think it would be right for me to meet the parents, since we are the goddess and consort after all.'

Finn smirked at Trinity. Trinity looked at Daniel. Daniel shrugged his shoulders.

Trinity fished into her bag, suddenly getting an idea. 'You'd better take this with you, so you can make a start on your studies. It's Gydion's grimoire. I think you should begin with page eight.'

'Page eight. Got it,' Daniel repeated as he looked in wonder at the Archmage's deep red leather-bound spell-book. 'Right, let's get going!'

'I'll be waiting here for you here,' Trinity said as she gave Daniel a hug under the watch eye of Finn. 'Be careful.'

'I think you have more reason than me to be careful with Tristan about,' replied Daniel.

'I'm serious, Daniel. I'm talking about what Aradia said.'

'Aradia?' Finn was surprised to hear the name. 'How do you know Aradia?'

'I'll tell you on the train.' Daniel took out his platinum ticket to check he was heading the right way then waved to Trinity and Tristan before setting off for the FTN station with his two companions. 'I'll see you soon, Ariest,' he whispered.

Trinity watched Daniel for a few moments before returning to her table in the tavern. She ordered some food and drink from Eveline before her mind started to drift to her friend and the fact that he'd be with Finn for the next few days, knowing that she'd be aggressively pursuing her man. Could she really call Daniel her man? She'd revealed her feelings and they'd shared that kiss. Remembering that made her smile.

'Don't worry,' Tristan said as he put his hand on Trinity's knee. 'I'll look after you. We can fill in as the consort and goddess.'

She lifted up his hand and placed it on his own knee. 'That's ok, I can take care of myself,' she said. She hoped Daniel wouldn't be gone long and also wondered what was keeping Gydion, she was desperate to tell him about what had happened with Daniel.

Chapter Six

Darkness. Silence. Eerie. Stillness. These were some of the words that went through Gydion's mind as he stepped through his portal that brought him from Fungal's castle and into Salamida.

The realm was like no other he had been to before. He could see as normal, but there was no light source anywhere in the sky, he couldn't tell if it was day or night-time. But that was the least of his worries, because this was the home of the Essence vampires known as the Shade.

He wondered if they had become aware of his presence as soon as he had arrived, but he had sensed no stirrings as of yet; in fact, he could feel nothing at all, as if there were no life on Salamida.

Gydion didn't have the time to give it much thought; ideally, he wanted to be in and out of the realm as soon as possible and without incident. Unlikely, he knew, but it was always good to have hope.

It was hope, after all, that had kept Daniel's mother Tina from falling into hysterics when Gydion had returned to the Welsh family home and explained what had befallen their only son. And it had been hope again that Eric harboured, when he was told of the possibility of the Shade being on Earth realm, hope that Gydion was wrong. It had taken all the mages of his old home to turn back their advance and what chance did his new home have with none?

The Archmage, who had by now dispensed with his Earth outfit and replaced it with his dark grey robes with their gold embroidered edge, looked perplexed. He had cast a spell of levitation on himself, intending to get a fix of his position, but nothing had happened. Flight enchantment, again nothing.

It must be the realm itself, Gydion mused as he looked about himself, *something to do with the physics of the place, no doubt. In time I could undoubtedly overcome this little hindrance, but time is a luxury I may not have a lot of, so I will need to work a little outside the box.*

Gydion cast a quick spell of Earth Control on the ground he stood upon. It suddenly began to rumble and quake and a column of rock formed beneath him before slowly elevating him into the air.

Since he couldn't sense anything by magical means, Gydion needed to try and sight something visually to get his bearings, and from this vantage point that was going to be an easy job.

Well, well, well, the old mage thought to himself as he spied something in the distant. *A light? Here? And a flickering light at that, which could suggest a fire and possibly sentient activity, maybe even a homestead.*

He stroked his black beard as he mulled things over in his mind. He knew that he didn't really have any choice but to investigate the light; after all, he had seen nothing else around, but that still didn't mean he liked the idea of putting all his eggs into one basket, so to speak.

Gydion held his hands out beside him and with his fingers outstretched, transformed the column of rock into a free-floating bridge that he began walk along toward his destination, the flickering light.

After a few hours of walking Gydion was glad to finally be nearing his destination.

Just because I have the vigour of a man a fraction of my age, does not mean I enjoy walking, especially when I am surrounded by such an uninspiring locale, he thought as he looked out at the darkness to emphasise his point. *Why walk when you can fly, I say...*

All of a sudden, he stopped in his tracks and cocked his head to one side.

What is that sound? Almost like a slow rhythmic rushing of wind. It could almost be the beating of wings, if I were to hazard at a guess. But if those are indeed beating wings then, judging by their slowness, the wingspan must be immense! Perhaps a Roc, or a Garuda would fit the bill, or even a dragon. Whatever it is, one thing is for sure, this makeshift bridge is no place for any sort of battle.

Gydion was a key proponent of the whole battle mage idea, the concept that the students of magic, whom traditionally were only taught rudimentary defence with their staves, should be trained in fencing. As such he had taken it upon himself to become proficient in tactical knowledge by learning from Queen Rhiannon's most highly decorated warriors, Eric Mondragon and Grimgaard Thunderbeard, the Dwarf. But he didn't need to call upon this learning to know that staying where he was, in the open on an elevated platform in a hostile realm, would be tantamount to suicide.

The Archmage broke out into a sprint. As he ran, he mentally lowered the rock bridge until it had been reabsorbed back into the natural landscape of Salamida.

It wasn't long before Gydion reached his goal, the flickering light he had seen from a distance. It was indeed a fire, but was more of a bonfire in size now that he was able to see it up close. He noticed that the flapping sound he had heard seemed to have vanished. Curiosity tugged at the back of his mind as adrenaline pumped through his body, and he hoped that he might have a chance to investigate the cause of the sound later. For the moment, however, he would put it on the back burner while he dealt with his primary reason for being on Salamida; to see if the Shade were being controlled and directed and, if so, by whom.

The flames danced and flared magnificently, and as Gydion approached them, it soon became apparent to him that it was magically generated since it gave off no heat. It also gave support to his theory that there was indeed life on Salamida other than the Shade, the several yurt shaped abodes further strengthened this belief. The homes not only looked to be out of place in the bleak wilderness that surrounded them but they also seemed familiar to Gydion.

They all appeared to be deserted as he checked them one by one looking for clues. The dirt and dust that had accumulated suggested that they had not been lived in for some time, and who ever had, seemed to have left in a hurry.

Plates of rotten food sat untouched in the kitchen, waiting for the diner that won't return. Clothes and toys were strewn across the floor after hastily being dragged out of drawers and chests. Jewellery boxes were turned over with the choices, sentimental pieces taken.

What could have caused such a panic, Gydion pondered. *This wasn't a planned evacuation; this was people running for their lives. I wonder if I could...*

Gydion's thoughts trailed off as he hurriedly began picking up random items before discarding them just as quickly as one by one, they failed to meet his requirements. Eventually he halted his search as his eyes came to rest on the jewellery left on the dresser and, in particular, a necklace with a tear-drop shaped orange gem.

He had been looking for something that had been handled in the last moments of the owner's time here, and that had, hopefully, left traces of their aura on the item. Gydion hoped that the jewels would be perfect for this, hoped that the woman they belonged to would have sorted through each piece as she decided what to take, hoped that he would be able to effectively 'see' what the necklace had seen that fateful day.

The Archmage clasped the necklace in his hands and spoke the ancient arcane words to cast the postcognition spell. The mists of time swirled across his eyes as the conjuration took effect, and within moments he could see what had been seen.

Chapter Seven

Daniel had learnt his lesson from his first trip on the Faerie Transit Network. This time he made sure he was in his enchanted seat before the train made a move. Although he was half tempted to make Finn have the full experience of the FTN, as he had, Daniel eventually thought better of it and made sure she was safely in her seat also.

Because he had been tumbling all around the carriage last time, Daniel didn't get to see the full wonder of his magical journey. Now, from his seat, he certainly made up for that. He marvelled at the speed the train travelled; at every twist and turn, loop and corkscrew it made. Looked on in awe as they plunged through oceans and ploughed through lava seas.

Magic was all around the carriage in the form of faerie dust. It floated around, giving everything a multicoloured hue. Daniel looked at Finn, and she had a look of fascination that he thought might be on his own face. When he looked at Fungal, he expected the laird to be disinterested, and he did; he looked like he was in deep thought, hatching some sort of plot. Daniel was about to ask him about it when the hurtling train came to a sudden stop.

'This is us,' Fungal said. He leapt from his seat and bounded from the train. He began to lead the way to the ticket hall.

The ceilings of the platforms were vaulted in a gothic style and when the boggart saw his compatriots take an interest in the architecture, he couldn't help but fall into his self-boasting spiel.

'When I first saw the faerie sidhes beginning to fail here on Earth realm, because people turned away from magic in favour of science, I knew it was an opportunity,' began Fungal. 'Sure, I could have gone into mining like Ganygu, but anybody can go into mining. And pretty much everybody has. The only reason Ganygu are top of the pile is because of their underhand tactics; a bit of intimidation here a bit of arson there. But I got plans to knock them off their perch.' He cackled manically and then, as he remembered he wasn't alone, he cleared his throat and continued.

'As I was saying, it's all well and good mining away in Ariest but what if your clients here on Earth? Do you wait in line to use a sidhe to transport your goods? Or do you pay a mage an extortionate fee to teleport you over? I gave everybody a third option; the Faerie Transit Network.'

They stepped onto one of the FTN's glorious steam powered brass spiral escalators and Finn couldn't help be impressed and swell with pride at her uncle Quinn's work. She had seen the blueprints thousands of times, but she had always wanted to see the real thing in action for herself. Now was her chance, and she examined every bit of it and watched for each hiss and puff of steam. She was in engineering heaven.

'You know that London Postal Railway, that mail rail?' Daniel nodded at Fungal's question. 'That was going to be my first line, but it wasn't big enough for what I had planned. I did turn it into my Faerie River Network when I expanded, however. Then I discovered all these disused stations. I had already made the old British Museum station my home and then I made it my flagship station.'

Daniel may have been impressed with the platforms and Quinn's steam escalator, but when they stepped into the main thoroughfare of the station his jaw almost hit the floor, much to Fungal's delight.

The station's floor was made of multicoloured granite and at five types of marble, veined from light grey to black. The chandeliers were made of gilded gold. Pillars were decorated with gold and bright blue majolica panels and marble bas-reliefs. Enormous marble benches with sculpted armrests, at either end, that resembled the tops of Roman Corinthian columns lined the walls. On the ceiling were several mosaics and the walls were adorned with ornate frescoes all showing scenes featuring Fungal. And to top it all off was a large marble statue of Fungal, hands on hips, chest out, wearing a top hat and chomping on a cigar.

'No' bad eh?' Fungal grinned from ear to ear, pleased with himself.

Ganygu may have the money, although with the success of the FTN fungal wasn't far behind and he had the fame too. As such, as the trio walked through the hall all manner of fae imp came to get a glimpse of the laird. And he loved it.

'Master Fungal!' The boggart laird's assistant, Lowack, fought his way through the crowd. 'It's good to have you back, sir.'

'Yes, it is.'

'The mage is here, but he says he won't finish the work until he has the rest of his payment.'

'Fine, I'll deal with him shortly. How is the new fresco coming along?'

They were led to a new work of art. A scene depicting the battle of Almedia against the shade. However, Finn notices something not quite right.

'What the vekt is this?' Finn couldn't believe what she was seeing. Fungal was shown blasting the Shade to pieces while he stood protecting the people of Almedia. 'You weren't even there! I remember you disappearing as soon as things kicked off!' Finn then noticed a little purple haired figure with two guns, in the corner of the fresco, cowering in fear. She pulled out a gun and in a matter of fact tone said, 'Change that now or I'll blow you head off.'

Fungal gulped, then shouted at the artist. 'Ye heard the woman! Change it!'

'Do you know how long it takes to change a fresco?'

'Do you know who I am?' Fungal dragged the artist away and when he was out of earshot he whispered in the artist's ear. A few moments later, he gave the artist a wink and sent him back to work. 'Are ye happy now?' He said to Finn. A cough from Lowack reminded him that he had somewhere else to be. 'Now if yous will excuse me, I have some pressing business t'attend to. Why don't you drop by on your way back t'Ariest?'

With that said Fungal and Lowack made their way to his office, deep in conversation, while Daniel and Finn headed to the exit.

The exit from the station was a large bronze door engraved with the image of the FTN logo, Fungal. Daniel pull the door open and allowed Finn to walk through. 'Welcome to Earth,' he said.

Daniel smiled as he closed the door to the British Museum FTN station. On the station side it might have been a big bronze door, but on the street side in was a dark-blue unassuming door with a Linden tree next to it. Daniel saw that they were on the corner of Bedford Place and Bloomsbury Square and decided to lead the way to Tottenham Court Road underground station to get the tube back to his home. He was looking forward to showing Finn his world, although he knew at some point, he would have to talk things over about the situation between her, himself and Trinity.

The first thing Finn noticed as she stepped out into a new world for the first time, was the peculiar smell in the air, then the blue sky with its single sun, and finally the white washed terraced buildings. 'Wow! This is so weird,' she said in amazement. She found herself looking at every person they passed. Every sight, sound and smell were something new for her to experience. 'What are those things that people are sitting in?'

'They're called motorcars, or cars for short,' explained Daniel. 'I guess you could call them our version of the horse in Ariest. Although we still have horses, but they're more for recreation activities and horse racing. And we have motor racing.'

'Strange.'

They walked past the actual British Museum with Daniel promising to show Finn artefacts from the ancestral lands of the council of three. It was shortly afterwards that he first started to get a dull throbbing sensation behind his eyes, which led to an acute headache. And he knew what was causing it.

It was the sun.

During His time on Ariest he hadn't thought about his photophobia. It had come to the point when he had even forgotten that he had any such condition. Hence the reason he had walked out of the FTN station without a care in the world, without any sort of covering or protection. Daniel had been a little excited to be visiting home, at least he'd get to see his parents again, but being back on Earth brought back the restricted life he had to lead and he became suddenly aware of all the stares and looks he was getting. The kind of looks that were a distant memory when he was in the faerie world.

They arrived on Charing Cross Road in seconds and as they waited at the traffic lights Finn looked around and took in all she could. The lights of the theatre, the call of The Big Issue sell, the buzz of the people, the noise of the vehicles, the height of the skyscrapers, the size of the cranes, the planes in the air. 'You lied Daniel,' Finn said wistfully, 'there is magic in your world.'

'HELLO? IS THERE ANYBODY in?' Daniel called but received no answer. The pair had arrived at an empty Welsh family home. This gave Finn the ideal opportunity to inspect a typical Earth home as well as get a few things off her chest.

'So, what did you and Trinity get up to at The Dog?' Finn being Finn went straight to the point. She wasn't usually one for the flowery build up.

'What?' Daniel almost choked on the juice he had taken from the fridge.

'What did you and Trinity get up to?' She repeated her question as she inspected the kitchen, Opening drawers and cupboards. 'You have history together. I know she has affections for you; and I've seen the way you look at her. So, I'd be surprised if nothing was done or said.'

'She talked about having a dream about me and about some of the things that Aradia told me.'

'Aradia of the Tolgarr? The grandmother of Crellis? They all think she's dead.'

'I have her safely in a gem. I promised to return her to her people.'

Finn briefly reminisced about her time with Crellis and his people. They were fond memories. She missed them. She missed him. But he chose duty over her. She couldn't help wonder if she would still feel the same about him if they were face to face, or if it was the memory of him that she still had feelings for. There was only one way she was going to find out.

'I'll take you to them,' she offered. 'They're a nomadic people so they move around, but they usually return to the same spots. I'll go with you,' she said. 'But this doesn't mean I've forgotten what you did with Trinity.' She jabbed him in the chest with each word for emphasis. I don't like being second choice.'

There was a jangling of keys at the front door and as it was opened, the voices of a man and woman.

'—and the sign fell off, then, with Justin's head down the pipe, Sam went in the cubicle and—'

'No, no, no! You stop right there, Eric Welsh.'

'What's wrong, Tina? You're a surgeon! You've seen plenty of things worse than someone getting a face full of—'

'Daniel!' Tina Welsh saw her son step out of the kitchen and she rushed to hug him. Then she saw Finn over his shoulder. 'And he's with a girl!' She called back to Eric. 'You must be Trinity.'

'Uh, no, I'm Finn.'

Finn couldn't believe her eyes. 'Vekt! Vekt! Vekt! It really is you!' She looked at him with wide eyes. Daniel could have sworn that she stopped breathing a couple times and that she might actually pass out. 'I can't believe I'm standing next to the legendary Eric Mondragon! The man that defeated the ogre giant, Daimalak! The man that stood alone against a horde of gnolls! The man that commands The Athanatoi!'

'Commanded,' Eric corrected.

'I read about them when I was Murias City,' Daniel interjected. 'It comes from Ancient Greek for athanatos which means "without death", right?'

'You went to Murias?' Eric was impressed. Not many surface-dwellers got the chance to go there, even before the ban. 'It's an amazing place isn't it?'

'It is! I met the king and kissed the princess,' Daniel said excitedly.

'You did what?' Tina and Finn both exclaimed at the same time, but for different reasons.

'So anyway,' Daniel attempted a swift change of subject, 'They are the elite military unit of Imperial City. Their number is always 1212; two generals, that's dad and Grimgaard Thunderbeard. Below them are ten commanders and each commander are in charge of 120 soldiers.'

'They're more than just soldiers!' Finn added. 'They're the best of the best, heavily armed horsemen in golden armour, all with silver faceplates. The 1200 have one face, the ten another. If one was killed, seriously wounded, or sick they are immediately replaced with a new one, maintaining the 1212 strength of The Athanatoi, so they seem to be without death because no one knows who's under the helmet.'

'How is that gruff old dog, Grimgaard, hmm? He must be relishing his position,' Eric laughed.

'Well actually Imperial City has been kind of quiet lately,' Finn replied. 'There are strange rumours going around, that there is some sort of madness there.'

'What do you mean?'

'I've heard that the people there aren't interested in doing anything, which is fine, until it gets to the point where you're not interested in eating or drinking. But these are merchant stories, mind you.'

'And what has Gydion had to say about it?' he asked Daniel.

'I haven't actually seen him yet,' Daniel answered, 'but I will; I've decided to study at the Mage Academy. I just wanted to let you guys know and say a proper goodbye.'

Tina was overjoyed for her son. She might have had reservations before, but she now knew that it was the right thing to do. As she hugged Daniel, could see the concern on Eric's face. Gydion had told them his plans when he had returned to tell them what had happened to Daniel. Eric was troubled by the idea then, and now it seemed that he was right to have those sentiments. 'You know what, Daniel, why don't you take Finn around Central London, let her experience what the city has to offer, while I sort out a spare room for her?'

'That's ok, I'll bunk in with Daniel,' Finn waved Tina off, but when she saw the disapproving look on Daniel's mother's face, 'on second thought, maybe I'll take that spare room, after all.'

'I don't think London is ready for Finn,' Daniel said with more than a hint of trepidation.

Chapter Eight

Everything he could see was now facetted and with an orange tint as his perspective switched to that of the gold set gemstone. It was a peculiar and unique experience for Gydion to be a part of. Since it was an inanimate object, his view was limited to whatever happened directly in front of the necklace. He compared it to what it must be like to peek through a keyhole; people, a man, a woman and what Gydion assumed to be their children walked back and forth pass the gemstone at irregular intervals, since it was located in the bedroom it didn't see much of the family. He wished he could have used the plates in the kitchen but the smell of the rotten food would have turned his stomach.

Eventually the necklace paid dividends, as it was finally picked up and inspected by its owner. And what Gydion saw left him in a confused state. The female had pallid skin, yellow eyes and no nose, as such, just six slits for nostrils. She had a ridged forehead, her elongated cranium tapered back and up into a point. The skin on her skull was opaque and it was almost possible to see her brain within. It wasn't her appearance that caused the Archmage's perplexity; it was the fact that he knew that she was from Naavina realm, no wonder the style of homes looked familiar to him. But why would they be on Salamida?

At last Gydion saw the Naavinian swing her head round, something had obviously startled her. Was this what he had been waiting for? There was no sound to this vision, but luckily the female still kept hold of the necklace as she held open her shades and peered through the window.

His view swayed from side to side, no doubt replicating the motion of the gem in her hand, Gydion presumed. The movement didn't impair his vision of events, however, and he could clearly see what he could only describe as a huge black hole in the sky above. It grew slowly in size, as it seemed to swallow up its surroundings.

Suddenly, portals seemed to open up everywhere. Frilled necked lizard like creatures with spikes protruding from their heads down their back to their tails came through them. Some came out dragging their serpentine bodies with only a pair of front legs, others bounded out on all fours, some walked through upright, their long tongues flicking about, tasting the air. Some even flew through the portals on leathery wings.

Wyvern, Gydion whispered to himself. He had encountered this offshoot of dragon before, but never in such huge numbers.

Hooded shadowy beings followed the Wyvern out of the portals; their faces were hidden but horns on their head made little peaks in their cowls. They numbered less in total than the Wyvern but that made them no less dangerous; in fact, it made them more so in Gydion's eyes. He knew that in any pyramidal hierarchy, the higher up you go as the number of persons lessened, the control that number commanded increased, as such, the hooded beings were the ones pulling the strings.

They issued commands, pointing out directions with their black scaly arms for the Wyvern to follow. Any curious Naavinian that ventured to close was mercilessly cut down. One of the hooded numbers then removed its hood. Even Gydion was taken aback by what was revealed. It had no head, just a huge round eyeball floating above the body.

It swivelled around as if looking for something, the huge iris occasionally dilating and undulating as it did so. Gydion wondered what it could be searching for, then it froze as it seemed to find it.

The creature moved closer to the home the Naavinian female was in. She understandably backed away from the window but in doing so Gydion's view from the necklace became obscured and the next thing he could see was a chain of crackling energy shoot up into the black hole.

It seemed to come from the ground near where the creature stood. The venerable mage wished the Naavinian would move nearer so that he could get a closer look at what was happening outside.

Just then, Naavin seemed to be in the throes of an earthquake but, just as the tremors grew in intensity, Gydion was dragged back to the present.

He had placed enchantments around his body to protect it while his spirit was away, so for him to be forced back without warning could only mean one thing: someone or something was near his entranced body.

'After all these years, this is how we are reunited; with you going through another woman's things? How is that supposed to make me feel?'

It was a familiar voice. It was a voice Gydion hadn't heard in a long time, a voice that still stirred emotions within him. It was the voice of Sayyidah, the wife he had banished to the far reaches of the known realms.

Gydion was face to face with the rival that became his lover, the lover that became his wife, and the wife that ultimately became the betrayer of Ariest. Yet he still could not bring himself to hate her.

Sayyidah stood before him in a white diaphanous lace halter neck dress, which plunged down to the gold rope belt she wore around her waist. It was simple yet elegant and harkened back to her roots growing up in Ptolemaic Alexandria. He knew that she wouldn't have been able to wear such things then, in those days it was reserved for the new Hellenistic upper classes of Egypt, the Greeks.

She didn't wear it now out of longing for the old days or because she thought herself equal to that long dead ruling class. No, she was beyond their equal, she was a goddess to them; Gydion had seen it with his own eyes when they had travelled back to that time. She wore it simply because she could. And it was that trait which had driven her throughout her life, the strong belief in herself and what she could do, and made her into the woman she was today, for good or bad.

She had grown up with nothing, from a poor village to living on the streets of the great coastal city. Nothing had been given to her as a child; she had had to fight for everything. More affluent children would deride her not knowing that they were only fuelling her determination.

From nothing, she briefly had everything, until the man she once loved and trusted, above all others, took it all away from her.

'It has been a long time, husband, although that is a concept that has little meaning for us.' She spoke in the ancient Hellenic language. 'I hope you do not mind speaking in this tongue, I do not get much chance to exercise my linguistics these days,' she said with a hint of sarcasm. 'You look well, still barely touched by the passing of the sands.'

'As do you,' Gydion replied truthfully.

Her eyes seemed to shine at his compliment, although she tried to hide her delight. He remembered that she was partial to the odd flattering remark and could imagine her being bereft of them on this realm, but before he could continue Sayyidah suggested that they leave the deserted abode for her own home.

'I once lived in a place such as this, when I was first forced to reside here,' Sayyidah explained as she led the way out, 'but that was before I discovered what this place really was.'

'And what *is* that? I saw a strange vision a moment ago.'

'All in good time, husband. Have a little patience. We should at least be comfortable for such a momentous reunion; do you not think?'

When they finally left the Naavinian home there was an ornately decorated carriage waiting outside which Sayyidah climbed into. Gydion would have liked to find out where Sayyidah could have obtained a carriage of such craftsmanship from, but he was more intrigued by the animal that pulled it. A giant shire horse, at least twenty hands high stood there with a harness over its muscular shoulders. It had a shiny black coat and instead of the usually white 'feathering' around its feet that a horse of this breed usually had; this one had flames fluttering in the windless air.

Sayyidah bid Gydion to enter the carriage. He did as he was asked and, upon closing the door, the horse set off at a tremendous pace. The bleak, barren landscape flashed past them as the mage looked out of the carriage window. Behind them he could see the trail of fire the amazing steed was leaving in its wake. Then he saw their destination come over the horizon. A crease of disbelief developed on his eyebrows and he swung round to question his estranged wife.

'Is that...?'

'Shhh,' she quietened him with a finger to her lips.

With the speed the horse was travelling at it didn't take long before they were close enough for Gydion to answer his own question. They were headed toward his own Sanctum, his tower, or at least a building that looked exactly like it.

They soon disembarked and walked the rest of the way up to the tower. It had no entrance and no visible windows, just as Gydion's own stronghold was without them. Sayyidah made the gestures and chants, familiar to Gydion, which opened the portal at the tower's base to permit entry into its hidden secrets.

Salamida was turning out to be a most bemusing place and Sayyidah was the only one here that had the answers, but Gydion was adamant that he too would discover them in due course.

She led the way into the study and immediately poured Gydion a drink.

'I hope you still like Scottish liquor.'

'Of course,' he replied as he took the drink. Her hand lingered slightly longer than was necessary, their fingers just barely touched, before she went back to make her own drink. 'How did you survive here?' Gydion hoped he might have some luck if he cut straight to the chase.

'Survive? I have not survived, I have only existed here, but I am glad that I have been blessed,' Sayyidah said as she held up her arm and admired her flawless olive toned skin. 'In a realm with no Sun, I was half expecting to lose my tone, become pale and gaunt. What do you think?'

'Yes, your skin still looks as perfect as I remember.'

'I was talking about my existing in a place with no Sun!' she snapped. 'Did you send me here to die a slow death?'

'Of course not!' Gydion was incredulous at the very idea. 'I sent you here because... because I could not bring myself to execute you. That is what the Assembly voted for, but I could not do it.' He shook his head as he made his regretful confession.

'So, you stripped me of my magic and banished me here. How humane of you.' Again her comment was filled with sarcasm but it did not last long as she spat the next venom laced comment out, 'If roles were reversed I would have killed you in a second!' She jabbed her finger at him for added emphasis.

Neither of them spoke as the weight of Sayyidah's words hung heavy in the air. Gydion did feel guilty but to hear her say that she would gladly end his life and to deliver it so vehemently shocked him.

'What happened to you?'

'You did! You betrayed me! Betrayed yourself!'

'What?'

'You once craved knowledge as much as I. Your thirst and hunger excited me, and we had tremendous adventures travelling the realms in our search. But once you became Archmage you betrayed our love.'

'You betrayed our realm! When you betrayed *us,* people died!'

'When you betrayed *me,* I died.'

Again, they took solace in the silence that descended. They both used the opportunity to calm themselves and to take more sips of the warming liquid.

'You know the responsibilities that came with the role.'

'What of your responsibilities to me. It seems to me that you are selective in regards to which responsibilities you do and do not adhere to, or else I would not be here.'

'I loved you. Even after knowing all you had done, I still loved you.'

'Did you hope you could somehow redeem me?'

'One day, perhaps.'

'I hoped the same of you; that you would one day remember the past and join me. I am who I am, it is you that has changed.' She took the final sip of her drink. 'Nothing was ended between us we are still bound by the laws of marriage. It could be as it once was, just you and I.'

She stared down into her empty glass like it was a reflection of the meaningless life she now led. Gydion had never seen her look so vulnerable, so innocent. He suddenly felt sorry for her and wanted to wrap his arms around her and hold her tight to him, and that is exactly what he did.

She nuzzled her head into his neck and he could smell the aroma of fruits and flowers rise from her long jet-black hair. He kissed her on the head. Decades had passed since they were last in such an embrace and sensations came flooding back in an instant. She raised her chin, and they looked deeply into each other's eyes. All their emotions were bared and visible in that moment. She could feel his hot breath on her lips and she quickly moistened them with her tongue just before Gydion leant forward and pressed his lips against hers.

They kissed like they were determined to make up for lost time.

If Gydion had chanced to open his eyes at that moment he would have seen the look that briefly crossed Sayyidah's face.

Eventually she broke for air and stood up. Taking Gydion by the hand Sayyidah led him to the bed they had not shared in a long time.

Chapter Nine

Finn was reluctant to leave her guns behind. She didn't like the idea of going out without them, she told Daniel that it made her feel naked. They finally got her to relent when Eric told her she wouldn't need them and Daniel explained that she could get arrested for carrying them.

'You don't understand,' she tried to explain later to Daniel as they arrived at London Bridge, 'those guns are a part of me, a part of who I am, they're my babies. You might as well have asked me to rip off my leg and leave that behind.'

'That might actually have been easier,' Daniel teased.

'This place looks amazing,' gasped Finn as she looked up at The Shard building. 'It makes the Council of Three palace look tiny. Is it a glass palace?'

Daniel scoffed. 'Nah, it's mostly offices where people work but it also has restaurants and a hotel.'

'Vekt! This is nothing like The Dirty Dog. I'm going to tell Mavis that she needs to up her game.'

'Come on,' said Daniel as he took Finn by the hand.

'Where're we going?'

Daniel pointed to the top of The Shard. 'Up there,' he replied.

'What? I'm not walking up there, Daniel!'

'You don't need to,' he replied with a smile.

After a few seconds in the elevator, the pair stepped out onto the 72nd floor. The platform was open to the elements; the designers had made a point of not having their viewing floor encapsulated like other high rises to go the feeling of flying.

Finn was certainly experiencing that, never having been so high in her life before. It was like she could see forever. All the buildings, different shapes and sizes, with patches of greenery here and there. She couldn't believe how vast the city was, and Daniel had told her that there were bigger, something she could hardly get her head around.

Something else that was beyond belief for Finn was that even up this high the clouds were still beyond her reach. She turned to Daniel excited about being so high up, but seeing Daniel with his hood up and with his dark glasses on tempered her enthusiasm.

'We don't have to stay if it's causing you trouble, being exposed to the sun up here, and all.'

'No, I'm fine. I've been here before so it's ok. Besides I wanted you to see it.'

'You've been here before? With Trinity?'

'Contrary to what you think, Trinity and I haven't done much things together.'

'But you want to?'

Daniels silence spoke volumes to Finn.

'I get it. She's a perfect little princess, what's not to like?'

'But I like being with you too,' he admitted. 'You bring something different out in me; it's hard to put a finger on it. I've been so reclusive and closed off, especially around girls, and then to suddenly have two, that like me. Even now I find it a little odd since no girl has ever looked twice at me before, well not in a good way anyhow, and I just wanted to hold onto those feelings. I think of both of you as friends, I don't want to hurt either of you.'

But Finn knew that, even with all his magic, that would be a hard thing to avoid.

'I'm hungry,' announced Finn.

'Ok, cool! Now you get to try some London cuisine! First stop...'

'Leon?' Finn frowned as they stood outside the restaurant.

'It's named after one of the owners dads, but forget the name, it's all about the food; tasty and healthy.'

After she had sampled some of the food on the menu Finn had to admit that it was pretty tasty, not as good as Eveline mind you, but still pretty tasty, especially the little custard tarts with the flaky pastry.

After they'd finished there, they went around the block into Borough Market where Finn's eyes lit up.

'This is just like Snack Street back home! Just a little smaller maybe, but the principle is still the same. She tried a bit of everything and made sure she got a bag of chocolate and cinnamon coated hazelnuts to bring back to Eveline, as a gift she claimed, but secretly in the hope that the talented Ariest cook would be able to recreate it and keep Finn's new craving satisfied.

Daniel continued his whistle stop tour of central London crossing the Thames and taking in the Houses of Parliament, Buckingham palace, Hyde park and eventually onto Oxford street. Finn was bewildered by the amount of people she had seen so far; to think that she still hadn't seen the same person twice on their trip.

They ploughed their way through the busy shopping street, being buffeted this way and that whilst Daniel held Finn's hand so as not to lose her in the crowds. Time was getting on but Daniel had one more stop to make on the way home.

'And this is it, my school,' Daniel revealed.

'Wow. It's pretty big,' Finn remarked. 'No wonder you have so many hobthrusts here.'

'You know, there was I time when I couldn't even see them,' Daniel smiled as he reminisced back to that fateful day with Trinity in the library. She had said that people stopped seeing Fae when they stopped believing in them. Well there was definitely no denying that his eyes had been well and truly opened to the world of magic. 'I'm sure the Mage Academy must be pretty special though, better than this, anyway.'

'Probably. I've never seen it but it's in imperial city so it must be pretty impressive since those High Bourne elves wouldn't have anything aesthetically displeasing near them.'

Hearing this piqued his interest mightily. As much as Daniel had been impressed with Murias City and Almedia, he knew that there was much more Ariest had to offer, good and bad. His curiosity fuelled his hunger for knowledge. Not just knowledge gathered from books but knowledge from experiences too. He had been told about the High Bourne by Nyriel, and Aradia had spoken to him about the Tolgarr, but he still felt the need to encounter them for himself.

'I had some good days here, not many to be fair, but I'll still miss the place,' Daniel said.

'I guess it is kind of the end of an era for you,' replied Finn.

'It's true it kind of is. Onwards and upwards to better things.'

All of a sudden, popcorn kernels began to rain down on the pair accompanied by voices Daniel knew all too well.

'Well, well, well,' Bobby Brinkmeyer smiled wickedly. 'if it isn't our good friend, Daniel Welsh. I knew you couldn't hide forever. Providence would finally deliver you to me.'

'"But I'll still miss the place",' mocked Jack Thompson. 'You're a joke!'

Willis Jeffries added his two cents. 'Have they finally kicked you out so us normal people don't have to look at your freakish face?'

Daniel tried to ignore them as best he could. He took Finn by the arm and started walking in the opposite direction of his tormentors. But to no avail.

'Are you kidding me? It looks like Ghostface has got himself a little girlfriend,' said Bobby.

'She looks a bit of a mess if you ask me,' laughed jack.

'What did you expect? It takes a freak to love a freak!' Willis retorted.

Daniel could feel Finn flinch at that remark.

'Why don't you use your magic and shut them up?' She whispered. 'Show them you're not that same person anymore.'

Daniel simply shook his head and carried on walking as the popcorn continued to bounce off his head. He wished he could use his magic on them but he wasn't even sure he'd be able to cast a single spell. His mind was filled with a whole gamut of emotions; fear, anger, embarrassment, all negative emotions that hindered the flow of Essence and the use of magic. And even if he did manage to overcome them what if he lost himself in that Essence euphoria again?

No, it was better to ignore them; small minded people get bored quickly. Unfortunately for them, people with fiery tempers reach their limit quicker.

'It's time for you to pay for that little sucker punch now, Daniel,' said Bobby. He threw his cup of fizzy drink at his victim, which hit him in the back of his head and it exploded everywhere, causing the three bullies to laugh their heads off. 'So that's what you look like with a bit of colour!'

Finn pulled her arm free of Daniels hold, which caused him to swear under his breath because he knew what was about to come; they were going to get a lesson on how to get beat up by someone that loved to scrap.

Daniel looked on as she gave them the chance to apologise, which they laughed off. Again, she told them to say sorry, and again they refused. Then Jack made the mistake of trying to push past her which resulted in him receiving several back-hand slaps, each one accompanied by her lecture of having better manners.

Bobby and Willis watched in astonishment as Jack slumped to the ground holding his reddened cheeks. A moment later Willis made a move to grab Finn but she was too quick as she took hold of his wrist instead, yanked him towards her several times and shoulder barged him each time before flipping the dazed and confused boy over her shoulder like a rag doll and left him in a heap on the floor.

Only Bobby Brinkmeyer was left.

After Seeing his cronies despatched with such ease Bobby wasn't about to take his opponent lightly and didn't intend to hold back either, girl or not. He just as well might have done because as he threw his first big right hander, she easily slipped it and doubled him over with a punch to his stomach.

'All you had to do was say sorry to Daniel then we would have avoided scenes like this,' Finn said matter-of-factly.

'I - I'm sorry,' he stammered.

'And...?'

'And what?'

'And you won't trouble him again or I'll come back again.'

'No! No, I won't trouble him again.'

That's when Bobby saw the wrinkled-up noses on the faces of the recovering jack and Willis, and felt then the warm dark patch that was spreading across the front of his jeans. It was the same look that they and he himself had given Daniel, now he was subject to it but instead of enduring it he ran away. With their leader gone and humiliated the remaining two helped each other and also left.

Daniel was more than a little happy to see Bobby get a taste of his own medicine, even though he knew his mum wouldn't be entirely happy with how the situation was handled. He wished, however, that he could have been the one to do it, to put Bobby in his place once and for all.

The way people reacted to his albinism had shaped the person he had become: guarded, reclusive, some people took it as meekness. Now he knew that to become the person he wanted to be he would have to take back control, not let others dictate who or what he could become.

And that included prophecies!

Chapter Ten

It had taken a lot of courage for Trinity to confess her feelings to Daniel. It had been a major hurdle for her to overcome. The feelings had been there for so long but she never quite knew how to express herself, or what to say, not until two things happened. Firstly, the forest dream and secondly, seeing Finn getting closer to him.

On both occasions she felt as though her affections were truly being tested; she could either persevere and ignore the dreams relentless warnings to renounce Daniel and declare her fondness for him or she could do as the forest wanted, forget him and not reveal her love for him at all.

Trinity had made her choice. She couldn't envision a life without Daniel in it. But now she was faced with an even greater test. Having told Daniel how she felt about him only to see him leave for Earth shortly after, with Finn.

Mornings in The Dirty Dog were a far cry from the rambunctious evenings the tavern was known for. Sure, it still had the one or two drunkards that were a permanent feature of the establishment, almost like furniture, but the clientele that frequented at this time were less interested in the drink.

Deals were being made in The Dog all the time, legitimate and otherwise, so if you didn't fancy being taken for a ride you made sure you kept your wits about you. Basically, the only thing you would wash your food down with would be a nice glass of water.

It wasn't just scoundrels and cutpurses that made it their inn of choice; there were also the shady Nobel's and merchant guild masters that felt somewhat safe there conducting business on neutral territory.

Eveline set a plate of breakfast down in front of Trinity then she returned to her seat at the counter next to Tristan. She watched a forlorn Trinity absentmindedly play with the food for a moment and sighed. 'That girl is in trouble. She's got it bad.'

'I agree,' Tristan said between mouthfuls of food. 'I sometimes get like this.'

She stared at him with an eyebrow raised and her head cocked to one side. 'Excuse me? When exactly have you been like that?'

'Oh, a lot of times! That downtime between quests is a killer. The danger of questing puts fire in your belly and when you don't have it you miss it.'

'So, you think she's depressed because she misses adventure?'

'No doubt.'

'And this is why I sometimes wonder why I am still with you,' she exasperated. 'You are such an idiot sometimes. She's pining for Daniel, you dolt! It's obvious.'

'Nah, trust me.'

Eveline rubbed her brow. She could feel the first twinges of a headache coming on.

'Fine, don't believe me! I'll go prove it then,' he said as he stood up and went over to Trinity. He grabbed her arm and dragged her out of the tavern.

Trinity rubbed her arm where Tristan had gripped her. He didn't release her until they had arrived at Union Park, next to Union Plaza and she wasn't particularly happy about it. All she wanted to do was wallow in her heartache and wait for Daniels return, not be manhandled by a self-centred show-off.

A shady man suddenly stepped out from behind a tree, threw open his cloak and made them an offer. 'You need a steppin' portal? I can get you from 'ere to Corivel or Treimatox in the blink of an eye and the price is very reasonable. What d'ya say?'

Trinity had barely calmed her nerves after the street dealers unexpected appearance when she suddenly heard shouts coming from the nearby town's guardsman.

'Oi! We already told you, you can't deal here without a permit! Oi!'

'Oh-oh, gotta go,' the shady man said as he sprinted off with the town guard in pursuit.

Now that they were alone in the park Trinity took the opportunity to question Tristan. 'So, why are we here? Why am I here?'

'Eveline seems to think that you have this long face because you miss Daniel, I told her it's because you're bored,' he stated, 'so I've brought you out here to take your mind off things and keep your sword arm sharp because adventure is always just around the corner.'

The young Druid rolled her eyes. She couldn't believe this guy. But, in saying that, she could do with the practice. 'Fine,' she submitted, 'let's get this over with.'

Tristan drew his sword and Trinity summoned her Schiavona. They went round after round, their swords dancing around each other. Swordsmanship however is just like magic in the sense that you need to concentrate completely on what you are doing. One stray thought and you might miscast your spell, or you might allow your opponent to slip your thrust and slap your behind with the flat of their sword.

'Touché!' he yelled with a grin.

She glared at Tristan. All she really wanted was to find out what was happening back on Earth with Daniel and Finn not have to deal with Mr Misogynist invading her personal space whenever he could.

He was handsome, that was easy for Trinity to admit to, but she really didn't know how Eveline put up with the rest of him.

Tristan was the better swordsman but the rounds of sparing would have been much closer calls if Trinity's mind hadn't been elsewhere. The fact that he got uncomfortably close, at every opportunity, also disrupted her concentration and furthermore annoyed her.

The flashpoint came when in a heated exchange of parries and thrusts Tristan eventually had Trinity pinned against a tree. 'Do you know,' he whispered, inches from her face, 'that if it had not been for that Shade you and I could very well have been the Goddess and Consort?'

'I guess I should be thankful then,' Trinity replied as she struggled to free herself.

'Forget about Daniel, move on. You and I make a much more believable couple.'

'This was your plan to take my mind off of Daniel? By telling me that you're a better choice?'

'You'll see for yourself,' Tristan responded as he leaned in to kiss the startled Trinity.

Trinity hadn't expected him to attempt such a thing but this was the final straw. She had endured All the butt slapping, derogatory comments about Daniel but Tristan trying to kiss her had tipped her over the edge. She had had enough and she intended to let him know in her own inimitable style. Being a Druid Trinity could become any animal she had seen, even from a magazine, and she knew exactly what creature she needed to become to get her point across to the disrespectful egotistical lothario.

Tristan's lips were nearly upon her but he never had the pleasure, as right before his eyes she transformed into a 3000lbs Giant Short-Faced Bear, the largest bear that ever lived. She stood over 14 feet tall on her hind legs. Tristan's grip was broken and he fell to the ground in a heap. Trinity dropped down to all fours; even like this she still stood taller than the average man, and she brought her face within inches of the fallen Tristan's. She bared her teeth and the let out a hellacious bellowing roar.

When she had finished, Trinity transformed back to herself, stood over Tristan and said, 'The next time you try that I'll eat your face off.' Then she headed back to The Dirty Dog. She had worked up quite a bit of an appetite. To say she was looking forward to finishing her breakfast would have been an understatement.

I guess Tristan was good for something after all, Trinity sniggered to herself.

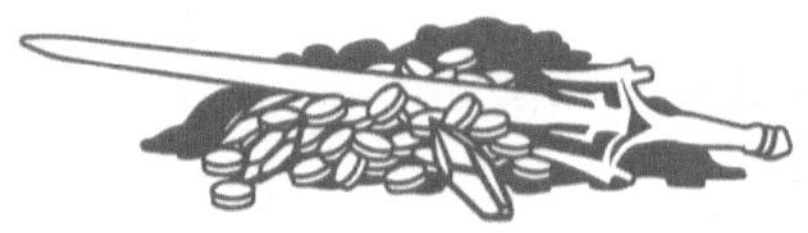

'I WAS JUST TRYING TO take your mind off things,' laughed Tristan, still dusting himself off as they returned to The Dog.

'Whatever,' Trinity dismissed his explanation, 'just go tell Eveline to bring me some more eggs will you.'

'Ok, but I may have a genuine distraction for you. I'm to go to Hyasda's Herbs and Alchemy store later. Sometimes she sends me on errands to find specific ingredients usually in dangerous areas. Maybe you should come with me.'

Trinity was non-committal as she sat down and waited for the eggs.

Just then the tavern door opened and two strangers, a woman and a man, strolled in. They appeared to be in their late teens and were dressed in garb which suggested they were from the hot, harsh southern territories of Ariest, as did their dusky completions, and this was confirmed when the woman walked to the counter spoke with a Semitic accent.

'I would like to speak to the proprietor of this establishment,' the woman said in a soft voice.

Eveline turned to call Mavis whilst Tristan, ever suspicious eyed the travellers. He watched as the male looked around the tavern then made some hand gestures to his compatriot.

'You're right,' she replied with a smile, 'this is big. It must be busy at nights and should be very lucrative for us.'

'I'm Mavis, this is my place. So, what do you want?'

'My name is Teresa Bint Ishraq and he is Jarl Gálvez,' she began with a flourish. 'We are travelling minstrels from Sisoara looking to make a bit of coin while we—'

'Not interested,' Mavis dismissed and turned to head back to what she was doing before she was interrupted.

'Of course, we would give you a cut of our takings, for the privilege,' Teresa continued, 'say 70/30?'

Mavis stopped dead in her tracks. '70/30?' Ever the business woman, any transaction where she would get the biggest share of the cake always piqued her interest. That didn't stop her negotiating further however. '70/30 And you buy your own drinks.'

'70/30 and we'll drink water,' Teresa responded.

The tavern owner thought for a moment and then broke out into a smile. A deal had been brokered. 'Welcome to The Dirty Dog!' She shook their hands and introduced them to Eveline and Tristan.

'Jarl, was it?'

'My partner cannot speak,' explained Teresa to Tristan. 'He does his talking with his music. Perhaps you would like a small sample of what we have to offer?'

'Excellent idea! I should make sure that you are up to the standard of my clientele.' As soon as Mavis had finished that statement Eveline shot her a look of disbelief.

Tables were pushed aside by Tristan, and a space was created for the entertainers. While this happened, Jarl, had swung his bag off his back and taken out a long slim case, which he handed to Teresa, in it was a flute. He then pulled out a 10-string lyre which he strummed and plucked to test its sound. In a few moments they were ready to begin.

Jarl began the performance with a few chords before Teresa joined the melody on her flute. The music was wonderful! Mavis was happy with the deal she had made but it wasn't until the girl from Sisoara began to sing that the tavern owner really saw the gold coins in her eyes.

Her voice was like nothing they had heard before, it was ethereal, otherworldly, even the well-travelled Tristan sat up and took note. The other patrons of The Dog stopped what they were doing, even merchants deep into their bartering paused to pay attention to the singing. It was a mesmerising, hypnotic sound and everyone was enthralled by it, everyone that is except Trinity.

As Teresa continued to sing, Jarl walked among the people in the tavern lightening their loads of money, jewels and whatever other valuables they had, unchallenged by anybody. Mavis didn't even flinch when Jarl pilfered the small coin bag she had hidden in her bra.

The thief moved towards his final victim, the red-haired girl that sat alone. As he got closer, he scanned her from head to toe, focusing on any rich pickings, the diamond stud in her nose, the bracelet on her wrist, and the one around her ankle. That's when he realised that unlike everybody else in the establishment, she wasn't even watching his partner at all, she was eating.

'That's pretty disappointing,' Trinity said as she finally finished her breakfast. 'You guys are actually really good, but then you turn out to nothing but petty thieves. That's a shame. So, you're sound mages? You use your music and singing to enchant and mesmerise your victims, then you move on to the next town.'

Teresa had joined Jarl, bringing his lire with her. 'And why didn't it work on you, might I ask?'

'You both have quite a bit of Essence but you don't control it well, as if you've never had any formal training. As soon as you came in, I could feel it, and when you started playing and it amplified, I knew something was up. So, I took the necessary precautions,' Trinity explained as she showed them her magically sealed ears as they returned to normal.

'Ah, of course,' Teresa smiled, 'well, played. You seem to know a little of our abilities but they go well beyond simple mesmerism.'

The singer started again, a different melody this time, which garnered different results. Trinity suddenly felt severe nausea, so bad that she dropped to the ground and wretched. Her mind was in turmoil. Her eagerness, bordering on arrogance, to stop the criminals made her overlook the potential dangers they could present. She had shown her hand too soon and now she was paying for it.

Damn it, Trinity! What's wrong with you? Sweat dropped down Trinity's face as she berated herself. *You slipped up, girl. Get your mind back in the game! Think, think, think, what do you know about sound attacks? Ok, sound attacks can be used to hypnotise, obviously, and cause vibrations, which is probably what she's doing to cause this motion sickness. But the highest practitioners can use it to cause internal haemorrhaging and death. Let's hope she's not one of those, and end this quickly.*

As Trinity struggled to cast her spell through the nausea she immediately came upon a new problem. Her voice had been muted; Jarl had retrieved his lyre and was playing.

'Oops, did you think I was the only one that was a sound mage? What a mistake to make. Let's get this over with Jarl. This is a big city, we have a lot of coin to make here,' smiled Teresa.

Good, the nausea is passing, Trinity discovered. *It seems the vibration spell needs continuous singing. That's her mistake.*

Trinity didn't need to recite a spell or use hand gestures to transform into animals, just a clear mind, and with the motion sickness gone, that's exactly what she had. In the blink of an eye she had turned into a red Mozambique spitting cobra and sprayed her venom at Jarl, hitting him in the eyes. He fell to the floor in a silent scream and his music ceased.

'Jarl, my love!' Teresa rushed to aid her fallen comrade. The venom had reddened his eyes and seeing this infuriated the young woman. 'Do not worry, I will make her pay for this dearly.'

But it was already too late. With no hindrances holding her back, Trinity, didn't intend to be caught out again. With quick and precise gestures, she cast a spell to gag her and another to bind Jarl's hands. She then created a cloud within the tavern which floated above everyone in turn and rained on them, the magical properties of its water dispelled the mesmerism that Teresa and Jarl's music had put on them.

After Trinity had explained to Mavis what the southern pair had planned, the tavern boss sent word to Eamon Wolff.

'And who might Eamon Wolff be?' Trinity asked Eveline as Mavis returned to her room in the back.

'Eamon Wolff is the thief Guildmaster, and also Mavis' ex-husband,' explained Eveline. 'He was making it in the thieves guild, she got this tavern because she wanted to go legit, and they went their separate ways. But she still has his protection, which doesn't bode well for these two.'

'Because they tried to rob Mavis?'

'Because they didn't follow protocol. It's custom to announce yourself to the guild, if they had, they would have known that The Dirty Dog was a no-go area. That's a major no-no.'

'Forget about them, Trinity, their days are numbered now. Since you are warmed up for action and adventure now why don't we go and see what Hyasda has to offer? Then Daniel will be well and truly off your mind.'

Trinity reluctantly followed Tristan, still wary around him. She knew that what he said would never happen, and what he didn't know was that she was expecting to see Daniel again very soon. This little distraction would be welcome for the time being though.

Chapter Eleven

The next morning, or what could be considered as such on Salamida with its perpetual darkness, Gydion stood by the window and watched Sayyidah as she slept. He had never expected that reconciliation would be a possibility between them, but once he had seen her, the old feelings had rushed back, in truth they had never left him.

Looking at her sleeping peacefully, he couldn't help but feel like nothing had changed, like the war had never happened, like he hadn't banished her. Just to be able to pick up where they had left off was perfect...perhaps too perfect.

Maybe it would have been better if he had brought Trinity along after all, then perhaps things would not have escalated so fast. *Good grief! I had almost forgotten Trinity! And why have I come to Salamida? It's like something is clouding my memories.*

Gydion closed his eyes and took several deep breaths. He internalised his Essence and used it to cleanse his body. Something definitely was trying to block his memories, but who had done it? Sayyidah?

As if aware that she was in someone's thoughts, the Egyptian mage slowly roused from her slumber. 'Good morning, my dear. I hope you slept as well as I,' she said with a stretch and a smile.

'Yes, I did, thank you.'

'Then what are you doing over there? Come.'

Gydion walked over to Sayyidah and took her outstretched hands as he slid onto the bed next to her. He ran his hand through her dishevelled hair and drew her close to him.

'We need to talk,' he said before leaning in to kiss her.

'If we must.'

'We must. I know nothing about this place.'

'Very well,' she replied with a petulant sigh. 'What do you want to know?' She draped herself across Gydion's lap and waited for his reply.

'I want to know everything.'

'*There* is that thirst for knowledge that I loved in you,' she smiled up at him as if she had been expecting him to be tempted by her offer. 'Fine, I will tell you what I have learnt, but I still think Salamida has many secrets still to reveal. In fact, I am not even sure if this area *is* the original Salamida.'

'What do you mean?'

'This place is like no realm I have been to before,' she enthused. 'Sometimes I think it is alive, sentient. It grows! It absorbs other realms into itself!'

Gydion was astounded. He had never heard of a realm actively seeking to expand itself. Was it even possible, he wondered, then he remembered what he had seen and couldn't explain, 'The Naavidian homes?'

'Yes, that was a relatively recent addition.'

'When I did the post-cognition spell, I saw Wyvern searching for something.'

'From my understanding, it uses them to find where the mystical heart of a target realm, where its energy resonates the most.'

'The ley lines.'

'Exactly; it seems to take it, add its mass to its own and feed on the energy.'

'Much like the Shade feeding on Essence,' Gydion mused, 'who also just happen to reside here. So, if you are correct, Salamida is in effect an Essence vampire, only on a planetary scale.'

'And we could tap into that power; become omniscient, become like gods, *more* than gods!'

'Is that even feasible?' he asked suddenly alert from his contemplation.

'I have found ancient texts, older than anything Master Penwyll had in his possession, they suggest it *is*. And it was actually attempted but was stopped before the spell could reach its conclusion.'

'By whom?'

'His name was Baelthorn. It is written that four of the Tuatha, the four that would become the elemental gods of the winds of Ariest...'

'Boreas, Eurius, Notus and Zephyrus?'

'Yes, they combined their strength to defeat and imprison him.'

'That must have been an epic battle.'

'It was. Apparently, many of the known realms were created by the fallout of the conflict, including Ariest.

'I need to see these ancient records. I need to find a way to stop this... this whatever it is before it can send more Shade to Ariest.'

'There is Shade on Ariest?' Sayyidah was shocked by Gydion's revelation, then she paused as things became clear to her and she sat up. 'That is why you are here, because you suspected... me.'

'I had to investigate. I had to be sure. You must understand why you would be the principal suspect.'

'And yet you still made love to me even though you did not trust me? I suppose you are just like any other man in that respect. Am I supposed to be flattered by your weakness? Flattered that my feminine whiles still hold sway over you?'

'No, I made a mistake, I was wrong to accuse you, I see that now. Even I am not infallible.'

'Well I guess some things have changed. I cannot remember you ever giving an apology before...such as it was.'

'Put it down to the wisdom garnered through old age.'

'So, what was your 'mistake' down to? The petulance of youth?'

'I suppose when you are over two thousand years old there is not much that could *not* be described as such.'

'Then it is lucky for you that I have a penchant for younger men.'

'Then I am forgiven?'

'For now.'

'Then we can leave for the temple so I might study these texts?'

'All in good time,' she replied as she caressed his face, 'there is no need to rush. Unless of course there is somewhere more important you need to be?'

Gydion thought hard for a moment as if trying to remember something, but nothing came. 'No, there is nowhere I need to be, except here with you.'

Once more Gydion sank into the arms of Sayyidah, and once more she couldn't hold back the sinister smile that crept across her face.

'This is it, we have arrived,' Sayyidah told the expectant Gydion.

The Archmage had been sitting silently whilst they had been travelling to the temple in Sayyidah's carriage. He had felt his mind being assaulted again and it had taken his complete concentration to fend it off, and it only seemed to be getting stronger.

'Are you ok?' his wife asked.

'Yes, I am now. Maybe something in the air is affecting me.'

'Come on, the quicker we can get to the texts the quicker we can return home.'

She took his hand and walked toward the temple. It looked completely out of place surrounded by the cracked granite and dark mountain ranges that made up the desolate landscape of Salamida.

To Gydion's eye it looked similar to an ancient Babylonian Ziggurat. It was built in seven receding tiers on an oval platform and reached some ninety metres into the blackened sky. It seemed to be made of solid gold except for the silver structure placed on the buildings flat top. On one side were a series of golden ramps leading up to different levels and one long path, at a shallow incline, taking you ultimately to the summit.

'What you seek is in the shrine at the top,' Sayyidah explained as she began the trek up the ramp.

At the peak the silver shrine stood proud in the forsaken landscape. But Gydion still didn't understand why it would be there at all. Did the Shade have gods they worshipped? Were there other unknown races living on Salamida? The mysteries surrounding this realm just kept on growing, and Gydion was intent on finding answers.

The shrine had an open archway as its entrance. There were strange symbols and hieroglyphs surrounding it that were beyond even Gydion's understanding. He traced his finger around the ciphers and prepared to cast a spell, so that he might translate their meaning, but before he could Sayyidah rushed him along stating that she thought he was here for an ancient tome, not to read graffiti. He was tempted to cast it anyway but she took his hand, headed towards the archway and the pair duly entered.

Inside, Gydion and Sayyidah were greeted by the sounds of moaning voices. It seemed to be thousands upon thousands of them, some human some not. To Gydion's well-travelled ear the sounds were from citizens of several different realms, but there was no body anywhere; the sounds just seemed to come out of the air.

'What is that?' Gydion asked.

'Apparently the sounds of the dead, or that's what I've been told.'

'Told? By whom?'

Sayyidah didn't reply just smiled knowingly as they walked into a marble large chamber. It was empty except for a single door opposite them, but as Gydion examined the room, the door suddenly slowly opened and a thin bald man emerged.

'That 'whom' would be me,' he stated. 'My name is the Keeper and I urge you now to turn around and leave this shrine, or your voice shall join those of the ones who have trespassed and fallen.'

Gydion looked from the keeper to Sayyidah and back again to the newcomer. 'I mean no disrespect; I just came here to learn more about Salamida. I was told there was a book...'

'There is. I am the Keeper of the Book of Secrets and none have seen its pages for millennia and none shall while I live. Your friend knows this.'

'Sayyidah?'

'You said you wanted to know more? Well, he has everything you need, everything *we* need. And if he does not relinquish it then we shall have to take it by force.'

'You have tried this before,' Keeper said to Sayyidah, 'several times, in fact, and you have failed each time. And it will be no different now. You should turn around and leave now. No more lives need perish because of your futile ambitions.'

'We should go Sayyidah,' a stern Gydion stated. She had obviously hidden certain information from him and he didn't like it; after all, if she had hidden the fact that she had attempted to get to the book before and the presence of the Keeper, what else was she hiding?

Gydion began to make his way back to the entrance, an action that distressed Sayyidah enough to make a desperate choice. She couldn't stomach the thought of being this close to her goal again and falling short yet again. And now that her hand had partially been exposed, she knew that there would be many questions for her to answer back at her home. She looked at the impassive Keeper and then at the quickly departing Archmage before she made the rash decision to charge the protector of the Book of Secrets.

The Keeper was astonished to see the unarmed woman rushing towards him. In all the times he had seen her here she had never been so reckless, always sending a companion to attack him, and when they had been promptly defeated, she would leave. Why was this time different he wondered?

No matter, he had a job to do, a job he had been honoured to be chosen for, and a job with a simple mandate; protect the Book of Secrets and defend the shrine. He had been unwavering in his task to date and that wasn't about to change now with this attack.

As Gydion walked down the passage he suddenly heard Sayyidah scream and then silence. He turned and ran back to the chamber room only to find her unconscious body crumpled against the wall, the smouldering traces of a magical attack rising from her.

Chapter Twelve

The dream: a succession of images, ideas, emotions and sensations that involuntarily occur in the mind during sleep. Some believe they are manifestations of one's deepest desires and anxieties, a connection to the unconscious mind. In many ancient civilisations' dreams were always held to be extremely important for divination. Ancient Hebrews believed dreams were the voice of god. But one interpretation rang truer for Daniel than the others. That of Herodotus who in his The Histories wrote, "The visions that occur to us in dreams are, more often than not, the things we have been concerned about during the day."

He sat on the edge of his bed in the familiar surroundings of his own bedroom and sighed. He could have sworn that, since his introduction to Essence and the world of magic, his dreams had become more vivid.

The setting of Daniel's latest foray into the land of nod was Almedia. He had walked arm in arm with Trinity one side and Finn the other. Everyone was happy and smiling. They arrived at a landscaped park area where they lay beneath a large tree and talked and laughed.

All of a sudden, the sky darkened and Bobby Brinkmeyer appeared. He terrorised the citizens of Almedia and destroyed their property. Eventually the people turned to Daniel to save them but he couldn't. He couldn't use magic; he was too scared.

Then a dryad materialised from the trunk of the tree and began to berate Daniel. Trinity and Finn joined in, laughing at him and calling him names.

'You are such a coward,' Finn laughed.

'A huge giant failure of a human being,' added Trinity.

'They say that the apple doesn't fall far from the tree, but in your case, it couldn't have fallen any farther,' the dryad chimed in.

Daniel looked at them in horror. He tried to shut out the hurtful comments they threw at him but failed. He tried to run away but everywhere he turned they were there pointing and laughing.

'To think that we both liked you.'

'We were ready to fight over you.'

'You're not good enough for either of us.'

'We don't need you anymore.'

'You're no mage.'

'You're a disappointment to your father.'

Those last words of the dream reverberated in Daniel's mind as he woke up.

They may only have been in his dream, but if he was being honest with himself, he thought those same words on an almost daily basis. Even before he knew his dad was a fae legend. He always noticed that his father had a kind of aura about him; people always liked being in his company, they listened to him and valued his opinion. And it was another thing when it came to physical activity.

Daniel was nothing like his father. It bothered him a little in the past; a son always wants to emulate their father and make them proud, but now it irked him more than ever, now that he knew the status his dad held in his past life.

Suddenly he became aware of sounds that emanated from the garden. Curious, Daniel went to his window to investigate. Down below in the backyard he could see Eric and Finn sparring. Typical; just as he was feeling down about not being the child his dad would have wanted. He couldn't begrudge Finn though. She must be in heaven, he thought, knowing how much she was in awe of his dad. It must be like having all her Christmas's at once. Daniel smiled at the thought.

After having a quick shower, whilst he was getting dressed, Daniel spied his satchel and remembered the spellbook Trinity had given him; Gydion's very own grimoire. He took it out, and on closer inspection, was a bit surprised by its unassuming appearance. The book was nothing like the Book of Azul. Whereas that one had been thick, hard backed, with a big golden clasp, this one was more akin to a small leather journal with a thin strap wrapped around it to hold it closed.

The dark red cover was embossed, front and back, with runes and other esoteric symbols. Daniel untied the book and lay it down in reverence. He took a deep breath and prepared himself to open the spellbook. He was about to see things that, to his knowledge, had not been seen by many. Things that Gydion had written, secrets he had in his mind. The moment wasn't lost on Daniel.

But he couldn't open it.

From every angle he tried, the cover wouldn't budge. He looked the book over again to see if there was another catch that he had somehow missed but there was nothing. Whatever he did, slap it, punch it, smack it, bang it, kick it, throw it, reverence had gone out the window by now and the book still wouldn't open.

Daniel slumped back into his chair, panting heavily and sweating.

'Are you quite finished?'

The unexpected voice shot Daniel up in his seat. His bedroom door was closed and that was definitely the direction the voice had come from, but there was nothing there, just that bloody book.

'What a dunderhead! Did you really think that the great Archmage Gydion would leave his book unprotected so that any dunderhead, like you, could get access?'

Daniel stared at the spellbook with his mouth agape. 'It was the bloody book. It can talk.'

'What a dunderhead! I'm the grimoire of the great Archmage Gydion, I'm not like ordinary books. Now pick me up.'

'Oh, right, sorry about that,' apologised Daniel.

'And so, you should be, Dunderhead. Now,' the book coughed and recited a set command after being placed on the desk, 'speak the magic word, or words, and you shall have access.'

'Huh? What magic word? She didn't say anything about any magic word,' Daniel said.

'Who didn't?'

'Trinity. She gave me the book - uh - I mean you, and told me to read page 8.'

'I see. And who might you be, Dunderhead?'

'I'm Daniel, Daniel Welsh.'

'I know that name.'

'Really? How?'

'I know a great many things about a great many things.'

Daniel saw this as an opportunity and swiftly asked a question. 'In that case, perhaps you can tell me about this Mortokai thing I've been hearing about?'

'I don't know anything about that,' the book replied, which prompted Daniel to roll his eyes. 'But I do know that the great Archmage Gydion and Trinity spoke of you often—'

'What did they say? Only nice things I hope.'

'—and Trinity did wish it, so I am willing to allow you access to page 8 and page 8 only, until you can tell me the magic word or words.'

Gydion's grimoire flipped its pages to the correct entry. It opened on a double page. On one side were the arcane words, the verbal component of the spell, followed by the runic lettering that denoted the hand gestures. On the other side was a description of the spell itself. There were scribblings around the edges, additional notes Daniel assumed. At the top of the page was the name of the spell; Astral Projection. 'That's what Trinity used when she came to me during the wheel run,' Daniel whispered before he continued to read the fancy script of the magic book.

Astral Projection

This spell is used to separate the astral form from the physical one. Once separated the astral form is invisible to all those you wish it to be and is also intangible. Astral bodies can be sensed by detection spells and forcibly pulled from the astral plane with a Summoning spell. The astral form can travel great distances at great speeds, or even instantly if you know the place well. I have added the Mind Vision conjuration here also since it aids instantaneous travel. You visualise where you want to be and send your astral self to that point.

Essence: personal

Element: arcane

Necessary techniques you must utilise to achieve spell success:

Relaxation

Concentration

Visualization

Remain mentally alert

Astral combat is used so as not to cause significant damage to the physical world around the combatants. Within the astral plane you can-

Daniel instinctively made to turn the page but the grimoire suddenly slammed shut.

'No, no, no, page 8 only,' the book reminded Daniel. 'Besides, at this juncture you have no need to learn about astral combat.'

After Daniel apologised for his instinctive page turning and explained how he zones out when he reads, the spellbook relented and reopened, much to Daniel's relief.

The would-be mage looked over the arcane words. A couple of them looked familiar, or rather some of their syllables did, Daniel having been taught them by Aradia. The others would be a guess at best.

Daniel sat cross legged on his bed with the book in his lap. He went through the runes and practiced the gestures. This part of the process he found easy. There was no need to worry about pronunciation or syllables, just follow the instructions, hold your hands here, extend and retract your fingers in sequence at the right moment. Simple.

When he felt he was ready, Daniel made his first attempt at casting the astral projection spell.

'Whoa! Stop right there!' The grimoire clearly heard enough. 'If I had ears they would be bleeding right now. What, pray tell, was that supposed to be? The words in spells are supposed to be lyrical, not whatever that was that came out of your mouth. Is this the standard of young mages these days? Who exactly is your master? No doubt it is that dunderhead, Master Monroe. He calls this training?'

'Well, actually, I - uh - haven't had any real training yet.'

'What? There was a time when an untrained mage would never dream of touching the Archmage's grimoire, and if they did they would instantly find themselves in a mystic cell to ponder what they had done. Oh, how I wish those days were back.'

'See? I'm not cut out to be a mage! Everyone is on my back about it, Gydion, Trinity, Aradia, even Finn. I'm destined not to live up to my father's reputation, nothing more.'

'I really don't see what the great Archmage Gydion sees in you, myself. It must be something though, so I'll help you. Repeat after me.'

Daniel did as he was told. Once he had heard the spellbook recite the arcane words, he now had the sounds for the words that were permanently in his photographic memory. He repeated them verbatim, much to the surprise of the book.

Again, after taking several deep breaths, Daniel tried to cast the spell. The mystic words flowed from his mouth. Each syllable accompanied by a hand gesture. All the while, concentrated on his Personal Essence Reservoir in his lower abdomen.

His muscles relaxed. He felt like he was going deeper down a spiral staircase into a world of relaxation. Daniel then started to experience a sinking feeling, as if he were slowly falling, but he was actually rising.

His astral form was free of his physical one.

'Wow! This is awesome,' Daniel exclaimed as he examined his translucent, glittery astral body. He noticed how sharp his vision was, like everything was in super HD with ultra-vivid colours. He floated down and looked at his physical body with its serene face and he smiled. 'Let's see what this astral body can do!'

The first thing he attempted was to see if he truly was intangible and placed his hand against the wall before he pushed. It went through as if it was not there and he nodded with appreciation. 'Cool!'

He followed this experiment by flying through the wall himself and floated down to where Finn and Eric sparred. 'They totally can't see me,' Daniel marvelled as he levitated around them. 'Maybe I should give that Mind Vision a try. So, to begin, you visualise where you want to be, picture it in every detail. Then you close your eyes, mentally send your body there, and when you open them, you'll be in... Westminster Abbey!'

He laughed as he floated above the famous gothic building, seeing it from an angle not many people got to experience themselves. It reminded him of when he floated, uncontrollably, over Almedia. 'I can go anywhere!' The realisation suddenly dawned on him. He could send his astral form anywhere, as long as he could visualise it. 'So that's why Trinity told me to start on page 8,' smiled Daniel, as he thought of Almedia then closed his eyes and reopened them to find his astral body had instantly travelled to Ariest.

'I'm never going to get tired of this! One minute I'm home, then Westminster and now I'm in The Dirty Dog by the look of things,' Daniel said as he took in his surroundings. He floated down through the floor, hoping Trinity maybe there eating. But there was no sign of her. 'Where could she be?'

'I'm right here,' Trinity said.

Daniel turned around to see Trinity's astral form floating behind him. He couldn't hide the delight that appeared on his face, and neither would he want to. 'How did you know I was here?'

'I've been keeping a little detection spell active just in case,' she smiled.

'Just in case?' Daniel scoffed. 'You orchestrated it!'

Trinity beamed. 'Maybe I did, but I didn't want Finn to have you all to herself, not now things are... different between us.'

'I thought you might have forgotten about that,'

'Are you kidding? Did you?'

'No way! Any regrets?'

'None. You?'

'The only regret I have is leaving you behind.'

Trinity smiled as she slowly reached out her hand. Daniel mirrored the action and they tentatively linked fingers. Neither said a word as they enjoyed the moment. Then Trinity suddenly had an idea. 'You haven't been to the Astral Realm yet have you?'

'The book only allowed me to read page 8. And speaking of the book you could have told me that it talked. He almost didn't let me read it at all,'

'Yeah sorry about that, it was a last-minute decision,' Trinity said, 'Grim can be a bit of a stickler sometimes.'

'Grim?'

'That's his name,' Trinity revealed. 'I'll give you the password before you go back. For now, let me show you this.' She smiled back at him excitedly as she held his hand tightly then closed her eyes and reopened them. 'Welcome to the Astral Realm.'

Daniel examined their blank surroundings in amazement. 'It's like everything has been erased, like we've blinked into nothingness!'

'I wouldn't exactly call it nothing...' Trinity replied. The emptiness around them suddenly became a tropical beach with a beautiful red sunset. 'The Astral Realm can become anything you desire. Why don't you give it a try?'

'Ok! So, I just will it to happen?'

Trinity nodded and the realm transformed into Daniel's bedroom. She looked at Daniel and smiled coquettishly. 'Are you trying to tell me something, Daniel?'

'What? No!' Daniel could feel his face heating up. 'It was the first thing on my mind - I mean - ahem - let me try again'

The Astral Dimension changed again.

Trinity looked out of the window before them and saw buildings whose walls were nacreous and iridescent with roofs of multi-coloured shells. The room they were in also had the same pearlescent floor and walls. Trinity had an incredulous look on her face, she had never seen anything like it. 'What is this place?'

'It's Pichini Palace in Murias City,' Daniel told Trinity happy to be able to show her something new. 'The medical wing to be exact. This is where I woke up after that incident with the kelpie.' He changed the scenery again. Four rows of gold-veined marble pillars suddenly appeared around them with a huge mosaic of Zephyrus under their feet. 'And this is the throne room where King Noi gave me the Book of Azul and Princess Nyriel kissed me.'

'Excuse me?'

'Long story short, she did it to keep my head on my shoulders.'

'Long story short, I'm going to take your head off your shoulders... if you don't kiss me.'

It was only then he realised that they hadn't actually kissed since reuniting, but his excuse was that he was still learning the ropes of being in a relationship. It was all new to him. Hearing it still made him chuckle inside, I'm in a relationship, with Trinity Evergreen! Kissing her now would be a reaffirmation of that declaration.

They stepped closer to each other. She looked up at him and he lost himself in her green eyes. He pushed back a stray curl of her auburn hair then he instinctively leaned forward and their arms wrapped around each other. Their lips met.

'And for future reference,' Trinity started when they finally parted, 'you don't have to wait until you're threatened to kiss me, I am your girlfriend after all.'

Daniel was about to reply when he was suddenly yanked away by an invisible force. 'What's happeniiinnnggg!' Then he vanished.

'Maybe it was too soon for him to hear the "G word",' smiled Trinity.

Chapter Thirteen

Gydion dropped to his knee and checked her pulse. It was there, weak but there. He brushed the strands of hair from her face and made his wife comfortable in the recovery position before he stood and faced the Keeper.

'That was unnecessary. She has no magic.'

'She has no right to be here. Repulsing trespassers is my duty, and that is what I have done. You should take her now and leave before the same fate befalls you.'

'You should know a couple things first; unlike Sayyidah I have magic and secondly she is my wife!' Gydion unleashed a volley of blasts at the Keeper who barely got his shields up in time to defend himself. The power of the attack was still enough to force him back.

'It has been a long time since I have faced such power. I commend you, but you still shall not pass.'

'What is in this book that is so valuable?'

'Nothing that you shall learn while I still live.'

'So be it.'

The combatants stood facing each other. They both flared their Essence to replenish their levels. Gydion stood unmoving watching his opponents Essence. It was somehow different to any he had seen before. Sure, it shimmered a golden colour, but it wasn't that; it was something else, but he didn't know quite what. What he did know was that the Essence level of the Keeper was comparable to his own.

It had been some time since his last duel, before he had returned to Earth in fact, but Gydion was able to keep up some semblance of practice, especially whilst training Trinity.

He had done the gentlemanly thing and allowed his opponent to replace his lost Essence but he knew of some mages that would use the underhand tactic of attack whilst doing such a thing. He was glad to see that his adversary was not such a man.

'This shrine is a place of great importance; I would not like it to be destroyed in the coming contest.'

'Then the Astral Realm shall be our battleground.'

The Astral Realm, the realm between realms. Also called the Spirit World by shamanistic magic wielders. It can only be reached by the projected Essence of beings. These astral forms are intangible and incapable of being harmed except by opponents who are themselves in astral form or by the most powerful of magic users. Combat here cannot be seen, heard or felt by those in the physical plane hence, as devastating and destructive a magical battle can be, there is no collateral damage.

The two combatants simultaneously slowed their breathing and entered a trance state; at which point their Essence forms left their bodies and entered the Astral Realm.

Gydion faced the Keeper, getting his combat spells ready to cast. Perhaps there was an element of battle rust on the part of Gydion because before he had time to react, the Keeper sent his first spell and wrapped the Archmage in mystic bands.

'Keeping things simple usually pay dividends,' the Keeper said smugly. 'I had expected more from you however, considering the power within you. What a waste. Now you must pay the price for not heeding my warnings.'

The Keeper silently spoke an incantation and his hands began to glow with power. He released a volley of arcane beams towards Gydion who just stood his ground. The beams grew nearer and nearer until they were about to strike the helpless mage. But instead of delivering a killing blow they passed right through him and the image of Gydion dispersed into nothingness much to the chagrin of the Keeper.

'So it would seem I have underestimated you after all,' the Keeper said as he searched for his opponent.

'All I want to do is briefly read the book so I can learn about this realm and protect my own against Salamida,' Gydion said. As soon as he had arrived on the Astral Realm, he had cast an Image Generation spell quickly followed by a spell of Invisibility so that he might study his adversary.

'Protect against Salamida? What nonsense! Salamida is a paradise.'

'What do you mean paradise?' Gydion asked incredulously as he kept moving so as not to give away his position. 'When did you last have a look around your paradise?'

'I have never left the shrine,' the Keeper admitted. 'My mandate is to this shrine only.'

'Then you know nothing of what is happening! This realm is feeding upon others, draining them of their life force!'

'Draining Essence? But that's not possible... he has been imprisoned, in stasis for millennia.'

'Who has? Who are you talking about?'

'No, this is a lie, all lies!' Angered by what he perceived to be Gydion's game playing, the Keeper released an arcane wave, which radiated in all directions from his spot.

Gydion wasn't worried about the approaching attack because he already had his shield in place, but as the wave struck him and was diverted by his defences it revealed his position, just as the Keeper had hoped and he unleashed another torrent of blasts Gydion's way.

His shield held but it was significantly weakened, another volley or two like that and it just might fail. It was time to show the Keeper exactly who he was facing.

A quickly cast spell and the ground beneath the Keeper turned to ice and encased his feet but before Gydion had a chance to follow up his attack, his adversary used a conjuration to lower his density so much he took on a cloud-form and floated free of his ice shackles.

With quickness of thought and knowing the weaknesses of being in such a manifestation, Gydion created a strong, mystical wind which blew the Keeper and began to disperse his body at a molecular level across the Astral Realm.

Against a mage of lesser ability this tactic would have worked perfectly but the Keeper was not such a mage. He was able to keep his mass together long enough to cast his own spell. Three ethereal servitors appeared around Gydion and instantly attacked him.

Their strength was phenomenal as they pummelled the Archmage to the ground. If he had not magically hardened his skin, he would probably be dead from the assault but even with this protection he was still taking damage and he couldn't withstand the incessant battering for much longer.

Since he was using his arms to defend himself the best he could, meant that Planetary and Realmic spells were not accessible to Gydion, but that didn't mean he had nothing.

During his travels through the infinite dimensions, Gydion had come across many mystical artefacts; skulls, wands, rocks, rugs. One item in particular had fascinated him for the simple fact that it was more than just an unassuming relic.

He had found it during his time at O'nio. When he had first seen it, he had thought it was just your everyday shiny stone, but when he picked it up he found out that it was actually a container and had a sentient being inside it, a mauve-coloured faerie, and that it had a name, Cuthala. But the most interesting thing about this fae was that she was a Screaming Mimi and she made the most piercing scream imaginable when poked. Which is exactly what Gydion did.

He took the stone from inside his cloak, opened it just a crack and, after using a Personal Energy spell to close his ears, he gently prodded the faerie in her stomach. She let out an almighty piercing scream. The decibel level was at such a high frequency that the servitors soon began to vibrate under the stress and within moments they had dispersed.

Gydion thanked Cuthala and put the stone container back into his hidden pocket. When he stood up, he saw the Keeper on his hands and knees, recovering from the sonic attack. Extreme sound can be very distracting to a mage since it takes tremendous concentration to recall the incantations, gestures and precise breathing to cast spells.

'Are you ready to yield?' Gydion demanded.

'You are a fool to think that I would be so easily beaten,' the Keeper replied as he got to his feet. 'You shall only gain what you desire with my de—' The rest of his sentence was cut short as a look of wide-eyed shock and pain descended across the Keeper's face. 'My – my body.'

Gydion knew immediately what his opponents strained words meant. The major failing of astral battle was that it left the host body completely unprotected, something must have happened to his.

The Archmage returned back to his own body as fast as he could and when he opened his eyes a most gruesome tableau greeted him. The Keeper's body lay on the ground in a puddle of blood, his torso cut open. A jagged edge of the bloody flint stone that lay beside the body. There were droplets of blood leading towards the door the Keeper had been guarding, which was now open, and the print of a small hand was on the wall beside the frame.

He turned quickly and discovered that his wife was no longer at the place where he had left her. 'Sayyidah, tell me you did not do this,' he said under his breath, as he shook his head with disappointment. Gydion did the only thing he could now and walked through the doorway.

Chapter Fourteen

'You know you don't have to do this, right? I'm fine! I don't need any distraction from anything.'

'You can say what you like, Trinity. I'm doing you a favour; unless, of course, you want a heart to heart with Eveline over a cup of linden tea.'

Trinity wasn't sure she'd want that either, to be honest. The last thing she needed to hear was about how great their relationship was, although, judging by the way Tristan made a move on her, she had serious doubts that it actually was; unless it was one of those weird relationships she'd watched a documentary about on TV. She didn't want any more ideas planted in her mind of Finn exploring her friendship with Daniel, either. Trinity had had more than enough experience of girls gossiping when the boys are away back at school.

No, she wasn't overjoyed with the idea of being alone with Tristan again, but it was the lesser of two evils. And he had been behaving himself since she warned him off, so I could've been worse.

The more and more she saw of Almedia and life in Ariest, the more trinity began to feel comfortable in this realm. She could recall her initial reservations about coming here when Gydion first told her and they increased when it was revealed that she would be making the journey alone, whilst he went to Salamida.

He had said they were going home; she had felt they were doing no such thing. But now, the longer she was here, the more she got that tell-tale sense that she belonged here.

Trinity and Tristan passed some of the buildings devastated during the battle of Almedia and she was amazed at how quickly things were moving. Quinn Jesson along with his automatons had helped with the clear up, and now the Gillygon Conglomerate had begun building work on some of the properties.

'Careful, Og, don't strain yourself. You're the brawn and I'm the brains of this operation. If you get injured, they'll just strap me to the back of another ogre,' a goblin said from a wicker seat the ogre wore on its back.

'Me careful, Wizglop. Me much careful,' replied Og as he picked up a large container of rubble.

'That's what I like to hear, buddy,' Wizglop said. 'This is an important contract. I don't know how Gillygon got it - let me rephrase that - I don't know who Gillygon bribed, threatened or killed to get it but what I do know is that this Almedia, not some backwater village like Elkim. We're going to make some serious coin! Just think of all the dances you can get at the ogre showgirl club.'

'Me no go there. Wizglop know me married with children.'

'Yeah, nineteen of the little beggars, can't forget that. In that case, just think of all the dances that *I'm* going to get at the club,' cackled the goblin.

Trinity cocked her eyebrow at hearing this. She struggled to imagine an ogre showgirl and struggled even more when she tried to imagine that showgirl with a little goblin.

Before her mind could grind to a halt from overwork, Tristan, announced that they were almost at their destination. Trinity couldn't help but notice, as they turned into the street, that it was surprisingly untouched by damage.

'Wow!' Trinity exclaimed. 'I can't believe this area escaped all the carnage, especially since it's on the Eastern Gate route.'

'Hyasda may be old,' Tristan replied, 'but she is no slouch when it comes to the mystic arts. With my own eyes, I saw her repel Shade, single handed.'

'Really? Then why didn't she aid us in the final battle? We could have done with her help.'

'Because she *is* old. I'm sure she would have helped more if she were physically able.'

'Hmm,' Trinity nodded slightly. 'It's a little odd that my dad has never mentioned her. She must have had an incredible master.'

'None that she mentions,' came the reply. 'From what I can gather she trained herself. Mostly.'

'I see,' scoffed Trinity. She knew such a thing was incredibly unlikely. The Mage Assembly had strict rules. If you have sufficient Essence to become an Adept you must follow the path or have it stripped from you.

'This is it,' announced Tristan. He opened the door to Hyasda's Herb & Alchemy, accompanied by the twinkle of a bell, and a myriad of fragrant aromas struck Trinity.

A call came from the back. 'Is that you, Tristan?'

'Yes, Hyasda. Who else would it be? It's not like business is booming, after all.'

'Don't be so rude. Business is doing very well, why do you think you're here?' The old woman came out, leaning heavily on her staff. 'Oh! You have company.'

'Yes! This is Trinity, the daughter of Gydion. She's in need of some adventure so she's going to be coming with me.'

'Hello,' Trinity said. She had been curious of all the scents and paraphernalia and inspected many of the different bottles and the cornucopia of ingredients throughout the store. 'You have a very interesting shop here.'

'The daughter of Gydion, you say? My, my, my, come to grace my humble little shop.'

'So, what is it you would have me do?' Tristan asked his aged benefactor.

'I need a new supply of Solecuss Root,' she answered.

'What? That's it?' Tristan was not only deflated, but also a little embarrassed to be taking Trinity on a gathering hunt and not the big adventure he'd been promising. 'Fine, let me get a few things and we'll be on our way.'

Tristan disappeared into the back rooms whilst Trinity returned to browsing the items of the curio shop. 'Do you know my father?'

'Everyone knows the great Archmage,'

'You have a lot of interesting things here,' she said. 'A *lot* of interesting things.'

'Thank you,' she wheezed. 'I like to stock many things because you never know what a customer is going to need.'

'I can imagine. You must get plenty of commissions.'

'The people of Almedia keep me busy.'

'Do you get many requests from outside the city?'

'Now and again.'

'Tristan told me that you held off The Shade during the battle.'

'I did what my frail body would allow. Not as much as you young ones I'll admit.'

'Still, that is impressive power for one to have, to turned The Shade away. You should be in the Mage Assembly with that ability.'

'Such things are not for the likes of me.'

Trinity continued to browse the store in silence for a few moments. 'So, perhaps you can help me with a little problem...well actually it's a problem a friend of mine has. Maybe you know him. His names Fungal.'

'Fungal, you say? Hmm, can't say that I recall knowing any Hobthrusts by that name. What problem does he have?

'Well, the problem is that he got a mage or some other wielder of magic to create a fourteenth century castle in his FTN office. It seems that this person, whilst working a reality warping spell, took it upon themselves to add a corridor of portals. Being a person of incredible abilities yourself, I thought you might know someone that could have taken up the job?'

'I'm sorry, dearie, I wish I could help. I don't get out much to socialise in my condition.'

'Really? The thing is Fungal said that the person that performed the spell was an old crone.'

'Did he now? Well, there are many old practitioners of magic on Ariest.'

The two magic users locked eyes. Neither one deviated their gaze. Trinity's mind raced as it tried to make sense of the situation. Tried to process and analyse the information. Uncertainty and weariness permeated within her. She couldn't do anything without concrete proof that Hyasda was that same person Fungal talked about. And, even if she was, what could she really do against someone with such power.

Just then, Tristan returned and the palpable tension immediately dropped a few levels.

'Perhaps you're right,' Trinity admitted. 'I'll ask around a bit more.'

'You do that dearie,' replied Hyasda. 'And if I should hear anything, I'll be sure to tell you.'

'Much appreciated.'

The youngsters said their farewells and as there made their way to the store exit, Hyasda picked up a bottle from her many shelves and discreetly disposed of its contents. 'Just a minute, Tristan,' she called. 'I seem to have run out of Lunar Weed also.

'Already? But I topped it up just the other day.'

'Yes, well you know Eamon Wolff, he's always wanting some potion or other. It's actually kind of time sensitive so I don't suppose you'd mind collecting the weed first.'

'Fine,' Tristan relented, 'we'll head to the Beltane forest first.'

Hyasda watched Trinity and Tristan leave her store. Once the door had closed, she magically locked it and quickly turned towards the back wall where she spoke the magical words to open her hidden sanctum. The old crone entered and the wall closed behind her.

ANOTHER PINE CONE WENT flying as a disgruntled Tristan kicked the woody cone in frustration. He had promised Trinity fun and excitement yet she now sat under a Linden Tree apparently sleeping.

Trinity suddenly stirred and smiled broadly. Whenever she was amongst nature, she always felt revitalised, as if the aura and energy of the forests recharged her own. That wasn't the only thing that alleviated her mood, however.

She had just spent time with Daniel on the Astral plane.

The dynamic between them had changed so much in such a short amount of time. It wasn't that long ago that they were meeting for the first time at high school. There had always been a connection, even then, but neither of them had known what it was or had the courage to make that first step.

Then there was the moment she had told Daniel about magic, and their friendship grew and grew from there, until the moment he was swallowed by The Shade, and she came face to face with her feelings towards him. Remembering how she felt when Daniel fully Awakened, and it became apparent that he was still alive brought a smile to her face. Thinking that you've lost the chance to tell someone you love them forces you to confront your fear of rejection, and she had faced her fear, eventually, and there wasn't a rejection in sight.

Tristan watched Trinity as she stood up and stretched. 'Did you have a nice sleep?' He took a small glass ball out of his bag and whispered a spell and a white light immediately shone from it.

'Relaxing is not sleeping,' Trinity replied. 'What's that for? I didn't know you knew magic.'

'A little. That Lunar Weed Hyasda wants only comes out during a full moon, this spell she taught me replicates it. She would happily have me to put down my sword for a spellbook instead, but that is not for me.'

'How often do you do these little jobs for her?'

'Whenever she needs me to.'

'What is the story between you two?'

'I owe her my life. She rescued me.'

'Rescued you? From what?'

Before Tristan could answer, Trinity held up her hand to stop him. She was in her element, almost as if she were one with the forest. As such, any threatening aura that passed through a forest, touched a tree, brushed through grass, trod on moss, was felt by the Druid. 'We're not alone,' Trinity whispered to Tristan.

The swordsman didn't react to the information he had just been given. He carried on with searching for the elusive weeds, only he paid more attention to their surroundings. Something was indeed off. The woods were deathly silent.

Years of combat had given Tristan a honed battle sense and combat reflexes and it was those skills that saved him now as a knife flew silently from the brush, missing his head by inches. He shone the light in the direction the weapon had come from.

Trinity was about to fire an eldritch bolt at the same place, when another assailant jumped down on her from the branches above.

With great skill and agility, she was able to roll through and regain her feet before unleashing her bolt at the unsuspecting attacker. Being the physical embodiment of the powers of nature, she liked to nickname it Nature's Wrath and it struck with all the fury the name suggested, slammed the attacker against a tree and left him slumped on the ground with a smouldering chest.

After a series of blocks, strikes, grapples and reversals, Tristan finally got the better of his assailant and took a closer look of him. 'Vekt! They're Shadow Dancers!' Before he could explain the implications of his discovery to Trinity however, he was set upon by three more of the deadly assassins.

He barely had time to draw his own sword before they attacked. It was like fighting a person who had three arms; if he parried one the other two attacked, if he blocked two, then the third would strike. He needed to reduce their number fast.

Tristan called out the magic words that illuminated his glass ball. A beam of white light shot up into the sky and, as he had hoped it would, caught the eye of the assassins, giving him the split second that he needed to, in one fluid motion, despatch two of the assailants and face up to the third.

Whilst her comrade had been tackling his three would be assassins, Trinity had been dealing with her own. She defeated them, easily manipulating the nature that was all around, and which she had a particular affinity for.

Things went well for the pair until more Shadow Dancers seemed to materialise from the forest. Fatigue and the superior numbers began to take their toll and shift the tide of the battle. Then Trinity felt a nick in her neck. It was a tiny dart, almost as small as the sting of the bee that it felt like.

Trinity glanced over at Tristan and saw the warrior hold his neck before he collapsed to one knee, still he attempted to hold back the assassins.

The sting must be laced with poison!

Although it didn't have the same fast effect on her, it did slow her down, and with Tristan out of the picture all of the Shadow Dancers now focused their attention on Trinity.

She felt several more stings as blows rained down on her from all directions. She was losing consciousness fast. But then, on the verge of blacking out, she heard renewed combat, flashes and the acrid smell of lightening. As she was dragged up off the ground, the last words that Trinity heard were that of a female.

'I *told* Gydion that it was too early for her.'

Chapter Fifteen

Ordinarily Gydion would have enjoyed exploring the ancient ziggurat but, unfortunately, his mind was filled with one thing only, the actions of Sayyidah.

When he had reunited with her again, he hoped that she had once more become the woman that he loved, justifying his decision to go against the council and spare her life, and for a time he believed that she had.

The time they had spent together, talking, touching, kissing, had told him that he was still intoxicated by her. Even the smell of her hair ignited memories of the passionate youth they once shared. The good times... but also the bad.

Gydion would be lying if he said that he hadn't been thinking about bringing her back to Ariest, hoping that she would want to return, wishing that they could start over.

But the vicious death of the Keeper could alter those plans, if not destroy them completely. He had to be sure of her innocence before making the mistake of accusing her again, after all, she herself could be in trouble; perhaps someone else killed the Keeper and took Sayyidah as prisoner.

Unfortunately, Gydion soon discovered that his worst fears had been realised.

He had been following the trail of blood droplets, allowing them to lead him through the ancient structure. They led him down into the core of the ziggurat, it's very centre by the Archmages estimations, where he eventually found Sayyidah.

She stood in what Gydion could only describe as, much to his bemusement, a cavern, complete with stalactites and stalagmites. He found it strange to find something so chaotic within the obvious order of the ziggurat, but then again nothing had been as it should be since he arrived in this strange realm.

A huge, craggy column of obsidian rock dominated the centre of the grotto. Gydion couldn't tell if it was originally from the ceiling of the cave or if it was shooting up from the ground, like a jet back geyser frozen in time.

'Sayyidah?' She continued to face the rock formation and didn't reply to Gydion's gentle call. He took a few tentative steps towards her. She seemed to have her arms clutched across her chest. 'Are you all right?' he asked, fearing that she may be injured.

'You want to know if I killed the Keeper?' As if in reply to her own question she held up her left arm; it was covered in blood up to her elbow. 'When he said you would have to kill him to read the book he was not lying, for it was stored within his body.' Sayyidah held up her right hand when she heard Gydion's sigh of disappointment and revealed the blood covered Book of Secrets. 'What I do, I do for you, my love.'

Gydion didn't know how to react. He would be lying if he said he wasn't intrigued by what esoteric doctrine lay between the covers of the tome, but he was distressed by the lengths Sayyidah was willing to go to retrieve it. Although he hadn't been privy to her plans, he still felt some guilt since it was his astral battle that had given her the opportunity to mutilate the poor man.

'Forget him, Gydion. If it truly is your wish to learn about Salamida then he had to die. He knew what his job entailed when he took it.'

'That still does not make it right.'

'Really? Even if this book holds the knowledge to save millions of lives? Spare one life and condemn millions? You had no such qualms when it came to being rid of me, my love.'

She was right; he knew she was. This was the same rationale he had used to stop her, although he had not gone so far as to end her life as she had the Keepers, the motivation was identical. No matter how it made Gydion feel perhaps what she had done could not be avoided, perhaps it was a necessary evil that had to be committed for the better good.

Gydion stood behind Sayyidah now and placed his hands on her shoulders. He gave a reassuring squeeze to let her know that he was with her and stood by her and the decision she had made, then he moved his hand along her arm until he took hold of the book of secrets.

Again, Sayyidah smiled with sinister triumph and again it was obscured from Gydion. She was so close to her ultimate goal it was making her giddy with excitement, but she had to keep it bottled inside, exposing herself now would be disastrous. For decades she had been devising her plan and now it had almost come to fruition. The time was almost at hand. The time when everyone would feel the wrath of a woman scorned.

She didn't turn to watch Gydion read the book; she didn't have to. She could imagine him in her mind hungrily digesting the words as she heard him flip over each read page.

He is no doubt revelling at learning the truth about the Tuatha, Sayyidah mused. Learning that they, the first race, mighty dragons once worshipped as gods and still treated as deities by their elemental descendants. Learning that when the four ruling brothers, Boreas, Zephyrus, Notus and Eurius decided that the time of the Tuatha was at an end and a new age dawning, were set upon by one of their own, an ambitious dragon god named Baelthorn.

It would chart the battles of the Great Upheaval, retell the skirmishes, the realms that were created from the cosmic fallout but, crucially for him, it would omit how one was able to stand against four for so long and almost win.

'It does not say anything about Salamida,' Gydion finally stated.

'*That* is the true secret of the book and such esoteric wisdom cannot be obtained so easily.'

'Why did you not say so earlier?'

'Because there is but one way to reveal them and I did not think you would be willing.'

'And why is that?'

'Because it would involve you returning my magic to me.' She could feel his sceptical gaze upon her. 'As I said,' she continued, 'you would not be willing.'

'But you must surely realise why.'

'And you must realise that the Book of Secrets was created by the four brothers of the ruling family and the elements they controlled.'

'Water, air, fire and earth.'

'And it would take all four to reach the truth.'

'An elemental key for an elemental book? That makes sense. All four brothers would be needed to open the seal, so that would suggest a deliberate action that they would all have to agree upon so it could not be accessed accidentally...but what kind of secrets would need that level of protection?'

Sayyidah felt that Gydion's mind was beginning to reason things out, restrain his enthusiasm, a situation that was detrimental to her plans. She had to keep his mind on the agenda, remind him why he was here and hope it was enough for him to throw caution to the wind.

'The secrets to save Ariest,' Sayyidah stated as she turned to face Gydion.

'Which beggars the question, how do you know so much about it?'

'What, do you think I have sat here idly waiting for the great Gydion to give me a reprieve?' she venomously spat, 'I have explored my surroundings, learnt what I can to survive here, done what I have had to do.'

'And what of the Keepers claims?'

'What do you want me to say? I am here because of you if you expected me to simply roll over and die then you were sorely mistaken.'

'To be fair, I think I have only ever expected the unexpected of you, Sayyidah.'

Gydion knew that there was only one real course of action for him to take. If he wished to learn about Salamida and the Shade he would have to do as Sayyidah suggested and return her magic. But that didn't mean that he couldn't take precautions.

As much as he wanted to, he felt that he couldn't really trust every word she said. She used them like they were chess pieces being moved on a board. Deception and manipulation were areas that she excelled at; she'd dangle her King in front of you just enough to draw you into making a mistake then the game was over.

It was hard to know the truth from the lies. The trick was to play her game but, crucially, figure out her endgame before she reached it, something he failed to do last time. But *then* he hadn't been expecting any betrayal.

'So how do you suggest we do this?' Gydion eventually asked.

'You return my fire and water magics and then, whilst holding the book, we each channel one through each of our arms—'

'Thus, imbuing it with all four at once... but I think *I* will keep hold of the fire spells along with air.'

'What, no trust, Gydion? Do you think I will set your robes alight and let hells fire consume you? And yet you had no qualms with entering my bed... is that why it was *so* intense?'

'I believe it was no more intense than the last time.'

'Perhaps you are correct,' she agreed with a coy smile as she had a moments recollection whilst Gydion began to make the preparations to cast the spell.

The conjuration Gydion had used all those years ago was the Spell of Transferral. It was an invocation usually used by dark mages to steal the magic from an opponent and involved a long laborious ritual to cast it. But Gydion had adapted the components of the spell for his own uses; instead of the magic energy being absorbed by a person, it could be stored within an inanimate object. An object such as the rough, uncut crystal he fished from the inside of his robes.

A deep-purple energy slowly swirled within the gemstone as Gydion held it up to his face and made the final decision to go through with the transfer reversal. But just as he was about to begin, however, he felt the numbing, probing assault on his mind once more, stronger than either of the previous times, and still he had no idea where it was coming from. He suddenly felt fatigued like his energy levels were dropping, however, as he flared his Essence and cleared the miasma in his mind, Gydion was once more rejuvenated, and cautiously began the ritual.

Chapter Sixteen

Daniel heard a voice. He couldn't discern what it was saying or who it was, it sounded so far away, but as his astral body returned to his physical one and he became more aware of the immediate world around him, Daniel knew it was Finn that was shaking him.

'Ow,' he said rubbing his head after the jarring return of his ethereal form.

'What are you doing? It's like you were having the sleep of the dead.'

'I wasn't sleeping. I was travelling the astral realm.'

Finn looked at him with a blank expression. 'I see,' she replied. 'Maybe next time you should put a do not disturb sign.'

'I may just do that, especially with you around. Anyway, what have you been up to?'

'Well, your dad has been teaching me some moves. We're taking a break now, so I thought I'd check up on you, see how you are after yesterday.'

'How do you think?' He looked down, unable to make eye contact. 'I did nothing... just let it happen.'

'Your dad thinks you did the right thing.'

'You told him?'

'Of course,' Finn said as she sat next to Daniel. 'The way you went storming upstairs last night, your parents knew something happened.'

'Great! So, he knows I embarrassed myself in front of you.'

'What? No! I told you he said you did the right thing.'

'That's bull! When I told him about me punching Bobby you should have seen the pride in his face.'

'But that happened before he found out about you being a mage, right? He knows the abilities magic users possess, that they have the potential to make someone cease to exist. He was proud that you didn't. He also said something about great power and responsibility or some vekt.'

'Spider-Man.'

'What? You have Spider-Men here?'

'No, it's - forget it. You know, all I've ever wanted to do was make my parents proud. But I've seen the way you react around my dad, the way you look at him with reverence. How can I ever hope to be like him?'

'But he's a legend! He's fought wyverns, dire wolves, conquered many quests—'

'And I can't face up to one bully?'

'I didn't say that! Bullies are more powerful than you think. They latch onto a thing, something that makes you different to them, something that you don't like about yourself or they think you don't like and they keep needling you about it over and over again until you start believing it and then you start hearing it everywhere you turn thinking that everyone you see is saying the same thing.'

Daniel squeezed her hand. 'It sounds like you're talking from experience.'

'They tried to bully me once,' Finn admitted. 'No parents, not the most girly of girls, more likely to be in overalls than a frilly dress, but Uncle Quinn was always there for me. I didn't give a vekt what the bullies had to say after a while and I kicked every bodies ass. Why do you think I'm so good at fighting?'

'This is a different world, Finn. You can't go around beating up everyone that has a bad word to say about you.'

'You don't have to, Daniel. Just one.'

'Bobby?'

'No, yourself.'

Daniel stared at Finn with his brow creased in confusion.

'I've seen your courage and strength on Ariest, Daniel,' said Finn. 'You were swallowed by the Shade and you fought your way out. It may be a different world but it's the same you, Daniel.'

He thought about what Finn said. Could she be right? Is it really that simple? Could it just be a simple case of switching your mind-set? No, it must be more than that. On earth he was shy, that much he knew. On Ariest nobody looked at him differently so he felt more able to open up and be himself, his true self. But Ariest brought its own dilemmas, living up to the Mondragon name paramount among them.

What she said made Daniel look deeply into himself, at the person he was and the person he wanted to be, two sides of the same coin. It was true that his life on Earth and his experiences on Ariest had been completely different. They had shown him that he had the potential to be more. But he felt that he could never be that person on Earth.

There would always be another bobby. The easiest solution would just be to go to Ariest and never come back. However, was running away really the answer to all his problems?

'Hey, you guys better come down here!'

If Daniel and Finn had been listening a little harder, they may have discerned a hint of worry in Eric's voice as he called them from the living room. He stood in front of the tv watching a news report with folded arms and a stern look on his face.

'What is it, Dad?'

Eric didn't reply but simply pointed to the screen and continued to watch the news. Daniel was intrigued. What was so interesting that it held his dad's attention so firmly. After bidding Finn to sit down, he took a seat next to her on the sofa himself and turned his attention to the TV.

It wasn't what he was expecting.

A girl who lived in Swiss Cottage had gone missing in suspicious circumstances. Her bedroom windows were locked from the inside, as were all the other windows in the apartment. Her parents were downstairs watching tv at the time she had gone to bed and stated that it was impossible for anyone to have gone in or out whilst they were there.

'It's got to be the parents,' Finn said as she got up to find something to eat. 'What else could it be?'

'That's what I thought... at first,' said Eric.

Daniel picked up on the little throwaway comment. 'What do you mean "at first"?'

'I mean there have been others.' Eric pulled out a folder from the bookshelf and tossed it on the coffee table in front of Daniel.

Finn came back to the sofa to see what Daniel was looking at. She read over his shoulder the newspaper clippings that he spread across the table. There were seven other disappearances, all in similar circumstances. 'Vekt!'

'Exactly,' Eric agreed. 'Before Gydion left for Salamida he came here. He told Tina and myself what had happened to you, Daniel, and also about fungal and his corridor. He told me to look out for anything out of the ordinary...'

'There's nothing ordinary about these disappearances, that's for sure,' Daniel pointed out.

'... because he believed the Shade, one or more, could possibly use the portals to get to any and all dimensions.'

'You're trying to tell me that the Shade are here on Earth?' Daniel couldn't believe what he was hearing. These creatures terrorised Ariest, a place that readily had magic and killed countless people there. What kind of devastation could they cause here, in a world that had no defence against them, a world that didn't even know they existed?

'It seems that everything that we believed about the Shade was wrong. We always thought they were mindless creatures. That they did nothing but feed on people's Essence,' Eric said in recollection.

'I don't get it,' admitted Finn. 'What makes you think that isn't the case? Daniel told me that this world has no magic, no Mage Assembly, no Mage Academy so people here would not have developed huge amounts of Essence.'

'That's true.'

'So why come here? If I'm hungry, the last place I'm going to is somewhere with little food.'

'Exactly, you wouldn't. Unless you had to, unless you were told to, unless you were following someone's command.'

'But that still doesn't answer the question, why? What's so special about this place?'

Daniel had heard enough. He had listened to all the talk; why is the creature here? Who sent it? 'It doesn't matter! What about Sharon and David?' He pushed two paper cuttings forward, one about a five-year-old girl missing from St John's Wood, the other about another five-year-old, a boy from Great Portland Street. 'And now this nine-year-old girl from Swiss Cottage. We're the only ones that know what's really going on, the only ones that can do anything about it and what are we doing? Sitting around and talking. I've been inside a Shade, the bleak nothingness within them. Slowly being drained of your Essence. It's no place for a child. We're up against the clock here, they may be dead already, but if we waste any more time, then they will be for sure.'

The silence that followed his embittered speech made Daniels cheeks warm. It wasn't until that moment that he realised it was easier for him to defend strangers than it was to stand up for himself, by how carried away with emotion he had become, as he got things off his chest about the whole situation.

However, he needn't have felt embarrassed. The pride in Eric's face said as much and Finn beamed at Daniel too.

'That's us told, Finn,' Eric said as he squeezed Daniels shoulder. 'Don't worry, son, we'll save those kids and the others. We just need a plan.'

'Well, I kind of have a plan - of sorts,' revealed Daniel. 'It's actually quite simple to be honest. Do you remember how it came after me in the forest, Finn?' She nodded and Daniel continued. 'Basically, we have to offer it something more irresistible than anything around, namely me.' He glanced at their faces, tried to gage what they thought.

'That's the Daniel I know,' smiled Finn, 'brave and courageous. I told you Daniel, you're you wherever you are.'

Eric looked concerned. 'You're happy to be the bait?'

'Not really,' Daniel admitted, 'But I know that it can't really work any other way. Neither of you have the levels of Essence to pull it off.'

Eric nodded. 'The disappearances seem to be around central London so we should probably head there.' After seeing that everyone was in agreement, he moved to a display cabinet that Daniel knew had been in the family before he was born. 'When I made this,' Eric began, 'I never thought that I would be the one to open it again. I had left instructions, with a lawyer, about it, if anything were to happen to me, so you could open it, Daniel. Inside is your legacy.'

Daniels eyebrows creased. He was more baffled than ever. He had driven his cars toys into it plenty of times as a kid and at no time had he ever had so much as an inkling to suggest that it was anything more than a cabinet to display his parents favourite crystals.

Next to him Finn was beside herself with excitement. 'Oh my god! Oh my god! Oh my god! I know what it is! It has to be! There's nothing else it could be!'

Eric reached over the top of the display cabinet and pressed a hidden depression. There was a 'click' sound and the glass shelving front unit eased forward. He pulled it forward some more, exposing the hidden hinges that allowed him to swing the unit aside.

Finn shouted and almost gave Daniel a heart attack. 'I knew it!'

Inside was the golden armour Eric wore as commander of the Athanatoi, dust and time had not touched it as it gleamed as if it had just been made.

Hanging in front of the armour was two-handed, double-edged sword. The hilt was something to behold. Its golden pommel was intricately etched. Red leather wrapped the grip. Its gold cross guard was finely detailed to resemble the spread wings of a dragon. The ricasso or blade grip was wrapped in the same red leather as the hand grip and the long silver blade itself was fullered and glinted brightly under the light, also seemingly untouched by rust or grime.

'The Dragon Claymore,' Finn breathed reverently. Her mouth fell open and she stared at the blade with an unblinking, fixed gaze. The sword was just as big of a legend as Eric was and she imagined it in action, slicing this way and that, dispatching foe after foe.

Taking the sword down from where it hung, Eric gripped the hilt and held it close. 'Hello, old friend,' he whispered.

Daniel had to admit, with that amazing sword in his hands, his dad cut an impressive figure. The man, who he had known to be a construction foreman all his life, was gone. This was the first time he had been in the presence of Eric Mondragon, the hero, the legend.

And it was rather daunting.

Chapter Seventeen

Sayyidah looked on intensely with her dark eyes. She was barely conscious when he had cast the Spell of Transferral on her, after her defeat, and had only caught quick glimpses of him performing the conjuration. Some of it she recognised, having performed the ritual herself to steal the magic from another, something she had never confessed to Gydion.

Being familiar with the components of the original spell allowed the Egyptian to spot some of the changes Gydion had applied. She watched his lips move as he soundlessly recited his incantations, and reflected how pointless she thought the spell to be; why steal someone's magic only to imprison it, when you could have it for yourself?

As Gydion performed the necessary gestures for the ritual, a large diameter circle appeared on the ground around him, then a second smaller one within the first. Finally, runic lettering slowly wrote themselves inside the circles. When they were complete, they flared with bright magical power and a mystic gust blew throughout the cavern, fluttering the robes of the two mages, at which point Gydion thrust the stone towards Sayyidah and the purple energy held within it was sent slithering through the air like a serpent until it penetrated the chest of its rightful owner, who gladly welcomed it. Sayyidah's three meridians glowed, one by one, as they once more had magical energy flowing between them.

Although Gydion had been true to his word and only returned the Personal, Planetary and Realmic essence pertaining to water and earth spells, Sayyidah was ecstatic to be partially whole once more. It was like welcoming back an old lover, for in truth that's what it was; she loved nothing more than her magic and she was desperate to feel it now.

The Egyptian began to cast a spell and she couldn't help but smile broadly as she noticed Gydion adopt a defensive stance.

He had several spells prepared and ready in his mind just in case Sayyidah did try a foolish attack but he was relieved when she was suddenly propelled into the air by a watery vortex.

She just needed to let off some steam, Gydion thought. *Understandable really, considering she has been without for so long. I would no doubt feel the same as her.*

He observed her go from spell to spell and was a little surprised to see her do it so effortlessly. To be a master of the mystic arts involved continuous study, even an Archmage must reinforce his knowledge regularly. Sayyidah had been without such texts for decades, so seeing her go through the chants, gestures and movements with such perfection came as quite a shock to the on looking mage.

One minute she was making it rain, then hail then a freezing blizzard. Finally satisfied that her water spells were still up to par she decided to try her hand at a few earth spells; Boulder, Rock Shower, Golem all performed perfectly.

'That was impressive,' Gydion smiled as Sayyidah sauntered proudly over to where he stood.

Perhaps too impressive, Sayyidah thought, hoping she had not shown her hand to early.

'To think that you still perfectly recall all those spells...'

'Almost as if they never left me,' she said happily, then seeing Gydion about to press her further on the subject she cut him off. 'Now, shall we open the secrets of the book?'

He took a moment to think things through again. He was almost certain that things were not as they seemed but he had to play along and hoped that the throbbing in his head didn't impede him too much if indeed he had to implement his precautionary plans.

'Very well,' Gydion finally replied as he held out the Book of Secrets before him in both hands. His estranged wife took hold of the other end of the book and whilst looking into his eyes told him to begin.

They recited their spells, Gydion calling on the powers of fire and air, Sayyidah that of water and earth, all the while concentrating on diverting each element down either side of their body.

It wasn't long before the book responded to their elemental touches and began to draw the energy into itself before redirecting it in four coloured beams, red, white, blue and brown, towards the obsidian rock.

The elemental streams of magic swirled around one another, coalesced and separated until they struck the mass. Gydion was expecting it to explode at the impact, but instead it began to melt and become a black oozing puddle.

As the rock receded, it became apparent to the curious Archmage that something was inside. He soon concluded that it wasn't some*thing* but some*one* when two arms were revealed, then legs, torso and finally a head.

Although the ooze was still prevalent on the being Gydion could see that it was a male almost seven feet in height and stood with his hands clenched in front of his thighs in a strong defiant pose.

Then he opened his eyes, as black as a moonless night. 'Finally, Baelthorn is free!'

Gydion looked on in awe and trepidation as he realised that once more, Sayyidah was outplaying him. 'Goddess preserve us,' he whispered.

Gydion glared at Sayyidah with disdain. He had allowed his affection for her to cloud his judgement and she had used that knowledge to her advantage. She had tempted him with her story about the Book of Secrets being the key to unimaginable power. She had manipulated him into battling the Keeper, so that she might retrieve the tome by murdering the innocent man. Perhaps the book did have such mysteries, but what she failed to tell him was that it was also the key to releasing the fallen god, Baelthorn.

'Free! Free at last!' roared Baelthorn. 'You do not know how it feels to have the full use of my faculties once more and to be able to return to my true form after all these millennia.

Gydion could sense the power radiating from the huge dark-haired man that stood before him. Suddenly, the man transformed and, in his place, stood a magnificent black dragon. Its immense size filled most of the cavern; spikes ran down from the top of its head to the tip of its tail, which was the same length as that of its body and gently thumped the ground, its overlapping armoured scales were so dark that light seemed to be absorbed by them and when Baelthorn spread his vast leathery wings and flapped them several times, the gusts it created buffeted Gydion who had to cast a spell to strengthen his body against the winds so as not to appear weak before the dragon god. He wished, however, he could find a similar spell to calm his pounding heart.

# Chapter Eighteen

It was early evening; rush hour and Oxford Circus was as busy as always. The area had a long and somewhat checkered history; from being part of a Roman road, to being the former capital punishment site of prisoners from the notorious Newgate Prison, now demolished. From attracting street traders, confidence tricksters and ladies of the night to being the home of the UK's first department stores, Oxford Street and Oxford Circus had established itself as the busiest shopping street in Europe.

Now it was to be the site of a confrontation the likes of which no London street had witnessed before.

Daniel, Finn and Eric arrived on the famous street and moved within the Niketown foyer, off the street, where it was quieter, so that they might go over their plan one last time. Although it was a simple strategy, go to a populated area and attract the Essence vampire, it wasn't without its elements of risk and it also revealed another dilemma.

'We've been so focused on destroying this Shade that we've all forgotten a very important detail,' said Eric.

Finn glanced at the hero as she excitedly checked her guns, eager to get them firing again. 'What's that?'

'We can't fight the Shade here. We can't use our abilities in public view or expose them to magic,' Eric said as he clutched the wrapped-up dragon claymore. 'We need to lure it to somewhere less crowded.'

'This plan is getting crappier by the minute.'

'It was your plan, son.'

'Don't remind me,' he sighed. 'I think I know a place, though. The Brewer Street underground carpark. Once we sight the Shade, I'll make my way there.'

'You think you can outrun it?' Finn was concerned about this new twist in the plan.

Daniel shrugged. 'No idea. But I'm good at running so I'll treat it like my other bully. More importantly, you two need to keep up. You can't be too far behind because as soon as I get to the carpark, I need it to swallow me and not just drain me then and there. Don't forget that this needs to be a two-pronged attack.'

'Don't worry, we'll be there,' his father reassured.

'Of course, we will! Eric and Finn, the new legendary duo, have got your back!' She kissed Daniel on the cheek and whispered, 'For luck, not that you'll need it.'

The trio stepped back out into Oxford Circus and waited.

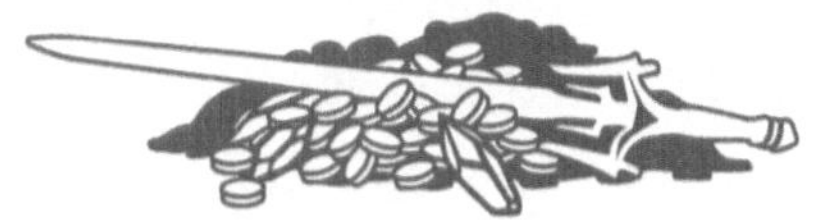

OFF OXFORD STREET WEST, not far from the Double Tree hotel, was Bryanston Street. Inside the multi-storey carpark, on that street, was a white ford transit van. None of the staff knew how long it had been parked, it just kind of appeared there one day. Nor did they know who owned it, but its fees seemed to be covered indefinitely. They assumed that someone must have been attending to it, however, because it never appeared to have a speck of dust on it. So, the staff no longer payed it any mind.

Even if they were to watch the van on their CCTV nothing out of the ordinary would appear on their monitors. At that moment it was bouncing and rocking with ever more vigour, yet through the security cams all seemed passive, neither did they pick up the light that was shining through the gaps of the van.

Just as suddenly as all the activity with the van begun it stopped.

The door at the back opened and a female with a feline appearance pounced out. Sleek red fur with black and white stripes covered her whole body. She had pointed ears and large green eyes with slit pupils and her teeth were sharp with pronounced canines. Her ears twitched and her tail gently swayed as she sniffed the air, her superior senses to took stock of her surroundings.

'It's all clear,' she said over her shoulder in a language not of this world. She was satisfied that no one was nearby.

The next being to emerge from the van was some 8 feet tall with equine hind legs, the heel bones of which extended beyond the hock joint and were exposed. 'Another dreary realm? What joy,' he said.

'Do not worry, Borion,' a boy child with sallow skin and sunken cheeks said as he jumped down from the vehicle. 'It will be a quick operation as always, will it not, Ferin?'

'That is up to you, little one,' Ferin replied. The final person to exit the vehicle stood tall and had the air of command about him. His white hair was pulled back and tied into a single long braid. He stroked his long white goatee as he surveyed the area, his eyes blinked with four lids. 'Can you feel our target, Jostin?'

The boy closed his eyes a moment to concentrate. 'Yes, I can. Not far from here, maybe less than a Cuton.'

'Music to my ears,' Borion smiled.

'Mine too,' Katrin said as her tail caressed his cheek.

Ferin looked at his comrades. Looked at his band of refugees, his family. They had been through a lot together and they would go through a lot more. Starting with the elimination of their target. 'Let us begin.'

The four travellers stood in a circle. Ferin put his right fist into the middle followed by Borion, Katrin and Jostin. He then bit into the index finger of his left hand until a drop of his indigo blood appeared at which point, he touched the back of each fist with it before putting the finger to his forehead.

For the next part of the ritual they had performed so many times before, the group's leader closed his eyes and spoke some words of magic. A third eye opened on his forehead where he had placed his bloodied fingerprint. Ferin continued to chant as he reopened his eyes. All three took on an ice-blue colour. The same colour suddenly pulsed through his veins, from his forehead down his right arm and into his fist. From there it spread up the arm of the three that touched his and into their foreheads, opening a third eye on each.

The ceremony was complete. They now each had a portion of Ferin's magic.

'Let's make a move,' Ferin commanded. One by one they began to imbue an artefact, which they each wore on their left wrist, with arcane energies. Once completed they all began to vanish, to camouflage and meld into the environment.

ONE THING THAT WAS reliable about the weather in London, was that the weather in London was unreliable. The rain poured down relentlessly. Daniel was soaked through and he cursed his lot as he looked over at his dad and Finn, still standing in the Niketown entrance. They had been joined by several other people, all desperate to shelter from the rain.

Finn mouthed "I'm sorry" at her bedraggled friend.

'If I could, I'd get him an umbrella,' said Eric with regret.

'I know,' Finn replied, 'but since we don't know where the Shade will pop up it would be too dangerous because an umbrella would block his view. I'm sure Daniel knows that too. I still feel sorry for him though. I wish this creature would hurry up.'

It was a sentiment echoed by Daniel. He didn't know how long he had been waiting but, the way time worked, he had a feeling that it wasn't as long as he felt it was. Fortunately, he honestly didn't mind the rain. He leaned his head back and closed his eyes. He liked to feel the pitter patter on his face, it was almost therapeutic.

His mind was cluttered with thoughts; about Trinity and Finn, about the legend that was his father, Eric Mondragon, about studying to become a mage, what that looked like, about Bobby, about The Mortokai.

Daniel opened his eyes. As the cold droplets made him blink, he wished the rain could wash away all his confusion and self-doubts and give him clarity of thought.

That's when Daniel thought he saw it. Out of the corner of his eye, the shadows above the Microsoft store seemed to ripple. He straightened up and focussed on the area.

Eric, who had been keeping a firm eye on his son, saw the change in demeanour of Daniel, saw him become more alert. 'It may be time,' the warrior said to Finn as he followed Daniel's gaze.

'I'm ready, commander,' Finn replied.

It was something Eric hadn't been called in a long time and he was startled to hear it again. He turned to see Finn grinning up at him and he smiled back before they both watched and waited for Daniel to make a move.

They didn't have long to wait.

Just as Daniel was beginning to think that his imagination was playing tricks on him, above the H&M's store he saw the shadows ripple. A feeling of fear came over him. All along he had hoped they were wrong about The Shade being on Earth, but seeing it here, now, remembering what it was like inside the creature, made his blood run cold. He began to wonder, what could they possibly do to stop it? It was no point fighting back. They should just let it do what it wanted. He should tell his dad not to bother.

However, when he looked over at his dad and Finn, he could see them frantically trying to gain his attention as they ran towards him. He couldn't hear what they were shouting over the noise of the people, the traffic driving on the wet tarmac and a strange sound of rushing wind. But as they got closer, he heard them.

Run.

He woke up from the miasma that had descended upon him and saw the wide maw of The Shade beneath him, drawing on his Essence. Daniel reacted instantly and ran across the road, zig zagging through the traffic.

It wasn't the time for manners as Daniel barged pass several people on his way down Regent Street towards Piccadilly Circus. The rain had forced some of the people not prepared for the changeable London weather, to take shelter, but there was still enough on the streets to be an obstacle. He was literally in a race for his life and he wasn't about to lose it for the sake of etiquette.

Daniel was beginning to think that this was the worse idea that he had ever come up with. How could he ever hope to escape from a creature that could use the shadows to travel. Beside him, he could see it, moving swiftly from dark recess to dark recess. Occasionally it would reach out an elongated arm and then withdraw it. The creature was toying with him.

'I'm sorry,' Finn called out to Eric as they chased Daniel.

'For what?'

'This!' Finn suddenly drew her guns without breaking stride and started firing at The Shade. She knew Eric had said not to expose themselves to the public, but Daniel wasn't going to get away. She had to do something.

With her phenomenal sharpshooting ability, shot after shot from Finn's steam powered guns struck home against The Shade, forcing it to retreat momentarily and giving Daniel valuable seconds.

People whooped and hollered, wondered if they were, unbeknownst, part of some guerrilla filming or if she was a cosplayer. Eric slowed down to make sure no one had captured it on their phone and that nothing too serious was being discussed, then he heard someone ask about her crazy guns. At which point he looked up and saw a sign. 'She got them from Hamleys,' he replied before he set off after Finn, who had kept up her pursuit, completely unaware of the stir she had caused behind her.

Having reached Piccadilly Circus, Daniel navigated through the perpetual crowds and headed left, up Shaftesbury Avenue, London's West End theatre district. It wasn't long before he was making another left onto Great Windmill Street.

He neared his goal.

At the end of this Street was the Brewer Street Carpark. Daniel hadn't seen anything of The Shade since Finn started shooting it. Even though it went against what they had all planned, keeping a low profile and all, he was glad that she was a rule breaker because if she hadn't, he knew he wouldn't have made it.

Daniel checked behind him as he crossed the road and ran into the carpark. There was no sign of Finn or his dad, so he stopped just inside the entrance momentarily. He just hoped that they were nearby because even though he couldn't see the creature, he knew it wasn't far.

'Come on, come on,' Daniel impatiently willed them on. His heart pounded; partially from the run but also because he knew The Shade could descend at any time. Then he saw Finn around the corner shortly followed by his dad.

This was it. The final countdown. This was where they turned the tables and fought back. Daniel just needed to find a suitable battlefield; level two only had a few cars. Perfect!

Unfortunately, it was the perfect environment for The Shade also, and it wasted no time in claiming its prize. Elongated arms extended from the darkness above and grabbed hold of Daniel's wrists. They pulled him up into the air as a black, shapeless mass slowly formed below him. A large mouth opened up and began to feast on the Essence of the terrified youngster.

Daniel felt like he was fading fast. He could feel his Essence draining away more rapidly than it had before. He seriously doubted that he would be able to hold out for Finn and Eric to arrive.

Then he turned his head and saw the reason why he was being drained so quickly. Daniel saw ripples in the darkness. They had all assumed that it had been one Shade that was involved in the disappearances but, in actual fact it had been three.

Chapter Nineteen

Sayyidah looked angrily at Gydion. 'You should be kneeling before him instead of fooling yourself into thinking you are his equal!' Sayyidah spat.

'Allow him his moment of defiance, my love,' roared Baelthorn, his booming voice echoed around the cavern. 'Let him believe that he is significant, after all, he was your leader and lover once, that should afford him some benefits, but rest assured he shall kneel and worship before his returning god like everyone else.'

'You are no god to me, Baelthorn. To me you are nothing more than someone whom over reached and was put in his place by his siblings.'

'Why do you provoke me, mortal, when you know I can kill you so easily? Do you wish to feel the wrath of the black wyrm? But to reward the one that has released me from my purgatory with death would not be fitting of the benevolent deity that I am.' The ancient being reverted back to its humanoid form and drew Sayyidah towards him. 'And you, my dear, I have yet to reward you for your endeavours, either.' Baelthorn kissed Sayyidah with ferocity. Gydion could barely hide his discomfort at the display and this gave the would-be god pleasure.

'Do not look so hurt, Gydion, for she was to be mine long before she had ever heard your name, but she was a rebellious girl then and was bewitched by another before she was finally taken by your Master Penwyll to become a mage, but this was always her destiny.'

'Her destiny? How can that be? The Tuatha are unknown in our realm.'

'You doubt me, mage? Your myths and legends are littered with dragons. Only the unenlightened do not know this. In ancient Egypt there was a cult to me, the Cult of the Black Wyrm, and it was then that the young Sayyidah was given to me.'

'A sacrifice by a cult no doubt long dead, yet you still claim their offering.'

'The true believers of my cult knew I would return one day, my priests still called to me, and now I have, with your unwitting help. And as your reward you shall spread the word as my special envoy, along with Sayyidah and reintroduce the Cult of the Black Wyrm to your realm.'

'Envoy? I am very happy with my present role so I will not be the envoy of anything.'

'This was not an offer, little mage. You are in no position to refuse me.'

'I told you he would not accept, Lord Baelthorn. His sense of righteousness would not allow him to abandon the people of Ariest.'

'I am their Archmage, it is my duty to stand up for them.'

'As you did when Sayyidah led an army of Shade to that realm. You defeated them, eventually, and banished the woman you called wife here. Ironically the same mistake my siblings made.'

'Why would you turn against your kin?'

'They turned against me!' Baelthorn spat in a rage. The dragon lord regained himself before he continued, 'In the chaos ether, before form took place, there were many entities. We battled for supremacy of our realm and the Tuatha finally won out. In the ensuing peace my brethren rejected any form of hierarchy instead choosing equality. I fought like no other in the chaos and was rewarded with nothing! So, I decided to take what I deserved.

'We Tuatha believed there was nothing beyond our realm, but I found that to be untrue. I discovered a portal that brought me to this marvellous dimension, Salamida. It is a living entity, older than the Tuatha and, just like black dragons, it is an essence vampire much like myself, but it feeds on the power of worlds, through their ley lines, not individuals.'

'So, you thought to usurp the power of the realm and use it for yourself? This does not sound very godly or divine. To me it sounds like someone hungry for dominance, a control freak, so to speak.'

'Still you persist.'

'I do. For the simple fact that I do not think you can do anything about it. No self-respecting 'deity' would repeatedly take this affront. And yet you do, like a powerless common... lizard.'

The angered Baelthorn unleashed a rage filled force bolt at Gydion, just as the Archmage had hoped he would. If Gydion was to escape he had to know what he was faced up against. Luckily, he had been proven right in regards to not trusting Sayyidah with her full powers and from what he remembered about the Tuatha civil war and the punishment meted out against Baelthorn when he was defeated, he too would be weakened. The question was, by how much?

The shield Gydion threw up was struck hard by Baelthorn's bolt. Two or three more such attacks would be enough to bring it down, he surmised. The dragon lord must have succeeded with his spell and had indeed been syphoning power from the realm. Was he at full power? Probably not, thought Gydion. But he knew one thing, if he was to get out of this situation, he would have to come up with something quick.

Baelthorn's hands glowed red as he began to draw upon his powers once more. 'We had hoped you would see the light and join us, but since it is your wish to be extinguished, so be it. Feel the full might of a god!'

Just as the dragon lord was about to unleash his eldritch barrage Sayyidah threw up her hand. 'Halt!' she commanded.

It would appear that things are not as they seem, Gydion thought to himself as he looked from Baelthorn to Sayyidah. *Which one of you is the master pulling on the puppet's strings?*

'You have had a small taste of what you are up against, Gydion. In your heart of hearts, you know you cannot win. Join us, do not force my hand and have you destroyed.'

'Perhaps you have not heard but I am the Archmage, I am no slouch in the power department.'

'Is that so? For all your vaulted power and ability, husband, you always seem to miss the small things and that is why you will never defeat me.'

'I seem to remember defeating you before.'

'Is that what you think? I conceded that battle so that I might win the war. It never ended for me, Gydion, I just made a tactical withdrawal and allowed you to think you were victorious, but in truth you have been out played for some fifty years. Whilst you lived your life with your apparent guilt of sending me here, I have been moving my pieces into position waiting, biding my time, until the moment to play my hand. Do you know the first move I played? It was so long ago and even now you do not realise.' She leaned closer, her lips gently brushed Gydion's ear as she whispered, 'I am not the true Sayyidah. She never left Ariest.'

Chapter Twenty

The plan had gone wrong. Horribly wrong. On a scale of how wrong it was, it would be right up there with Neville Chamberlain's "peace for our time" speech. But when things go wrong at this kind of level, casualties are not far behind. And Daniel knew that he was about to become one.

It had always been a dangerous plan, with plenty of risk on his part, but it had been a measured risk; that he had enough Essence to hold out against a Shade until Finn and his dad arrived. It most probably would have worked, but against three Shade it was a different story; his Essence was all but depleted.

The last time he had been completely drained of Essence, Trinity had been there keeping him alive, when he was in a coma, by sharing her own. But this time there was no Trinity to save him.

'I'm scared,' he whispered as tears began to well up in his eyes. 'I don't want to die. Not now I've found a new life to live. Not now that I have Trinity.' Daniel began to violently struggle against the restraints, unfortunately it was too little too late. His energy left him as he closed his eyes and slumped over.

This time Daniel was done.

'Daniel!' Eric screamed as he charged onto the parking level. The sight of the lifeless body of his son falling into the mouth of The Shade caused him to lose his composure and throw caution to the wind. Instead of remaining with Finn, Eric dived into The Shade after his son, leaving Finn to battle alone.

'So, it's just you and me now,' Finn grinned broadly. 'I hope you're ready to get a beating because you're going to pay for what you did to Daniel.' Finn's bravado suddenly vanished as she saw not one but two Shade descend from the dark shadows of the carpark ceiling. 'Oh vekt!'

WAS THIS DEATH? Daniel wondered as he opened his eyes and found himself in an empty void. *No angels with trumpets, no devils with pitchforks. Just emptiness?* It was like being in a black hole. *Where am I?*

'Everywhere and nowhere,' replied a voice, a glittering light show accompanied each word. 'You are in the space where one second ends and the next one begins.'

'Who said that? Who are you?'

'Everything and nothing.'

'Why am I here?'

'To make a choice.'

'A choice?'

'Live or die?'

'What?'

'You have yet to accept our gifts.'

'Gifts? I don't know what you mean.'

'And because of that, you are on the verge of death.'

'I'm dying?'

'Search your feelings, you know it to be true.'

Daniel could remember the carpark, The Shades. But it seemed so long ago, as if it were a distant memory. How long had he been here?

'Why do you care if I'm dying or not?'

'We are the sum total of all magic and protect the many realms from mystical imbalance. Order cannot *be* without chaos. Chaos cannot *be* without order. The balance must be maintained. We created the realms and allowed our children the capacity to entreat us when they need our aid. You are our Mortokai. You are a bridge between us and all else.'

'So, I *am* this Mortokai?'

'Only if you accept who you are.'

'I still don't understand. Why me?'

'Because you were born different. You are the synthesis of the human world and the faerie world, of the physical world and the abstract. We are magic. The Mortokai is one with magic.'

'I have heard many things about The Mortokai. People fear the name.'

'Small minds always fear what they do not understand.'

'They have prophecies that say it will destroy everything.'

'That is down to you. Accept our gifts and what Mortokai becomes will be your decision. We shall not interfere... as long as the mystical forces of order and chaos within a realm are balanced.'

'It sounds evil.'

'Good and evil is solely determined by the perception it is perceived from.'

Silence reigned whilst Daniel tried to comprehend everything he was hearing. Magic wasn't just real, it was alive. But he was dying. He thought about his dad and Finn finding his body. It was becoming more and more difficult to remember things as his life faded away. One thing refused to die, however, his affection for Trinity.

He needed to live. He needed to live for her. Daniel didn't want to miss out on the joys of life now that his was just beginning. If part of life was about creating experiences then he had to live because his fell way short of what could be deemed a full life.

'It is time to choose, Mondragon. Do you accept death or do you accept our gifts?'

'What are these gifts?'

ERIC DIDN'T THINK TWICE about his actions. He saw the limp body of his son falling into the mouth of The Shade and he just reacted. Sure, he felt bad for abandoning Finn, but this was his son his only child and besides, he believed in her, believed that she would be able to handle herself against the creature until they destroyed its heart. She was plucky that way.

The way she idolised him reminded him of how things used to be back on Ariest when he was commander of the 1212, the legendary military unit. His fame rose even higher when bards wrote songs about the adventures of Eric, Grimgaard, Tavisum and Gydion.

He had to admit to himself that he did miss it, the admiration, the notoriety; he hadn't picked up the Claymore since coming to Earth. Not that he would change anything he had now for his old life, he loved his wife and his son.

Even though Daniel had described, to Eric, the pocket dimension within the Shade, right down to the white path, being in an environment that was monochrome was still a bit off putting. Everything was either black and white or a mixture of the two. Everything except for the hue around his body and Dragon Claymore, that is.

The enchanted sword was resplendent in its red, gold and silver. It was almost like a beacon against its colourless surroundings. Immunity to magic was just one of the many magical attributes the Claymore had and although it had been in Eric's possession for as long as he could remember he still believed that it could do more than he knew.

Eric scanned the bleak horizon of the Shade's strange inner dimension until he found Daniel and rushed over to him. His son, seemingly unconscious, lay sprawled out on the side of the pathway. As he approached him, Daniel became translucent and began to fade away.

The last of Daniels Essence drained away. The warrior was too late to save his son.

Three to one odds didn't faze Finn in the slightest, even if it was against The Shade. Her time on Earth had been the longest she had gone without shooting her guns, so she intended to relish every second of it now.

The young rebel-rouser could easily admit that she enjoyed experiencing what Earth's London city had to offer, but she could never imagine giving up her life on Ariest, like Eric did, in exchange. Having to put his sword and armour away and hide your past must have been difficult; she didn't think she could do that with her precious guns. She knew it must have been something really dreadful to make him up and leave everything. And taken a lot of courage. Finn wouldn't ask what it was, though, it wasn't her place to, her uncle Quinn had brought her up to respect people's privacy, especially those she respected. She still kept those values, others that didn't get that respect, however, were fair game.

Finn was in constant motion, jumping from car to car and sliding behind some for occasional protection. She knew she had to keep up the pressure on the Shade, keep damaging them with her enchanted bullets and give Daniel and Eric the time they needed to accomplish their side of the conflict.

Jet black elongated arms with long spindly claws shot around either side of the car Finn was crouched behind. She leapt into the air, narrowly avoided being skewered and sprang into action. Finn rolled over the bonnet of the saloon and let loose a barrage of gunfire, changing target from one to the other without missing a beat. The three Shade began reeling away in agony and vanished into the shadows.

Finn didn't drop her guard. even with the Essence vampires seemingly gone. She kept her guns at the ready as she slowly moved through the carpark, aimed at every shadow and dark corner, expecting the Shade to jump out at any time.

What she didn't expect, was what *did* happen.

Black tendril like appendages with lamprey mouths began to reach out of those shadows along the ground cast by the pillars and cars in the building. One, near Finn, began to wrap itself around her leg. After being momentarily startled, she shot at the base of the tendril and it quickly retreated.

'Vekt!' Exclaimed Finn as she looked around and saw all the tendrils wiggling about. She climbed onto a nearby car to stay clear of them. But things were about to get much worse. A blackness began to grow in the carpark level, spreading out in all directions, engulfing all light until an impenetrable darkness had completely filled it.

It was as if all light had been extinguished and Finn couldn't see a single thing. 'Vekting, vekt!' She groaned.

HOW CAN YOU DESCRIBE the feeling that you have when you see your only child dying before you, knowing that there is not a single thing you can do to save him? That was the sentiment going through Eric's mind as he watched Daniel fading away to become another victim of the Shade.

His son had told him that the last time he had depleted his Essence, Trinity had transferred her own Essence into him. If he knew magic, he could have done the same thing, but all he could do now was watch and think about how he intended to make the creature pay.

He tightened his grip on the Dragon Claymore and prepared himself to confront the Shade heart. It was almost over; Daniel had all but disappeared. Eric started to think about how he was going to break the news to Tina, explain to her that their son was gone. When, all of a sudden, the process began to reverse.

Daniel was no longer transparent, he became more solid with every second that passed, until he opened his eyes and sat up.

Eric was astonished and stared at his son with an open mouth. 'Daniel?' He touched his arm to see if he was real or not.

'Dad.'

'What happened?'

'I don't know,' replied Daniel. He saw the questioning look on his dads face and knew he would tell him everything he knew soon enough. 'Where's Finn?'

'Out there keeping the Shade busy.'

'By herself?'

'Sure, she can handle herself against it.'

'It's not just one Shade! There're three of them out there!'

'Oh my god!'

'We need to finish this,' Daniel said as he got to his feet. 'Quickly!'

The father and son duo ran off, down the white path, towards the beating heart of the Shade, knowing that time was a critical factor.

FEAR WASN'T SOMETHING that Finn suffered from too often, but she was big enough to admit that she was scared silly right now. She was in an environment the likes of which she had never experienced before and it was making her jumpy. Of course, she had been in the dark before but darkness was one thing this, however, was a complete and utter absence of light.

The only time she could see anything was when she fired her guns, which happened when she felt something brush against her in the blackness of flicked her hair. In those split seconds of light, she could see Shade clones moving about and every now and then she would hear something like wind rushing pass her ears.

She wracked her brain trying to think of a way out of her situation but she came up empty. Even if she could remember which direction the exit was, she would still have to contend with the Shade tentacles.

She was trapped.

All Finn could do now was hope that Daniel and Eric returned soon. She could feel her strength fading, knew the Shades was feeding on her and she hated the feeling of not being able to defend herself.

'You damn, vekting Shade! You couldn't take me on in a straight up fight so you have to resort to this crap? But that's ok, if *I* don't finish you, Daniel and Eric will make you pay,' Finn shouted out. Then she heard voices.

'This is it,' Jostin stated as the four, dimensional refugees came out of their camouflage.

'But there's somebody in there,' said Katrin.

'So, what do we do, Ferin? Wait for them to finish or what?' Borion turned to their team leader and waited for an answer.

They already knew the answer to that, Ferin didn't have to tell them. Their remit was extermination, if someone just happened to be rescued along the way then they can count themselves lucky. 'Are you sure there's three of them in there, Jostin?' The boy nodded. 'Then we shouldn't keep them waiting, should we?'

A third eye opened on the forehead of each of member of the team before they all turned an icy-blue colour. Katrin's Long canines and claws glowed with the same colour as did Borion's powerful legs.

'You ready to tear this up, baby?' Borion glanced at Katrin as he rubbed his hands together in anticipation.

The feline woman had already begun to dash towards the ebon blackness on all fours when she called back, 'You know I was born for this!' And she pounced into the wall of blackness.

'That's my girl!' With his huge stride, Borion quickly followed her.

'You know what to do, Jostin.'

'Yes, Ferin; wait here and use the arcane link to alert you if there are any intruders or if I feel any other Shade.'

'Excellent,' replied Ferin before he ran after his comrades. 'This will be over before you know it.'

Jostin longed for the day when he would be able to take a more active role in the elimination side of things instead of just being the sensory lookout. With Katrin teaching him hand to hand combat and Ferin instructing him in the arcane ways, he knew it wouldn't be long.

Just then, something caught Jostin's attention, something within the blackness. Ever since a Shade had all but drained Jostin's Essence and been killed, itself, during the process, the young boy had been able to sense or "feel them". With Ferin's magic transference, that sense became augmented. 'That's strange,' he said to himself. 'It's as if one of the Shade beings has some sort of huge Essence source within it. I'd better alert the others; this Shade could have abilities we're not aware of.'

Chapter Twenty-One

There's nothing better than having a long stretch after coming out of a deep restful sleep. And after Trinity did exactly that, and after her blurred vision had cleared, she began to wonder where exactly she was.

For all intents and purposes, it seemed as if she was inside a giant tree; the room was circular, filled with exquisite wooden furniture and there were hundreds, if not thousands of tree rings on the ground. One thing was for sure though, where ever she was, Trinity had a profound feeling of serenity and connectedness.

She bounded out of the bed she had rested on and discovered for the first time that she was barefoot, her sandals having been placed by the door. The wooden floor felt smooth and warm underfoot as the young Druid padded over to the large window opposite the door. The sight that greeted her was nothing short of astonishing.

Trinity found that she was indeed inside a tree, and *that* tree was just one among what she could only describe as a village of huge tree houses. Rope bridges crisscrossed the sky above and not far from where she was, she could see a tree with a massive trunk that seemed to be a sort of junction for the bridges so you could go up and down to different levels. And crossing those bridges and going about their daily routines were Woodland Elves.

'This must be the Druid Grove!' There was a distinct floral aroma mixed with the smell of fresh cut grass and it brought a smile to Trinity's face as she breathed it in deeply.

Three tiny flower faeries suddenly came fluttering around the window. 'She's awake! She's awake!' They said excitedly in unison. 'We must tell the Archdruid!' And before Trinity could ask a single question about the whereabouts of Tristan, they had fluttered off.

It wasn't long before there was a knock at the door, which woke Trinity from the serenity she experienced as the teen Druid gazed over the grove. 'Come in,' she bid.

Two elven guards, clad in green and brown, entered dropped to one knee and bowed their heads. 'At your convenience, we are here to accompany you to the Archdruid.'

Trinity was taken aback by the formality of the salutation. She always assumed that such deep bows were reserved for people of great importance. 'Uhm, sure, I'm ready now. Will my friend be there too?'

'He has yet to awaken,' the guard replied.

'And where exactly is he?'

The guard was reluctant to answer. 'I... think it would be best if you asked the Archdruid directly.'

'Then let's go,' Trinity responded.

The grove was an idyllic place, it was a portrayal of the beauty nature possessed, displayed at its utmost best. There were bubbling brooks which were spanned by quint little bridges, wildlife seemed tame and unafraid. Butterflies played in the air, as did flower faeries.

As Trinity was led down the paths of the grove, the elves, they passed, all took notice of her. There were many looks of awe, waves and more guards that bent the knee. Trinity thought that If she had known that this was the kind of treatment she would garner for being the daughter of Gydion, she would have made the Druid Grove her first stop on arriving in Ariest.

After going up a few levels in the junction tree and along a rope bridge they finally arrived at their destination, the sanctum of the Archdruid. Just as they neared the door, two other druids, a male and female, exited. They both gave Trinity deep flamboyant bows and then were on their way. She watched them retreat along the bridge, curious to know what the subject of the hushed conversation they were having was. Trinity shrugged her shoulders and entered through the door that one of the guards held open for her.

Inside, the rooms were filled with art of the finest quality. Paintings, statues, tapestries and pottery of various styles adorned the walls. For rooms that were supposed to be those of an Archdruid, they were nothing like what Trinity had expected. Gydion's sanctum, for instance, was more akin to a museum. Ancient books and arcane artefacts were the main decor there.

'You admire my art?' A female elf asked with an almost ethereal, musical tone. She glided barefoot down the stairs, behind Trinity, wearing light blue swaths of elven silk weave material which trailed behind her.

'I do,' Trinity admitted. 'It's impressive. There are many beautiful pieces.'

'All made with my own hands,' she stated matter-of-factly. 'When you live as long as we do, and you witness the fleeting beauty in others fade and extinguish in the blink of an eye, you seek other things that can hold onto that allure. I choose art.'

The elven woman stood before Trinity and cast a speculative gaze over the young girl. 'You know who I am, of course.'

'Archdruid Tavisum.'

'And you are Trinity. Gydion has done well with you; better than I ever thought he would, truth be told. But then again that man is the kind of man who would go to the far reaches to prove his point correct. Perhaps he was right with you, perhaps not.'

Trinity had no clue the elf was getting at, she just wanted answers. 'Where is Tristan?'

'Your companion is under armed guard,' said Tavisum as she sat down and offered another to Trinity.

'What do you mean he's "under armed guard"? Why?'

'You are lucky he is here at all. He is an outsider with a tainted aura. If not for you, we would have left him to the filth that are the Shadow Dancers.'

'Why would you do it for me? Because I'm Gydion's daughter?'

'No, because you're one of us.'

'I'm no elf.'

'True, but you are a Druid of the highest order. From a time when they ruled Earth.' Tavisum chuckled as she looked inquisitively at Trinity. 'You have no idea who you are, do you? No doubt Gydion's doing.'

'What do you mean?'

'I mean that you and I have met before. When Master Penwyll was the Archmage. Long before Gydion was even born. You went by a different name then of course. Lady Bianca Daumier.'

'That's not possible.'

'I'll admit, he did give you a very apt name, though, considering that this is your third life.'

THE BEATING HEART OF this Shade was faster, much louder than what Daniel had encountered before. Even the ebony lagoon bubbled and erupted more ferociously than what he had seen as he and his father neared it.

'It's scared,' Daniel thought out loud.

'What?' Eric shouted over the heart beats.

'The Shade,' Daniel shouted back, 'I think it's scared.'

'Of us?' Then the realisation hit Eric. 'It's you! It's scared of you! You were the first to actually destroy a Shade and not just put it into hibernation. It knows that you can kill it!'

'But that would mean that they have some sort of hive mind... what one knows, they all know!'

'Exactly! Which means that it's more dangerous because it's more prepared for you, it knows what you can do!' Eric held up the Dragon Claymore. 'Me, however, it knows nothing about.'

Eric began to advance on the tar-like lagoon with the intention of driving his sword into it. When, out of the blue, humanoid figures began to climb out of the Shade lake and charge at Eric and Daniel.

The hero warrior cut them down with his giant enchanted Claymore. Swinging left, then right, every Shade-being in range was being cleaved in two. Two became four. Four became eight. More and more kept coming in an endless stream.

Daniel looked on, fascinated by the way his dad fought and wielded his sword with such effortless ease. To think that he hadn't used it since fleeing Ariest impressed Daniel, it seemed like he hadn't missed a step at all.

But it also gave Daniel food for thought.

He was seeing the "legend" for the first time. Seeing the Eric Mondragon that Finn was so in awe of, that everyone on Ariest seemed to be in awe of. The Eric Mondragon that he would inevitably be compared with.

There seemed to be an inexhaustible amount of Shade humanoids, to the point where the landscape was almost alive with their movement. Daniel had watched his dad for long enough. It was time for him to get involved.

Luckily, the frost bolt was the spell that he now confidently knew he could cast, the one that he had the most practice with and the one that was most useful against a Shade. Well it would have been, if it had worked.

He knew he was doing it right, the hand gestures, the arcane words, the correct Essence reservoir yet, try as Daniel might, nothing happened.

Eric could see that his son was disturbed by something. To get to Daniel, he needed to push back the vast number of the ebon creatures, so he unleashed one of the Dragon Claymore's abilities.

Gripping the hilt in both hands, Eric thrust the magnificent weapon above his head, an action which summoned, ethereal replicas of the Claymore to also thrust out of the ground in an ever-increasing radius, impaling many of his assailants. Lightning was then cast down from the enchanted blade to the others, which created an electrical field killing many more of the creatures in a spectacular light show.

Eric finally got the chance to approach his son and asked, 'Are you ok, Daniel?'

'I can't seem to cast my spell,' an anxious Daniel replied. 'I don't understand it, I'm doing everything I did in Almedia against the Shadow Dancer. It's strange, it just won't work.'

Things suddenly got a whole lot stranger; the world literally turned upside down, inside out and back to front. They couldn't tell if they were coming or going. Communication between them became impossible as all that came out of their mouths was gibberish. The laws of gravity became temperamental and they began to float up into the air, or it could have been toward the ground. Either way, now that Daniel and Eric could barely get their bearings, the Shade serpent, unaffected by the madness that prevailed, finally made its appearance.

Daniel could do nothing to resist the creature as it wrapped around his body and began to squeeze. It locked eyes with him, it's face inches from the boy's, before the Shades giant maw opened wide and sucked on his Essence.

Then there was a moan of agony as the Dragon Claymore struck it.

The shadow snake loosened its grip on Daniel and, as the laws of gravity normalised momentarily, he fell to the ground. Eric was to feel the ire of the creature for his sneak attack, as it swung its head and slammed it into Eric's chest, leaving him sprawled on the ground.

Daniel went after the fallen Claymore, intent on finishing off the Shade heart with it. He reached out his hand to take hilt of the enchanted Dragon Claymore. As his fingers wrapped around it, he heard the voice of the Magic Entity in his head.

'The Mortokai has accepted the second gift.'

A volatile purple flame suddenly erupted around Daniel; his wide-open eyes mimicked the effect. His mind expanded and he could feel his Essence, not only in the three reservoirs Trinity taught him, but throughout his entire body.

Eric got to his feet and rubbed his aching body. It had been a long time since he had last been struck like that. He approached Daniel in sense of awe and wonder and couldn't help notice that the Shade reptile was hesitant to strike, perhaps out of fear.

'This is my birth right,' Daniel said as he admired the Dragon Claymore. 'And as the second gift, I accept it. This Shade did indeed learn from my encounter with the other, for all it was worth. Now,' he addressed the Shade in question. 'You will be my instrument. However, it is you communicate with your kind, you will let them know your fear, let them know your pain, let them know that they are now at the bottom of the food chain, let them know that The Mortokai is coming.'

Daniel held up his hand, fingers outstretched. As he slowly began to ball his hand into a fist, the Shade heart began to moan in agony. The creature began to crumple, as if it were folding in on itself, getting smaller and smaller until Daniel closed his fist tight and the Shade ceased to exist.

Eric had watched the whole thing. Seen his son do something he had never seen another mage do and with such ease. But the way he seemed to relish it, with a hint of malevolence and some enjoyment, troubled him. 'Son?' There was no response. He tried again, with more urgency. 'Daniel?'

'Yes?'

'Are you ok?'

'I have never felt better,' came his reply.

'What happens now?'

'We wait.'

'For what?'

'For the portal to reveal itself, and also for them.'

Eric turned and looked in the direction his son pointed. Coming towards them he could see several wispy objects floating beside some familiar faces; the missing children from his newspaper cuttings.

Although the plan hadn't gone exactly the way it had been formulated, Eric was a veteran of enough missions to know that they very rarely did. The fact that they had still somehow managed to partially obtain their objective pleased him. He just hoped that Finn was ok. She had been left to tackle the second part of the plan alone. He hadn't known that there were three Shade when he had dived in after his son but he was anxious to return now that's heart had been destroyed.

At that moment, a shimmering white ball began to swirl above where the Shade heart had been. The portal grew larger and larger until it was big enough for them to walk through, which they did with Daniel leading the way, his purple Essence still flickered around him.

FINN COULD HEAR ALL manner of sounds around her: chants, roars, stomps and general sounds of combat. Yet she got no response when she called out.

'What the vekt is going on!' Her curiosity was killing her. She was half tempted to jump down off the car and take her chances with the Shade tentacles in an effort to find out who was out there.

Fortunately for Finn, she didn't have to.

She heard a sound very familiar to her ears. It was the sound of a Shade's true death, the explosion of its petrified form. With the first Shade's death, the darkness that permeated the carpark level seemed to lift slightly. Whoever these people were, they looked nothing like the humans Finn had seen so far.

One seemed to be a red, partially feline woman. She moved exceptionally fast with incredible agility. Finn thought that she might actually be able to give the Shadow Dancer a run for her money. The next stranger was like a huge satyr, but instead of goat's legs, they seemed to be more akin to the hind legs of a horse and with the hardened bone sticking out which it used to attack as well as stomping the ground with its powerful legs which caused shockwaves. Finn determined that the one with the white ponytail and goatee beard was the magic user as she saw him let loose several spells. She saw the fourth one, a boy that she thought looked like he was in desperate need of a hospital, talking to the goatee guy.

Whoever these four individuals were, they had been fighting the Shades, which was music to Finn's ears because she was dangerously low on faerie dust for her guns.

The remaining Shades, depleted of Essence, couldn't withstand the assault on them for much longer and they soon lost cohesion, dissolved and seeped into the ground, which caused celebration among the strangers, Finn was less than pleased however.

'What the vekt do you think you're doing?' She yelled.

'Saving your backside by the looks of things,' replied the big one. 'You're welcome by the way.'

'Stop it, Borion. She's probably in shock at seeing the Shade and us. A quick wipe of her mind and we'll be on our way.'

'Praise be, Ferin,' Borion said with a clap of his hands. 'Me and Katrin can't wait to get off this dump.'

'You know it, baby,' she agreed.

'I might be able to help you with that,' Finn stated as she trained her guns on them. 'Nobody's wiping anything.'

'Well that's gratitude for you,' the feline said as she bared her fangs and claws.

'Uh-uh, down kitty,' Finn said with a shake of her head, 'unless you want putting down permanently.'

The air was thick with tension, neither side willing to stand down. Things were on the verge of kicking off. An ill-conceived twitch could be all it took to light the fuse. And the boy, Finn believed to be sick, detected something that could be such a twitch.

'Ferin! That energy I sensed within the Shade that exploded...'

'Yes, Jostin, what about it?'

'It's here!'

'What? How can it be, if the Shade is gone?'

'I don't know, but it's over there!' Jostin pointed at the portal that was opening.

'Is this your doing?' Ferin questioned Finn.

'No, it's not, but I know things are about to get evened up a bit,' smirked Finn.

The four strangers, had no idea what was coming through the portal, so they kept their guard up. They were a well drilled fighting unit; they didn't need to be told what to do. They kept half an eye on Finn also, just in case she tried to take advantage of any distraction.

Daniel stepped through the portal and surveyed the scene before him. He pointed the Dragon Claymore at the four unknown people and demanded, 'Who are you and where are the other Shade?'

Chapter Twenty-Two

Eric stepped out of the portal with the children, immediately after his son, but when he saw that things weren't quite safe, he told them to go hide. Instead of the two Shade he had been expecting, Eric saw four individuals, that were obviously not from Earth realm.

Finn's elation at seeing Daniel and Eric return quickly became tinted by trepidation as she saw that her friend was in the same powered but disconnected state he had entered the last time Daniel had battled the Shade. Although, this time he wasn't exhausted by it like he had been in Ariest, it seemed like he had more control. She had her suspicions as to why, the Dragon Claymore.

Being such a huge fan of Eric's, Finn had heard the stories and songs about him hundreds of times. And those songs and stories, more times than not, included facts about the mystical blade. Such as the fact that only someone of the Mondragon blood could wield it with ease, and that it was immune to enchantments and could cut through magical defences. But the most incredible thing was that it could increase the strength and abilities of its wielder, affectively taking them to the peak of their prowess.

'The Shades are dead,' Ferin answered. 'Just why does it concern you?'

'Because this is my world and your ignorance delays my work. All you have done is put the creatures into hibernation.'

'We know plenty about killing The Shade,' said Borion, 'we've been doing it for a long time and we're good at it.'

'It's true,' Eric stepped in, 'the only way to kill them is from the inside, by destroying their heart.'

Ferin and Jostin looked at each other. That's why the boy could sense energy inside the Shade. Perhaps there was some truth to their claims after all.

Just then, Katrin pounced on the unsuspecting Finn, disarmed her and knocked her to the ground. Daniel reacted instantly by unleashing a volley of eldritch missiles at her. She evaded some of them but there was just too many and she was struck over and over again.

Borion, seeing his mate with smoke rising from her crumpled body, let out a roar of rage and charged. He covered the ground with just a few of his exceptional strides and delivered a kick at Daniel, powerful enough to knock down a wall.

Yet, the young man didn't flinch.

The shield Daniel had erected reflected the force of Borion's attack back at him and sent him flying across the carpark.

'Impressive,' Ferin complemented. He tried to give an air of bravado but knew he was vastly outmatched even if he had once been the Archmage of his own realm.

We have our mission to complete, Ferin thought to himself, *and this may be our toughest test, but I promise you, Gydion, we will not fail you.*

'Gydion?' Daniel was more than a little surprised to hear a familiar name.

'How did you - wait, you know Gydion?'

'Yes,' replied Eric, 'I have quested with him and my son is his student.'

'His student?' Ferin exclaimed as he eyed Daniel, shocked that a student could already command so much power.

'Ferin is it?' Eric asked the stranger. 'What's your connection to Gydion?'

'He rescued me... rescued all of us... gave us purpose. Each one of us is the last of our race, the last survivors of Shade massacres, The Eims. Katrin is from Lo'Crae realm Borion is from Kkangea and Jostin is from Maeriis I myself am from the Te'fety realm, where the arcane is held in reverence and magic users live solitary lives in the pursuit of knowledge. But when the time came, when the one we called The Harpy Queen and Gydion called Sayyidah, brought those Essence vampires to my world, our understanding of magic wasn't enough to stop them.'

'They killed your entire race?' Finn was astonished but not as astonished as what she heard next.

'The extinction of my people fell to me,' Ferin admitted. 'I killed of my race. When Gydion rescued me, he rescued another of my people, a female named... Cera,' he stared at the ring on his little finger as he said her name. 'Gydion tutored me, progressed my magic, taught me the spells necessary to kill the Shade. I could have lived out my days with Cera, started our race anew. My mage ministry was gone, my vows now meaningless should have died with the ministry and yet I still clung to that life. I had a choice, a life with Cera as the father of my people or a life of vengeance.'

Silence can be golden, a blessing, but it can also force you to revisit decisions that, given a second chance, you may or may not repeat. Ferin had enough of such moments to fill a lifetime, but as he got older the visitations came more frequently, the choice made, more regrettable.

'We all have tough decisions to make in our lives,' Eric said thinking of his own past choices, 'we can't dwell on them, we can't change them, we can only forge on with the choice that we made and make it the best we can.'

'You're right,' Ferin said, as his resolve returned. 'Gydion set us on this path, brought us together, directed us to a portal corridor which we used to hunt down Shade, now we get to do it again,' he smiled and turned to Daniel. 'So, you're saying that Gydion was wrong about how to kill the Shade?'

'Nobody knew how to truly kill them then,' Daniel explained, 'the secret would die with anyone that had discovered it.'

'It was by chance that Daniel found out, to be honest,' Finn said.

'Or divine providence,' Jostin replied as he stared intently at Daniel. The boy, like all of his race before their extinction, had incredible sensory abilities. What he could see in Daniel was like no other mage he had come into contact with. Ferin and the people from Te'fety had two Essence reservoirs, other races had larger reservoirs. However, with Daniel, he couldn't sense any reservoirs at all.

Eric thought that it would be better if Daniel were to show rather than tell The Eims how to dispose of a Shade. To facilitate this decision Daniel radiated his Essence, just enough to reawaken the two that had fallen to the Shade hunters.

Daniel used his magic to make a duplicate of himself and took Ferin and Jostin into one dazed Shade whilst the other Daniel escorted Katrin and Borion into the second.

'I'm sorry about bailing out on you like that, Finn,' Eric said once they were alone. 'I just saw Daniel disappearing into the Shade and lost it. If I'd known there were three of them, here, I never would have...'

Finn who had been twirling her guns in deep thought cut in, 'Don't worry about it, Eric, I totally understand. Besides,' she nonchalantly fired a shot at both of the Shade, 'we have to worry about Daniel.'

A look of worry crossed his face. 'That change in him, that wasn't Daniel; that wasn't my son, he was so distant, so disconnected. And that was how he was before?'

'Yes, but it didn't last *this* long. I think it's because of the sword.'

'Goddess!' Eric exclaimed. 'Of course, it is. His spells wouldn't work until he held the claymore, which, not only put him in that higher state, but gave him the stamina and endurance to persist at that level.'

'What do you think will happen if we take it away from him? I hope he doesn't fall into that coma again.'

'I don't know, but we'll find out soon enough. My biggest worry is that he almost seemed to enjoy having the power. From being bullied and having none to having it all, it must be addictive.'

Finn's mind returned to the moment on Ariest when he had returned, before his collapse, the words he had said, that he had been everywhere and wondered what it must feel like to have that vast amount of power.

Before they could dwell on it any longer the Shades both exploded. Eric heard the children jump in their hiding place and he went to comfort them. They were happy to see his friendly face and they all gave him hugs.

'Don't worry,' he reassured them, 'we'll get you home soon... somehow.' He knew that would be the difficult part, the how, it wasn't as if they could walk into a police station, there would be hundreds of questions, the majority of which would be unanswerable.

Daniel and the Eims returned from their mission of discovery. The two Daniels placed their palms against one another's and, as they stepped forward, they merged together. Daniel was whole once more.

Although the Shade hunters knew that they would have to revisit realms they had already been to, so they could eliminate the Shades they, at the time, believed had killed, the Eims were actually excited about it. Especially Borion and Katrin. The Equilons from Kkangea realm and the Felitrini from Lo'Crae realm were similar in the fact that they were warrior races, from childhood they are taught to hunt and hone their combat skills. That understanding and spiritual connection made it easy for them to gravitate towards each other.

'We need to be going,' Ferin announced. 'We have a lot of work to redo. I'm sure our paths will cross again someday, Gydion always knows where we are.'

Katrin and Borion said their respectful goodbyes as did Jostin, who made a point to bow before Daniel and express his pleasure at meeting him.

'Eims!' Ferin called. 'Let's move.' With that final command, the four-dimensional refugees activated their camouflage and vanished from sight.

'Well, that was fun,' Finn said once she, Daniel and Eric were alone again. 'And I thought you said that there was no adventure on your realm, Daniel.'

'Things are changing,' he replied with a distant look on his face. 'Things have been set in motion that will alter this world forever. We must ready ourselves for when that moment comes, even you, father. Your self-imposed exile is at an end.'

'What is coming?' Eric asked.

'Something ancient, something hungry. We must all prepare ourselves. The Dragon Claymore is yours...' Daniel handed the sword back to Eric. 'For now.'

'What are we going to do about the children?' Finn asked. 'We can't leave them here.'

'And we can't take them with us,' retorted Eric.

'Children, come to me,' Daniel summoned. They slowly made their way to the young man with the purple flame. He spoke the little brunette girl in front. 'What is your name?'

'My name is Rosalyn Hargreaves and I'm four-years old,' she replied in a voice with little to no fear, surprising for one so young.

'Did you hear what I said to my friends, Rosalyn?' She nodded. 'That was for you, too,' he said before he bent down so only she could hear and whispered 'Prepare.' Daniel straightened up and addressed the children. 'I want you all to close your eyes and think of your homes, picture your bedrooms. Have you all done that?' When they all said yes, Daniel held up his hand and four beams shot out of his palm, struck each of the youngsters and transformed them into multicoloured shimmering spheres of light. The balls flew up, passed through the ceiling at tremendous speed and were gone. 'In a matter of moments, they will all be back home.'

'Excellent,' said Eric as he glanced at Finn. Even without the enchanted sword he was still able to do amazing feats of magic with just a wave of his hand. But Eric wondered for how much longer. 'Perhaps you could get us home in a similar way.'

'Of course.' On cue a tear in existence opened before them and quickly grew wider. Through it they could see Daniel's house, but Eric stopped them just as they were about to travel through the portal.

'We can't say anything about this to your mum, ok? I told her that we were going out for dinner.'

'Come to think of it,' Finn said as they started to walk through the magical gateway, 'I am kind of hungry.'

ERIC TOOK A DEEP BREATH just before he opened the front door of their house in Belsize Park. It turned out that he had good reason to be nervous. As they entered the living room Tina was already standing there with a stern look on her face.

'How was dinner?' She asked.

'Pretty, pretty good,' Eric replied with a smile. 'I would have brought you back some but I ate it all. You know me and my appetite.'

Tina unpaused the news report she had watched several times already. 'So, what's this? Dessert?'

The smile Eric had on his face vanished.

On the screen was CCTV footage from the carpark. The outside camera caught Daniel entering and a few minutes later Eric and Finn following. It then cut to Daniel being held in the air by the Shade although on film it looked as if he were floating before he vanished shortly followed by Eric. Finn began shooting before everything went black, with the occasional multicoloured flashes from her guns.

'I have to admit,' Finn beamed a broad smile, 'I look pretty vekting awesome!'

Eric tried to shush her and Tina rolled her eyes at the remark as the newsreader introduced a guest via satellite link up.

'...Danisa George is a New York Times journalist as well as a paranormal investigator. Danisa, welcome and thank you for taking the time to talk to us.'

'No problem,' replied Danisa.

'You've seen the extraordinary footage, would you say that this is now concrete, definitive evidence of the paranormal?'

'No.'

'But you can clearly see the young boy being held in the air but what I can only describe as a... sort of... shadow creature.'

'Which is your view of the events. Another view would be that the boy himself is causing the phenomena which would take this discussion out of the realms of paranormal and into that of the supernatural.'

'And what exactly is the difference between the two? What makes "paranormal" paranormal and "supernatural" supernatural?'

'That's a whole different debate because there's such a fine line between the two, but essentially paranormal events are beyond the scope of normal scientific understanding. Supernatural, literally means beyond or exceeding nature or the laws of nature including things characteristic of deities and other non-material beings. There is a lot of crossover, to be fair. Some things that are paranormal could be supernatural, some things supernatural can be perceived as paranormal.'

'This isn't straightforward, is it?' The newsreader laughed. 'Can you give us some examples?'

'Ok, so, although psychic abilities, telekinesis, telepathy, clairvoyance, extra sensory perception and the like are beyond normal scientific understanding and therefore historically paranormal, they would also be supernatural because they are abilities beyond which humans are born with, and therefore exceed the laws of nature. I can see you're still confused, so when in doubt go with Steven King. His first novel, "Carrie" is about a girl dealing with supernatural powers. Another of his novels, "Firestarter" is also about a girl dealing with supernatural powers, and yet some people call it paranormal because it has scientists and the other has religion so is therefore supernatural... go figure.'

'So, back to the video. What would your educated guess be as to what we are seeing?'

'I don't guess - I investigate,' Danisa stated flatly.

'Right... but you said earlier that it could be supernatural...'

'I don't know. It could be paranormal. It could be supernatural. It could be fake. Heck, it could even be magic, for all I know. Without investigation, it's all just speculation.'

Daniel, all of a sudden, began to feel faint and stumbled. Eric caught him before he completely collapsed.

'Daniel!' Tina looked into his eyes as she put her hand to his forehead to check his temperature. 'Are you ok? How are you feeling?'

'I'm fine, Mum. Just a little tired, that's all,' Daniel replied. 'I think I might just head up to bed.' He took a step towards the stairs and stumbled again.

Eric grabbed hold of his arm. 'Need some help?'

'I'm not finished with you, Eric,' Tina reminded her husband.

'I know. I know,' came his less than enthusiastic reply.

Upstairs, Daniel collapsed onto his bed. He was so fatigued he didn't even bother getting undressed, he just kicked off his shoes. Eric chuckled and pushed his son aside to sit down.

'You did good out there, Son. I never thought that I would get the chance to battle beside my boy.'

Daniel could sense that his dad was hesitant about something. 'What's on your mind, dad?'

'It's nothing much, really,' Eric replied. 'When you go back to Ariest, you're going to need some money.' He handed Daniel a piece of paper and a key. 'This is all the info you need to use the family vault. On the reverse is the location of the family estate, well, it's more of a castle.'

Daniel shot up. 'What? Surely that must be a crumbling heap by now.'

'Of course not! Well, I hope not. There was staff there and Grimgaard was supposed to be the executor in my absence. Hopefully it's all still in order. Anyway, you'll need somewhere to stay once you get to imperial city and begin your training at the Mage Academy.' Eric paused a moment as he tried to figure out how to deliver his next statement. 'Do me a favour, Daniel, when you get to the academy, study hard. Don't rely on this... other power.'

'To be honest, I don't have any real choice in the matter, dad.' He gazed at his hands. The solemn look on his face did nothing to hide the stress that was building up in him regarding his imminent return to the faerie world. 'You're still a legend in Ariest. No matter what I do I'll always be compared to you. I'll always be the great Eric Mondragon's son, always in your shadow. I'm afraid I'll never be my own man.'

'You have an amazing power within you, Daniel, something I've never seen before and I don't pretend to understand it. But what I do know is that you will do great things. Greater things than anything I did with Grimgaard, Gydion and Tavisum. All you need to do is train hard, never lose yourself and you'll cast a bigger shadow than I could ever dream of. Just remember this speech for your kids!'

'Thanks, dad.'

The father and son hugged each other tight. Although the words of encouragement were given and received with love, they didn't completely eradicate the hidden reservation they both felt.

'Oh, and since you want to be your own man,' Eric reached over to take back the key and paper, 'you won't be needing these.'

Daniel snatched the objects away from his dad. 'I can still be my own man with a little bit of a leg up. Besides, in all fairness, these are my university fees,' he joked.

'Fine, fine,' Eric smirked as he playfully pushed his son. 'Right, I'd better go down and face the music. Rest well, see you in the morning.'

As Eric left Daniels bedroom, Finn stood in the corridor, looking up at him with a broad grin on her face. 'I had to come up; Tina's face looked like thunder.'

'I've heard her colleagues call it her RBF,' he laughed.

'Her what?'

'Don't worry about it; I'm the one in trouble.'

'I heard what you said to Daniel; that was really nice. I - I wish I had the chance to have a relationship with my parents. Sometimes, anyway. If things...'

'Don't think about "ifs or buts" that won't change anything. Whoever brought you up did a good job, Finn, remember them, that's what matters. You're a great kid and I'm so glad Daniel has friends like you in his life, you've seen how it is for him here.'

Finn nodded. She had seen it first-hand. She wanted to say more. Say that she wanted to be more to Daniel but this wasn't the right time or the right person to be saying it to.

'Get some sleep, Finn, you two have an early morning tomorrow.'

'I don't know if I'll be getting much sleep,' she said excitedly, leaving her issues of love behind as she remembered the night she just had. 'I just fought Shade with the legendary Mondragon, with both Mondragons actually.' Finn sighed as she headed off to bed.

Eric joined Tina downstairs on the sofa. She still watched the news, the same report being repeated every fifteen minutes with the occasional new eyewitness phoning in to say how they had seen three people running down Regents Street, one of them having purple hair and funny looking guns.

'So that's a Shade, then?' Tina asked.

'Yeah,' replied Eric.

'You should have told me what you were going to do.'

'I didn't want to worry you.'

'I've been worried ever since Gydion told us that these creatures could be here. I've been worried because I knew that if you could do something then you would. It's in your nature, it's just who you are. I've kind of been prepared for it. But just imagine something had gone wrong? The first I could have found out about it could have been you or Daniel turning up on a table in my hospital. You should have told me.'

'I'm sorry,' Eric said as he held Tina's hands.

'I know you are,' she replied.

'The next time I do any heroics, I'll tell you,' he laughed

Tina put Eric into a wrist lock. You couldn't have a husband like him and not expect to learn a thing or two about self-defence. 'What do you mean "next time"?'

The only thing about having your husband teach you how to protect yourself, is that he would know how to counter your holds. In this case Tina didn't mind however, because after freeing himself, Eric and Tina began to kiss.

'THIS IS WHAT I WAS after,' Daniel said to Finn as he showed her the encyclopaedia he had just purchased. 'It's for Princess Nyriel. The books she has in her library about this realm are so out of date I thought it would be a good gift for her when we get back.'

His friend had been trying to make the unflattering hat his mother had loaned her, look halfway decent on her. Finn would rather rip it off and throw it to the winds, but firstly, it wasn't hers, and secondly, after the events of yesterday, wearing the hat to hide her distinctive hair colour, was a condition of her being allowed out. 'Argh! This vekting thing!'

'Calm down, Finn, maybe this will take your mind off of it.' Daniel handed her the plastic bag the princess's book had been in. He knew the one thing in a bookshop that could placate his companion... an encyclopaedia of guns.

Finn's face literally lit up as she flicked through the pages. Her mind was racing. The possibilities for her uncle's ingenuity were limitless. The young woman was now very anxious to get back to Ariest.

As she followed Daniel through the bookshop she continued to leaf through her new tome; pistols, machine guns, rifles all had her salivating. Until she saw a poster for an author who was having a signing of her new release that day and she came to a standstill.

Daniel, who had walked on, unaware initially that he had lost his companion, but returned once he had, to see what was holding

Finn's attention so much that it had taken it away from her beloved weapons.

'She looks so much like my mother,' Finn whispered when she felt Daniel's presence.

'I thought your parents died when you were very young?'

'They did, but there're in the family pictures uncle Quinn has shown me.'

Daniel looked at the poster. The authors name was NJ Kavanagh, a fantasy writer. He had to admit that, despite the authors dark hair, there was some resemblance between the two. 'She could be a distant relative of yours. Did your grandad have any siblings?'

'Yeah; two brothers and a sister.'

'Ever since I found out about the history of humans on Ariest I've been thinking about this. Because people tend to live longer on Ariest there are only three generations of Jesson's, Thomas, your dad and you. If your grandad was taken from here, during the early days of the industrial revolution, some 250 years ago, there could be ten or as much as twelve generations here. The same could be for your mother's side.'

Finn thought about Daniels possible explanation as she studied the poster. 'You could be right,' she shrugged. 'Come on, let's go.'

Daniel made his way to the exit, his head turning this way and that as his eyes drunk in the sight of all those gorgeous books, all that knowledge. Finn momentarily lingered at the poster until she finally made up her mind.

She picked up a copy of the signed book by NJ Kavanagh, headed to the counter and exchanged it for the encyclopaedia of guns Daniel had bought her. Having placed the book in the bag and wrapped it up, Finn walked quickly to catch up with Daniel.

Chapter Twenty-Three

The ancient Egyptian noted the dubious look Gydion gave her as he puffed on his pipe. She enjoyed seeing it vanish as she explained to him that when the war was turning against her, Sayyidah had cast a spell of duplication on herself.

Sayyidah never left Ariest. Sayyidah never left Ariest. The weight of the words reverberated around Gydion's mind as the realisation set in. The self-duplication spell was a simple spell to cast, but to create exact copies possessing an independent mind that was linked telepathically to the original, was a bit more intricate needing more time to cast and ideally in a ritual.

Gydion looked at the Sayyidah duplicate, remembered the time they had spent recently in one another's arms, and deduced that it must surely have been a ritual that was used. But that wasn't something that you could do at a whim during battle; it took time and preparation.

'She must have had it set up already,' Gydion thought aloud, 'as a failsafe of sorts.'

'Did you really think she would go into a confrontation without something to fall back on? Your adversary has had the advantage of planning and plotting for decades for a war that you did not even know you were participating in,' she said gleefully. 'You have lost, husband.'

'I have lost nothing. I still yet draw breath and as long as that is the case I shall fight.'

'Strong words husband but ultimately meaningless. You had your chance to end me before but you failed to do so. What makes you think you can do it now?'

'Because it seems as if the only way to finish this is with her death... or my own.' Gydion's lips moved imperceptibly behind the shield of his pipe. 'Of the two possible outcomes, I know which I would prefer.' He completed his spell and fired an arcane bolt from his mouth toward Sayyidah.

The aim of Gydion's bolt was straight and true. Sayyidah had no chance to avoid the point-blank attack, but Baelthorn made sure that she didn't have to as he conjured up a barrier to take the blow.

'Well look at that. Did you actually just try to kill your loving wife, Gydion?' She mocked.

'Like I said, it seems to be the only way to end this.'

'You have a lot of bravado now that you know she is but a duplicate of Sayyidah.'

'I will be exactly the same when I see her again.'

'And you think Baelthorn will allow that to happen? You honestly think you will escape here alive? Your God made you an offer and you refused, now you shall reap the consequences of your impudence and feel his wrath.'

'And I already told you that you are no God to me!'

Unbeknownst to his captors, Gydion had been replenishing his Essence levels, little by little, so that it didn't visually flare up and give them any forewarning. If he was to get out of here alive, he needed to strike first and strike hard.

His hands moved with rapid fluidity and he sent a ball of swirling arcane energy flying towards the "would be" god. The attack took Sayyidah by surprise but Baelthorn, the intended target, merely grinned. He was an entity that relished combat and the prospect of facing an opponent after millennia of being imprisoned excited him.

The dragon Lord raised his hands and an invisible force guided the energy blast away from him and into the ceiling of the cavern where it exploded causing debris and stalactites to rain down. Before they had even touched the ground Baelthorn was on the counter attack, opening his mouth wide and breathing black flames at Gydion. In defense the Archmage turned his back allowing his robes to take the full brunt of the fiery assault, yet remain unscathed.

'His cloak has been enchanted to protect against elemental attacks!'

'Not only that, my dear wife. It has been upgraded since last you or your maker saw it. Not only does it protect against but it absorbs magical attacks and converts it for my own use so that I might do this...'

Gydion's hands were but a blur as he cast another spell. As he finished, the air in front of Baelthorn began to shimmer and swirl and suck him into its black hole centre.

'My Lord, you must fight the pull! That is the banishment spell,' warned Sayyidah. *But how? I know from personal experience that the casting of this particular enchantment takes time,* she mused, *yet he did it almost instantly. It must be the energy he absorbed. It must increase his ability to cast as well as the power and potency of spells, but it cannot last forever. And I also know that for the banishment to be successful, the caster must concentrate on the target of the conjuration.*

Out of the corner of his eye, Gydion could see Sayyidah begin to cast. Although he had not returned the more obviously dangerous fire school of magic to her, Earth and air still had its own offensive capabilities. He knew that he should have dealt with her first but, even though he knew that she wasn't Sayyidah, she still had her face, she was a part of the woman he once called wife.

The stalactites and stalagmites suddenly broke off and darted toward the arch mage but they smashed harmlessly against his protective shield. Sayyidah screamed with annoyance at her failed attacked but seeing Baelthorn beginning to lose his battle against the void she quickly set about casting another spell. As she finished the intricate motions the ground shook.

Chunks of the surrounding cavern came away from their resting places, molded together to form a huge rock golem in front of Sayyidah. She immediately ordered it to do her bidding and it charged at her enemy.

He heard the booming steps of the golem closing in on him. Gydion hadn't been able to reinforce his shield after Sayyidah's initial attack, so all he could do was stand his ground. He knew he had taken a gamble hoping that Baelthorn would be easy pickings in his weakened state for the banishment spell but the so-called God still had more power than the arch mage had anticipated. Then Gydion felt the force of the golem as it slammed into him and sent him flying across the cavern. The spell was broken.

'Enough of these games!' Baelthorn's anger reverberated around the space. 'You have truly vexed me mortal, now you will suffer for it.'

Chapter Twenty-Four

Although it had just been a flying visit, Daniel was more than happy to of had the chance to say a proper goodbye to his parents and show them that he was safe and unharmed. He wondered how his mum was handling the whole situation. They had talked before about him going to Oxford or Cambridge and even mentioned universities in America, although she wasn't keen on that idea saying that it would be him moving to another world, but now he literally was moving to another world.

A world with different rules. A world with two suns. A world where magic existed.

'This is it,' announced Daniel as they arrived at the innocuous blue door in Bloomsbury square. He grabbed the old knob but couldn't turn it to gain entry. 'We just have to find out to get it.'

Tina looked sceptically at the dilapidated door with its flaking paint job and rusty door knob. She was about to ask her son if he was sure this was the right place when she suddenly slapped her hand over her mouth as a wrinkly faced, knobbly nosed, sharp toothed little man in a three pieced suit with pin striped pants and a bowler hat came pushing through them.

'Excuse me, excuse me, coming through,' he said.

'Out of the way,' Finn and pushed Daniel aside.

'Oh, I'm sorry,' Daniel said to the hobthrust.

'Quite all right,' the creature replied tipping his hat. 'If you're looking to use the FTN, you'll need to get a ticket from the ticket booth.' He pointed to the red phone box on the corner of the nearby park.

'Ticket? No, I already have one,' replied Daniel. He took the ticket, Fungal gave him, out of his pocket. Whereas the first ticket he had used to get to Ariest was gold, this one went through a kaleidoscope of metallic colours.

The well-dressed hobthrust stared at the ticket, then at his own gold ticket and back to Daniel's. 'That bloody Fungal.' He grumbled. 'I was the first to use his damn fangled contraption, but do I get any thanks or recognition for it? No! None!'

He continued to mutter as he touched the rusted door knob with his ticket. It instantly turned gold and gleamed as if it were brand new. Daniel and Finn winked at each other as they witnessed the secret procedure. The hobthrust then entered the previously old looking door and it slammed shut behind him before it reverted to its previous rundown state.

Once the episode was over, Tina could breathe again. 'What the hell!'

'I know what you mean,' laughed Daniel, 'I reacted the same when Trinity showed me the one at school but I had to use a gem to... wait a minute. That's right! I had to use a gem to see it. She said that humans couldn't see them anymore because we stopped believing,' he said as he turned to his mum.

'How could I not believe,' Tina replied with a shrug. I've been getting glimpses of things since your father first told me but I didn't pay it much attention and put it down to tricks of the mind. But now I've seen Gydion do things, heard about my son doing things and seen stranger things on tv. It's gotten to a point where it would be harder not to believe.'

Finn grinned at Tina's admission. 'Once we pass this door, you'll have your eyes well and truly opened.' She touched her ticket, the knob turned multicoloured and together they all entered the Faerie Transit Network.

THE SOUND OF PISTONS and gears being turned by the rhythmic escapes of steam immediately greeted them upon entering the fantastic transport system. Finn was her usual giddy self, the way she got around all engineering marvels, much the same way Daniel got when he came across books he hadn't read before. Eric and Tina were astonished by what they saw.

'How could something as vast as this have been built without anyone knowing?' Tina stopped Eric before he could answer her question. 'Don't bother, Eric, I know. Magic.'

'Maybe the excavation and hall area,' Finn corrected, 'But these moving stairs, all this brass work, the mechanisms, the cogs and gears, would have been done by my uncle Quinn,' she said proudly.

The warrior turned builder looked around the hall in wide eyed amazement. 'This place is pretty impressive,' Eric said, 'there's no denying that.'

Tina's wide-eyed amazement matched that of her husband. Not because of the architecture of the hall, she had hardly taken any note of it, but by the multitude of creatures that were filling it. All manner of beings great and small milled about the great space; some made their way to the train platforms, others to the exit and some were just admiring the British Museum FTN station, just like tourists.

Daniel suddenly saw a face he recognised. 'Waldo! It's me, Daniel. I made it back after all.'

'Waldo? -I'm-not-Waldo,' the selkie replied in its rapid speech. 'My-name-is-Aldo.'

'Oh, I'm sorry,'

'Are-you-trying-to-say-that- all-selkie-lookalike?'

'No! It's just that... you two... with that moustache... kind of... do.'

'That's-because-Waldo-is-my-brother,' Aldo replied before walking off.

Daniel stood there with a dumbfounded look until Finn tapped him. 'Isn't that Lowack? He should know where Fungal is.'

'Yes, I do know where Fungal is,' Lowack replied when the group approached him, 'but he is busy and doesn't want to be disturbed.'

'But surely he'd want to see his special freedom pass holders, so we can thank him again.' Daniel thought that having the kaleidoscopic metallic ticket might carry a bit of weight but he was wrong.

'Don't remind me,' Lowack's reply dripped with envy. 'I'm Fungal's assistant and I still have to buy my own tickets to get to work.'

A scoundrel knows a scoundrel and, unlike Daniel, Finn was a proud scoundrel. She had a better grasp of the kind of character Fungal was and Finn knew that he wasn't the kind of person to just give away two valuable unlimited tickets just to say sorry. Not for free anyway.

'We're actually here to pay the rest of what we owe for the passes. You didn't really think that he gave them to us for free, did you?' Finn said with a laugh.

'Fungal would sell anything for money,' agreed Lowack.

'I'm surprised he hasn't tried to sell you,' Finn continued to play up her role.

'Well, actually, there was this time...'

Daniel looked over the shoulder of the hard-worked assistant and saw a door open behind him. 'Here comes Fungal now.'

Beside the boggart laird was a tall robed man with a long half-goatee beard. He was bald except for the two long braided sideburns he sported. He bent over to discuss one final matter with the boggart before Fungal produced a small coin bag and placed it in man's open palm. He had full finger rings on his first and middle fingers and once he was satisfied with the weight of the bag, he secreted it into a hidden pocket in his robe. Business concluded; the tall man was about to leave when he felt he was being watched.

'Well, well, well, if it isn't Eric Mondragon. So, this is where you ran off to.'

'And what brings you here, Radek Zislaa?'

'Business,' came the short reply. 'I barely recognised you. These humble garbs are a far cry from the gold and silver regalia you used to wear.'

'These fit more comfortably,' Eric said brushing aside the snide comment.

'Indeed. Well, whilst you were falling from grace, I have become Archmage.'

'Don't you mean temporary Archmage?' Eric corrected. 'I've spoken to Gydion and he seemed to be in fine health, unless you know something that I don't.'

'No, no,' replied Radek quickly.

'Well, that's good, because he will be mentoring my son,' the proud father declared.

'So, this is Daniel the Shade slayer,' Radek said as he eyed Daniel up and down. 'The Assembly has heard much about you.'

'Did they also hear the calls for help from Murias City?'

'Politics are not for the young to understand.'

'Politics? They were supposed to be your allies! They fought side by side with you. Their people died along with your people and yet when they needed your help you abandoned them. I would never do that.'

'Well, my little Adept, if you survive at the Mage Academy and eventually become a Master and if you one day sit on the Mage Assembly you can do as you please, but until then, I think you should learn to address your seniors with more respect,' snapped Radek.

'Now, now, this is my establishment,' Fungal interjected, 'and I'm the only one allowed t'squabble here.'

Radek made a polite bow of the head to Fungal and began to dematerialise. 'The Mage Assembly will be watching you Daniel Shade slayer.' His eyes with their piercing gaze were the last things to vanish.

'Well that wasn't creepy at all,' Finn grimaced.

'I dinnae appreciate yous harassing my clientele. Even you, Eric Mondragon.'

'Well if you had a more wholesome character then Gydion wouldn't have asked me to make sure that your little corridor of portals was locked down.'

'He never did!' Fungal said in wide eyed panic. The corridor was central to his designs to topple Ganygu from his perch. Fungal's crafty mind worked overtime as he tried to think up an escape. He didn't want to reveal his true plans to Eric but he knew he needed to tell him something to placate him. 'You can't shut it down. I need the corridor for my new business venture. Fungal's... Fungal's... Fungal's Luxury Holidays and Adventure Tour,' he blurted out. 'Gydion was only concerned about there possibly being a portal to Salamida and I have my team working hard to find it. Let me show you.'

Fungal led them to the door he had entered from with Radek. He had played his part of the put-upon business owner perfectly, if he said so himself, now he just needed some visual aids to complete his hustle. And the corridor of infinite portals was just such a thing.

Behind the door the corridor of portals disappeared into the distant. Large wooden doors with metal ring handles lined either side of the magical passage. Pixies. Lots of pixies worked in what could only be described as a production line of activity surrounding the portal doors. Some were pulling off the boards Fungal had hastily put on them when he first investigated the corridor. Some were going in and out of the portals, the ones pixies returned from were given blank nameplates to be filled in later. After a short period, the doors through which pixies didn't return were marked with red warning signs.

'See!' Fungal threw open his arms in an exuberant fashion. 'I have it all under control. I had a bit of trouble with reality being warped but, thanks to Radek and his exorbitant fee, it's been stabilised.' Fungal walked them down the corridor explaining the whole process as they went until they came to a door marked Gilprain. 'The idea is to allow clientele to choose a destination, perhaps by questionnaire and process of elimination, all for a nominal fee, of course.'

Eric had to admit that it was a good idea but he wasn't totally convinced that Fungal could or would keep things totally above board. There had to be some angle but he just couldn't see it. 'So, you're planning to send people to Salamida for their holidays?'

'Of course not! We haven't even found that portal yet. And when we do, it will be treated like all the other portals to hostile environments. So, as you can see, I need this corridor to stay.'

'I don't know. Gydion was quite specific about it...'

'And what about you, Mrs Mondragon? Wouldn't you like to take a trip somewhere? Maybe to somewhere like this.' Fungal threw open the door for dramatic affect. It wasn't necessary, the landscape on view spoke for itself.

Tina and the others were amazed by what they saw. It was akin to the most pristine of tropical beaches, just not in the colours you would normally expect. Fungal took note of their expressions as he ushered them through the portal into Gilprain realm.

As they stepped onto the beach, the sand changed colour beneath their feet. It was blue under Daniel, amber for Eric, Finn and Tina had red and violet respectively.

'Look at that,' Finn exclaimed, 'that's pretty cool!'

'Apparently the sands reflect your mood,' Fungal, who had remained on the station side of the portal, explained. 'I'm thinking of marketing this place as a love getaway. What do you think?'

'It's lovely,' Tina said as she squeezed Eric's hand.

'And since Daniel will be at the Mage Academy, you'll have more time for just the two of you,' Fungal added. He could see that Tina was reticent but Eric was still a little hesitant. He needed one more sweetener. He clicked his fingers and a kaleidoscope metallic freedom pass appeared in front of Eric and Tina. 'Just in case you two ever feel you need to go on holiday or you'd like to visit your son in Ariest...'

'Or if I need a nice and easy way to keep tabs on you,' Eric added.

'So be it,' Fungal shrugged and lit a celebratory cigar.

'And if, in the meantime, you find the portal to Salamida be sure to seal it.'

'Isn't this a face you can trust?' Fungal replied, his cigar clamped within his big toothy grin.

They all headed back down the corridor of portals towards the British Museum FTN station. Tina and Eric were already making plans for their first portal holiday and an excited Tina's first proper visit to another realm.

Fungal held Daniel and Finn back momentarily before whispering to them, 'When you two have some free time come back and see me. I've just come up with a business opportunity that may interest ye both.'

Chapter Twenty-Five

Ariest never looked more welcoming to Daniel than it did now. He pulled back his hood and let the warming rays of the twin suns beat down on him without any of the fear. His trip back to Earth, short as it was, had highlighted how much he enjoyed not having to worry about the effects of being in the sun too long.

He was excited to be back because it felt like he was about to begin a new chapter in his life. The first time he came to Ariest it had been a mistake; this time it had been his decision. This was his ancestral home, this was where he fit in, where he should be.

Now that his parents had FTN freedom passes, just like him and Finn, he thought that maybe they might visit him here. He was sure that his mum would definitely want to see him graduate from Mage Academy, if they even had graduation. It would be more difficult for his dad to deal with, however, returning to the place where he had his darkest moment. How do you get over killing a son you never knew you had? Do you ever get over it?

Something else he was looking forward to was seeing Trinity again. Just thinking about her put a smile on his face. Things were never really sorted out between himself and Finn. The status of their relationship was never really laid out from his point of view. And, to be honest, it wasn't really a talk he was looking for to having.

Daniel turned to Finn and saw her glaring at him. 'What?' His hands were getting sweaty. Did she know what he had been thinking about?

'What do you mean "what?". I was asking you what you thought about Fungal's offer?'

Daniel had almost forgotten about that. Fungal had offered them roles as ambassadors for his burgeoning travel agency. Basically, they would go into these realms, learn what they could about it; weather conditions, indigenous people, language, currency, minerals and then report back with a viability rating.

'Well, it all sounds a bit tedious to me,' Daniel revealed, 'not to mention a bit dangerous.'

'Dangerous? Where's your sense of adventure?' Finn couldn't believe what she was hearing. 'I've always wanted to get out of Almedia...that's what I planned with Crellis. But that fell through. Going to your realm really opened my eyes to that idea again. You don't get too many opportunities to live your dream, and I'm taking this second chance to get out and make some coin, with or without you, Daniel.'

With or without him, Daniel could see how determined she was. She was strong willed, some people would call it stubbornness, but it was one of the things he liked about her. 'I don't think it would be a good idea you going off to these places by yourself, but...'

'I knew you wouldn't let me down,' Finn gave Daniel a big hug. 'You don't know how much this means to me.'

'But,' repeated Daniel, 'Fungal said we should go back when we have time, I don't know how this Mage Academy works, when do semesters start and end for instance, so I don't know when I'll be able to make it.'

'I'm sure Princess Trinity knows,' replied Finn.

They entered the vibrant and bustling city of Almedia through its eastern gate, Daniel was still impressed with the size of them and the city wall itself. They passed the guards on duty and were saluted. It reminded Daniel just how much of a celebrity he and Finn were at the moment.

The guards may have been the first to greet the returning duo, but the pair had already been spotted by Jimbo and a couple other kids that weren't at school. By the time Daniel and Finn had passed through both gates and entered the city they had formed an impromptu welcome committee.

'Well, boys, if it isn't our wandering leader and the scum that stole my consort position.'

'Don't you mean the guy that saved your life?' Daniel retorted.

Jimbo scoffed at the very idea.

'The gang's all yours now, Jimbo,' said Finn matter-of-factly as she dumped her bags and hugged her old friend.

'What do you mean? You too big to hang with us now that you're the goddess? Don't forget, love, that title only lasts twelve months. Once that times up, you'll be back to being the same old Finn: gambling, drinking, running scams and shooting off your mouth, as well as your guns.'

'And what makes you think I've stopped doing any of that as the goddess?' She grinned. Finn had always prided herself on not veering away from her standard, even being in a public position where most of Southwestern Ariest knew who she was couldn't sway her. 'What I mean is that I'm finally getting out of Almedia...well kind of. I'll be coming and going, but mostly going.'

Jimbo glared at Daniel. 'What's *he* done?'

'It's nothing to do with Daniel. I've been offered a job and I'm taking it.'

'I'm not sure Quinn will allow that.'

'I have a feeling my uncle won't have anything to say about it.'

Whilst Finn and Jimbo talked, Daniel watched the other kids go through Finn's bags. It was as if they could smell the chocolate coated hazelnuts and the other bags of sweets his mum had given her. As they rummaged through the goodies, Daniel caught a glimpse of the book by NJ Cavanagh and grabbed it out of the bag. He wondered what his friend had planned as he read the back matter.

'And what about Mr Wolff?' Jimbo asked. 'He sure as vekt won't be happy.'

'I don't owe him anything.'

'Maybe not, but he won't like seeing one of his best cash cows go.'

'He'll Just have to find himself a new one then.'

'I'd like to be a fly on the wall when you tell him you're quitting.'

'I bet you would. Anyway, I need to go see uncle Quinn, so I'll see you 'round, Jimbo. And make sure they share those Earth sweets around the gang.'

Jimbo took all the sweets off of the youngsters and gave his childhood friend a thumbs up and a wink. 'Oi!' He called to Daniel. 'Thanks.' He said reluctantly before rushing off with his juvenile entourage.

Daniel furrowed his brow as he looked down the street at the quickly disappearing boys. 'What was that?'

'From Jimbo? As good as it gets gratitude-wise,' chuckled Finn.

'And what about this?' He tossed the book towards her.

She caught it and looked at the author photo, just as she had numerous times since getting the book. Each time she did she became more and more convince that she was looking into the eyes of her supposedly dead mother. 'I need to know,' she sighed. 'I need to ask Quinn.'

'And what if the answer isn't what you want to hear?'

'To be honest, I don't know *what* answer I want to hear.'

'Do you want me to go with you?'

'No, it's ok. You go on ahead to the Dirty Dog, give these to Eveline and I'll catch up with you there.'

Daniel took the bag of chocolate hazelnuts she wanted the exceptional tavern cook to replicate, then gave Finn a big hug and kissed her on the forehead. 'Stay calm,' he told her.

In reply, she gave a sarcastic smile, before she took a deep breath and headed home, trying to decide on a way to bring up the subject.

He watched his friend depart. Daniel couldn't imagine what turmoil was going through her mind but he hoped that what she discovered wouldn't affect her too much. Either way, he knew, whatever the news, he would be there for her. As tough and strong as Finn liked to think she was, this could leave her in a fragile state, he thought, perhaps flaunting his relationship with Trinity in front of Finn might not be such compassionate thing to do right now.

Daniel headed off down the road, his mind deep in thought.

MAVIS WASN'T ONE TO miss out on a good marketing opportunity and Daniel saw evidence of that fact when he arrived at The Dirty Dog Tavern. By the entrance was a golden sign which read "Daniel Welsh, Shade slayer, stayed here."

He didn't know what to think of it. Sure, he wanted to make his own name away from the legacy of his dad, but he wasn't sure if having his name by the entrance of the dodgiest dive in town was a good thing or not.

Even if The Dog wasn't a five-star establishment the atmosphere that it had was very distinct; an old friend buying you a drink was just as likely to happen as someone punching you in the face. It had its own special charm. Daniel had to admit, he did like the place.

As he entered, there were a few hushed whispers, people recognising who he was, some were even in awe. Mavis' marketing drive must really be working.

'Daniel! It's good to see you again,' called Eveline. 'How do you like our new plaque? It came straight from the business mind of Mavis. She thought that she could cash in on you having stayed here and all. I thought it was a bit of a bonkers idea at first, but by the goddess it's only gone and bloody worked.'

Daniel smiled thinly as he looked around and saw so many people gazing at him and whispering amongst themselves. It was something that he had experienced his entire life, but whereas those hushed discussions had been derogatory and spiteful, these had been anything but. Someone actually came up and shook Daniels hand before filling it with a pint of mead, much to Daniels surprise.

'Come on,' Eveline whispered to Daniel, 'salute your fans.'

Daniel raised his pint in the air after Eveline's guidance, and the tavern patrons cheered and raised their own before downing the golden drink and the sound of glass mugs being slammed down rang out.

Mavis came out of her office to see what all the commotion was about and her eyes turned into Daniel shaped piles of gold when she saw him. 'If it isn't my good friend, Daniel "The Shade Slayer" Mondragon!' She him a big hug almost suffocating him in her ample body. 'It's so good of you to drop by to say hello.'

'Well, actually, I'm here to see if my room was still available.'

'Of course, it is,' Mavis replied so everyone could hear before continuing conspiratorially to Daniel, 'to be honest I've had to clear out the room because your friend hasn't been here for a few days and there's the small matter of an outstanding fee.'

'What do you mean? Trinity's not here?'

'She was missing you,' Eveline began, 'so we suggested that she should go with Tristan on one of his little quests, to take her mind off of things. That was a few days ago now though.'

'Do you know where they went?'

'No. They went to Hyasda, the alchemist. They must have left direct from there because they didn't return.'

'I'll just have to ask her where she sent them. Let me change then you can give me directions to the shop.'

Mavis cleared her throat. 'And the outstanding money?'

'I have money,' Daniel revealed, 'in a vault, but it's in imperial city.'

'Excellent!' Mavis rubbed her hands together. Nothing excited her more than getting overdue money.

Daniel was a bit confused by the landlady's enthusiasm. As he understood it, Imperial City was a few days ride from Almedia, so it wasn't as if she'd be getting the money straight away

'All banks in Ariest are linked to the central bank in Imperial City,' Eveline explained to Daniel. 'You have the combination, right?' He nodded, 'The bank isn't far from Hyasda's shop so you could pop in there first. Just come see me when you're ready and I'll give you the directions.'

NOW THAT SHE HAD BEEN to Earth and seen the homes there, Finn had more appreciation for what her grandfather had replicated on Ariest. Sitting in the lounge of the Jesson family home in Buxton Mews, she had placed her chair, in the corner, behind the double doors, where she contemplated things and tried to get her mind in order.

In her hands, Finn held the framed photo she had mentioned to Daniel, the one of her parents and her uncle. It had always been one of her favourites; the way they were laughing, it seemed so natural, a frozen moment of a beautiful day, trying out her granddad's new invention. She was convinced that the woman on the back of the novel and the one in the photo were one and the same. The hairstyle and colour may have been different and although the author was wearing glasses Finn was still certain that NJ Cavanagh was her supposedly dead mother, Niamh Jesson.

She was so anxious for answers that, upon returning home, Finn hadn't even taken the time to unpack her things, except for the book.

She had placed that on the table.

It wasn't long before Quinn returned, no doubt from working on Vincent, Finn thought. She watched him smile when he saw her bags, his niece was back. She watched that smile turn to curiosity as he noticed the book for the first time and continued to watch as his expression went through a gamut of emotions when he picked it up and examined it closer.

'I wondered how I would bring this up in a conversation,' Finn said from her hidden position. 'I mean, how would you begin it? When would be an appropriate time to say "I saw a picture of my dead mum and she's just released a book." And when would be a good time, in a discussion to, tell your uncle that you know he's been lying to you all your life!'

She didn't want to be hysterical and emotional; she wasn't one of those girls, but it was beyond her control. It was too much for her to cope with. Finn loved her uncle, he was more like a father to her, but now she felt betrayed by him.

'I hoped you would never find out,' said Quinn, resigned to having to finally share the secret he had kept for so long.

'Were you protecting me? Is that your excuse? Did you think you were keeping me safe? You told me she was dead! And what about my dad? Is he alive somewhere too?'

'I honestly don't know.'

'Do you know how it feels? To believe that you're an orphan, and then discover, after all these years, that your mum is alive and well?'

Quinn said nothing.

'Come on, uncle, tell me why you lied to me.'

Still Quinn didn't reply.

'Are you just going to stand there like your tongue's fallen out of your head or are you going to explain yourself?' His silence both frustrated and angered her, two emotions that often push people to hurtful lengths in an effort to get a reaction. 'Who knows what my life could have been like if I'd been living with my parents. I could have been Finnuala and not just Finn, I could have been a prissy princess like Trinity. But I never got the chance, because my uncle lied to me and told me my parents were dead. You took my future.'

'Your future?' Quinn had reached his limit. As calm and reserved as he was, even the mild-mannered tinkerer could only take so much. 'I took your future? I gave you a future! You really want to know why I told you she was dead? It's because I wished she was. And you should too... she didn't even want *you!*'

Finn felt a stabbing pain in her heart. 'You're lying... again! Why would you say that?'

'Because it's true.' Quinn leant on the table; his head bowed. It had been a heavy burden he had carried now he had some sense of relief at being able to share it. 'No more lies, Finn. You want to know the truth, then I'll tell you everything.'

Quinn went to a cupboard and brought out a bottle of sweet wine along with two glasses. This was going to be the first time that they had ever sat down to have a drink together, although he knew the kind of things that Finn got up in the city, the kind of reputation she had as a drinker and gambler. In bringing her up he had almost given her a free reign to do as she pleased, as long as she did them away from The Mews.

He filled a glass and finished it in one go, looking for the strength in fortitude that so many seek from alcohol. This time he filled both glasses and placed one in front of Finn. It wasn't her usual drink but she welcomed the opportunity to keep her Idle hands busy.

Quinn took a seat. 'The first thing you should know is that Niamh was my wife.'

Finn downed her drink and poured another. 'So, you're saying that you're my dad?'

'No, Martin's your dad. What I'm saying is that they had an affair.' Quinn watched his niece go through the cycle of finishing her drink and refilling it again. 'I don't know how long it went on for. He was always coming and going, doing jobs for that Eamon Wolff.'

'My dad was in the Thief's Guild?' Finn asked surprised that she had inadvertently followed her father down the same path.

'Yeah, he was supposedly good at it too. He loved the danger and adventure.' Quinn could see on Finn's face that she too could appreciated that the similarities between father and daughter were uncanny. 'Niamh was the daughter of my father's good friend, Andrew Fitzgerald. She was his only child. They had made an agreement that if anything should happen to either of them, the other would safeguard their family. To further cement the agreement, Martin and Niamh were betrothed.'

Finn listened intently as she heard her family history for the first time. 'But I thought you said she married you? What happened?'

'Your father happened. Martin being Martin. Shirking responsibilities and galivanting around the world doing goddess knows what. Understand that we didn't know anything about the pact our fathers had made, we just all grew up together as friends do, from kids up to teens. Then he started getting in with the guild. We saw less and less of Martin. As we got older affections grew between Niamh and myself. Then her father passed away and the agreement came into effect. We had no way of knowing where Martin was or if Martin was even alive or not, so the honour of marriage fell to me. I loved Niamh, more so than she loved me it would turn out, but we were happy for a time.' Quinn pour then last of the wine before opening another bottle. 'Martin wasn't at the wedding, in fact, we never saw him again until your grandfather's funeral.'

'Did he come back to help with things?'

'You're joking, right? He left everything to good old dependable Quinn. In his time away he had become worse; everything he had been when he was younger was magnified tenfold, especially his arrogance and womanising. Yet, Niamh seemed to like it,' Quinn reflected. 'I didn't see it at first...'

The anger that Finn felt had started to dissipate as she began to see that things weren't as black and white as she had originally believed them to be. 'Didn't see or didn't want to see it?'

The words resonated deeply in Quinn. He had suspected things but never believed it; they were his wife, his brother. 'I caught them... together,' he finally revealed. 'And embarrassingly I... I still took her back.'

'You mean they ran away?'

He nodded. 'For a few months. Then she came back. Apologised. Said she'd made a big mistake. Said he was irresponsible, that his lifestyle as a thief and adventurer weren't for her or his baby she was carrying. But that wasn't entirely true. As soon as she had you, she left... to be with him.' Quinn could see the scepticism on his niece's face. 'Take off the back of the picture. All the proof you need is there, written in her own hand.'

Finn did as she was told and found a folded piece of discoloured paper. She wanted to open the page, to see her mother's handwriting, but she hesitant. In her hand was the answer, the reason why her mother had abandoned her. And yet that reason had become moot. She was about to leave her uncle, after he had done so much for her, much like her parents had. It seemed like she was more like them than she cared to admit. But not quite. Unlike her parents she still valued Quinn. She may have been the daughter of Martin and Niamh but in her heart, Quinn was the only parent she had ever known or would ever need.

The unread paper was returned behind the picture and the backing replaced, then, as tears welled in her eyes, Finn stood up, wrapped her arms around Quinn and hugged him tightly. 'I'm sorry,' she said as he returned her affectionate gesture. 'I'm so sorry, for everything. For what I said... and for what they did to you.'

'Don't be silly. It's not down to the child to apologise for the sins of the parents.'

'It shouldn't be, but I still feel like I should. And there's something else. Now is as good a time as any to tell you... I got offered a job...'

'That's great!'

'From Fungal.'

'Oh.'

'Come on, you worked for Fungal.'

'Exactly! So, I know what he's like. But you're a grown woman so I won't stand in your way as long as it's not too dangerous.'

'Well, actually...'

'On second thought, don't tell me!'

'Thanks, dad!'

'What did you say?'

'Well, you and Niamh never actually got divorced, right? So that kind of makes you my step-dad.'

'I had all but forgotten that,' Quinn beamed. 'Because of the secret I thought that I would never get the chance to call you my daughter.'

'It's better late than never, dad,' laughed Finn. 'Although it wasn't said, I never felt less than a daughter to you.' She explained to Quinn that she had to go, having made an arrangement to meet up with Daniel. But first, Finn made a show of putting the picture of her parents back. Unbeknownst to Quinn, however, during the quick action, she had deftly retrieved the letter written by her mother and hidden it away in her coveralls. Then she bid her step father farewell.

Chapter Twenty-Six

Although it had been a few days since Trinity had last been in their room at The Dirty Dog, the elapsed time had not dispersed her distinctive floral aroma. It was a small comfort, as Daniel had been looking forward to reuniting with her, but it still brought a smile to his face as he entered.

As changed out of his Earth clothes and into his Ariest ones, he saw the communication shell that Princess Nyriel had given to him before she and Ch'tan left for the Shimmering Lake to avoid the fires of the Beltane Festival. Once it was over, he was supposed to contact them to let them know it was ok to return, but the whole reason they had come to the surface in the first place was to seek help from Gydion to destroy the Shade, but Daniel had done that. He could let them know and they could return to Pichini Palace and Murias City, after he had given the princess her present of course.

Daniel took the shell out and spoke her name into it. There was a series of bubbling sounds that emanated from the shell. It was some really strange magic, Daniel thought to himself, when he suddenly heard a voice on the other end. However, it was Ch'tan who answered and not the princess.

'We heard about you vanquishing the Shade from some passing merchants,' Ch'tan explained. 'The princess was overjoyed by what you did and contacted her father to tell him as further proof of you being a student of Gydion.'

'I'm sorry it took me so long to tell you what had been happening. As you can imagine, things got a little hectic. So, when will you two be arriving here? I have a gift for the princess.'

'Unfortunately, the princess has already been summoned back to court and I have been tasked with another duty to perform. On behalf of his majesty, King Noi D'Laani, I am to pay his respect to the Green Man.'

'The what?'

'He is the spirit of the forests, protector of the Goddess and patron of the druids. Perhaps you would like to accompany me, I believe it would be an eye-opening experience for you.'

'That would be amazing! I'll be waiting for you at The Dog.'

They ended the conversation and Daniel stared at the shell. Amazingly, the quality of it was better than the so-called modern mobile phones he was used to. A big tick for magic over science, he thought.

IT WAS LATE AFTERNOON when Daniel finally made his way to the Almedia bank. Rebuilding of the city by the Ganygu Conglomerate had carried on unabated whilst he had been away. He was coming to like living here in Almedia, the buzz it had was infectious, but he knew that he wouldn't be staying in this city much longer. He was destined to go to Imperial City to attend the Mage Academy.

He hoped that the capital of Ariest would have a similar atmosphere to Almedia but he doubted it. Most capitals tended to be overwhelming for first time visitors but at least he'd have Trinity there with him, and he was more than sure that Finn would take every opportunity to visit, especially since he had property there and he himself was really looking forward to seeing this new home. Things were moving at a pace for Daniel now, this was his new life going forward, and he couldn't wait to get it started. First thing to do with his new independence was get some coin in his pockets.

All of a sudden, Daniel could hear his name being called. He turned around to see Finn running towards him and then leaping on-to him when she was in range.

'I got to the tavern and Eveline told me you had already gone. So much for waiting for me, then,' she said as she punched Daniel on the arm.

'Sorry about that,' he replied as he tried to rub away the ache. 'Something came up. My friend, the one I was with when I first came to Almedia, is coming back and I wasn't sure how long you'd be with your uncle, so I thought I'd get things started.'

'Quinn is my step-dad actually,' smiled Finn. The look of be-musement on Daniel's face was something that she would have to get used to as more and more people found out the whole story. 'Basical-ly, that author is my mother, Niamh. And not only was she married to Quinn but she had an affair with his brother and after having me, ran off with him. What a lovely family I have, huh?'

'Wow, that's quite a story. How are you coping?'

'Don't worry,' Finn responded seeing the look Daniel was giving her. 'I've had a few drinks with my uncle...I mean my step-dad. I'm still getting used to saying that. Everything's fine,' she grinned. Finn ruffled Daniels hair before she linked arms and kissed him on the cheek before they continued on towards the Almedia bank, 'Serious-ly, I'm all right, but thanks for caring though.'

The facade of the bank was rather impressive, thought Daniel. It wasn't a particularly big building; merely two stories in height, it was wider than it was tall, but the front was styled like an Ancient Greek temple with its pillars, statues and coloured frieze of dragons.

'Are they the Tuatha?' He asked.

Finn looked up to where Daniel pointed. 'Yeah, that's right. No-tus is the red dragon, Zephyrus the blue, Boreas the copper one and the gold one is Eurius. They're the principle Tuatha deities although there are many others.'

They walked into the bank, there were only three customers queuing ahead of the two friends. There were paintings of small people, suited and booted, that Finn claimed to be gnomes. The only image of gnomes that Daniel had up to this point were of the garden variety that could be seen in some people's gardens.

Straight ahead was a stone masoned counter at the far wall, with four arched openings where the gnomes addressed their customers. There were only two gnomes working at that time on the counter, that Daniel could see, and a third explaining some banking matter to a potential new client.

As they waited, Daniel gazed around, noticing that it wasn't as lavishly decorated as the outside suggested.

Finn described to Daniel that gnomes and their Dwarf cousins were earth elementals with Boreas as their deity. As guardians of earthly treasures, such as minerals, metals and precious stones they also made perfect bankers. 'Although,' Finn added, 'banker gnomes can be very stoic compared to the others that I've come across. Complete opposites, really. The gnomes I've met in the guild, for instance, can be a bit obsessive and they have an enthusiasm, which although infectious, makes them a bit unpredictable, flighty, unreliable and a bit reckless. They can be excellent thieves, mind you, but vekt, once something glittery takes their eye, if you don't have a good grip on them, they'll be off, headlong, direct to the treasure, without scoping out the whole situation, busting the whole vekting...'

'Ahem,' the gnome banker interrupted. The pair had made it to the front of the queue without them even knowing it. The gnome looked down on them from the counter 'How can I help you?'

'Oh... I... uh,' stammered Daniel as he realised for the first time that he didn't actually know how the Ariest banking system worked. 'I... uh... would like to take some money out?'

'Certainly,' the banker replied.

Daniel's gamble was a success and he gave himself a little fist pump.

The banker continued expectantly. 'I assume you have the vault key and combination?' After being shown the aforementioned items the banker pointed to the last door on the right. 'If you go through door three, the cashier will see to you.'

As the pair made their way to the door to see their assigned cashier Daniel was intrigued, considering that his dad had told him that his account was at imperial city, he wondered what to expect next. It wasn't like the money in Ariest was a virtual thing that you could beam wirelessly over a computer system; here, if you had ten gold, you had ten gold. 'So, what happens now?'

'I don't know,' shrugged Finn.

'What do you mean you don't know?'

'I don't have a bank account! Are you kidding me? Have you seen the security of this place? Or should I say... lack of.'

'Now that you mention it...' Daniel trailed off into thought as he looked around and noticed that there were no guards of any description except for the three gnomes he'd seen.

'Exactly! And that's why I keep all of my money at home.'

'What? All of it?'

Finn shrugged. 'I have a big home.'

Still a little taken aback by Finn's revelation, Daniel opened the door, and shut it behind them.

A gnome in blue robes, who had been sitting at a desk reading as they entered, marked his place in his book and then sat crossed legged in front of them with his eyes closed. Whereas the appearance of the suited gnome was somewhat sedate, this gnome was anything but. His horseshoe hairstyle was spiked, he had an extra-long English moustache and classic goatee and all three were coloured bright green. Daniel and Finn were separated from the robed gnome by a large circle drawn on the stone floor.

'Please stand in the circle, hold hands and if the principal holder could think of your combination number,' the gnome said.

The two friends did as they were told and took a couple steps forward. The combination in question was a seventeen-digit alphanumeric 39409NH03703WT713, a cinch to remember for someone with a photographic memory.

'Ah, a very nice clear image,' the gnome commented. He began to chant and cast a spell. The circle they stood on began to slowly raise up and each part of their bodies it passed vanished.

The portal had reached halfway when a question in response to the gnome's statement popped into Finn's mind. 'Waitaminute! What if the image wasn't clear?'

'It's the customers responsibility to make sure it is. Unauthorised attempts to access vaults, even by mistake, are dealt with swiftly by security,' the gnome replied before they vanished completely.

'See, I knew they'd have some sort of security,' Daniel told to Finn. 'You of all people should have known that, come to think of it. I mean a bank with no protection would be a prime target for a thief guild to rob.'

'And who said they didn't?'

'What? When did they do it?'

'Well, they didn't. Well, they didn't succeed anyway. Well, not that we know of, at least. A group tried and were never heard of again.'

Daniel rolled his eyes. 'A veritable font of information as always, Finn.' Together they gazed around and marvelled at the bank's underground vaults. They were in a huge excavated oblong cavern which had levels built at every three meters, Daniel estimated. Sometimes he wished he wasn't so curious and this was one of those times as he looked over the protective barrier and into the seemingly bottomless pit.

'I wonder how deep we are,' said Finn as she looked up to see the levels of vaults extended up as far as she could see. 'You got to hand it to those gnomes and dwarfs, they sure know how to work stone.'

'Anyway, let's get this coin and get out of here.' Something suddenly dawned on Daniel. 'How *do* we get out of here?'

'*All you do is hold hands again and think of the circle you stood in at the Almedia bank and I'll bring you both back,*' the extravagant gnome's voice said in their head.

'What do you mean "back"? Aren't we there now?' Finn questioned.

'*Of course not,*' the gnome replied. '*All the vaults are beneath Imperial City. Each level has a thousand vaults and there are thousands of levels. That's why it's imperative to have the correct combination.*'

'Because they're coordinates!' Daniel suddenly exclaimed. 'The 713 is the vault number!'

Finn turned around and sure enough the vault they were standing in front of had the number 713 embossed on it. She couldn't help but think back to the story, which had become somewhat of a legend within the guild, of the four that had supposedly robbed the bank and how it could have been done. Even with this unconventional way of getting to the vaults, all it would need, she concluded was a skilled mage to port in.

Daniel approached the massive metal round vault door. The keyhole was smack bang in the middle and he took the key out of his pocket and slotted it in. Try as he might, however, the key would not turn.

It was the wrong door.

'*Oh dear,*' the gnome said disheartened.

'Are you sure it's the right combination?' Finn asked.

'Photographic memory, remember? You can see for yourself; I still have the paper.'

Finn looked at it and took a sharp intake of breath. 'Vekt! Your dad has a bit of a scribble handwriting. I mean, are those 3's or 5's and are those 6's or 0's?'

'*I think you two had better move whilst you decide,*' the gnome piped up again. '*When you have it, hold hands and think of it and I'll send you, but make it quick.*'

'What's the rush?' Finn scoffed. Then he heard what she thought was the sound of large wings slowly beating. Peered over the barrier and out of the darkness she could see flickering light getting larger and larger. 'I think we'd better do as he says, Daniel,' Finn said as she grabbed his arm and started to make a move.

It dawned on them that even though they would be in affect just running around a huge athletics track, they couldn't escape forever. And the realisation came before they discovered what was actually after them.

A creature that looked like a lion with a fiery mane, leathery wings and a scorpion tail with quills protruding from it, flapped its massive wings and flew straight up pass them.

'What the hell was that?' Daniel shouted.

'*That is one of our beautiful Manticores,*' the gnome replied in their head. '*He won't be alone.*'

As she heard that, Finn, saw the other creature climbing up, bounding from level to level until it reached the one they were on and stood where they had been at vault 713, where it roared and hissed. It had the body of a lion and its tail ended with the head of a snake.

'*And that is the Chimaera. A juvenile. It's goat head still hadn't sprouted yet.*'

Finn was suitably panicked at the sight of the animal. 'How's that number coming along?'

'I don't know. We're just going to have to do it by trial and error,' Daniel replied.

'I wouldn't do that...' the gnome began, but it was too late; Daniel had thought of a new combination grabbed hold of Finn and they both vanished to their new location.

'As I was about to say,' the gnome started, 'I wouldn't guess if I were you, because each time you get it wrong, a new Manticore and Chimaera will appear.'

'Vekt! You'll just have to try the key, Daniel,' Finn said reluctantly as she looked over the side and tried to find their assailants. She looked down and saw nothing but as Finn turned to look up, she threw herself back against the vault door as a fireball from the Chimaera just missed her head. 'You might want to hurry up!'

Daniel pushed the key in the hole, but again it wouldn't turn.

Out of the corner of her eye, Finn caught sight of the Manticore flapping its giant wings, holding steady as it flicked its scorpion tail and showered poisoned quills in their direction. The darts bounced off the vault door as Finn dragged Daniel to the ground to evade them.

'I've had enough of this dodgy around,' Finn said as she drew her guns, 'it's time to show these beasts who they're vekting with!' She stood up and noticed that a second Manticore had join the first. No problem, she thought, as she aimed each gun at one of the creatures and squeezed the triggers.

Nothing happened.

'The bank is protected against all unauthorised weapon and magic use,' the gnomes voice said in their heads.

Finn ducked down as another barrage of quills came her way. 'We need to move!' She said urgently and scurried off with Daniel in tow.

'So, it's not the first three or the first six,' Daniel told Finn as they crawled along.

'What if it's not just one number that's wrong? What if it's all of them? I mean all the 3's.'

'It could be. It's worth a shot,' Daniel agreed and reached out to touch Finn and thought of the new number.

They appeared in front of another door, number 715, where Daniel tried the key once more. He shook his head as the key failed to move again.

A fireball suddenly exploded above their heads. The pair were shocked into action and sprinted away from their assailant. Neither of them said it but they both knew that their chances were running out; there were now three Chimaera and three Manticore's after them.

Quills were striking the walls and vaults behind them and fireballs were exploding all around as they rounded the bend at the end of their level. Daniel came to a skidding halt as he saw the other two Chimaera running towards him and Finn. The creatures opened their mouths and they each shot a fireball at the frightened friends.

Daniel and Finn threw themselves against the nearby vault to avoid the deadly projectile. The numbers were against them now, however, as the three Manticore's took their chance to attack. The quills peppered the vault door and the two teens couldn't dodge them all; several of the darts found their target and pierced their skin. Finn's left leg immediately began to go numb, as did Daniels right arm.

All of a sudden, three fireballs exploded into each other, temporarily blinding Daniel and sending him reeling backwards into Finn who toppled over the barrier.

'Finn!' Daniel was desperate to check on his friend's safety that he put his own to the wayside and, still half blinded, he dragged his partially anaesthetised body and peered over the barrier. Finn held on for dear life. The fuzziness of his vision was clearing but not before more quills struck him. The poison was taking affect, the numbness was spreading.

'Well, I've had a fun life,' Finn said resigned to her fate as the three Manticore's with their fiery manes came up behind her. 'I'll be waiting for your dad in the ever after... to kick his vekting butt for having such vekted up handwriting!'

Daniel wasn't ready to give up, though. All he needed to do was reach out and touch Finn. The number sequence he had in his mind could be wrong but at least it would give them another chance instead of certain death at the hands of the Chimaeras and Manticores if they just stayed here without taking the gamble.

He almost had her. Daniel stretched his deadening arm out. Finn urged him on and gave her friend encouragement. The tips of their fingers almost touched. But the Chimaeras attacked. The blast wave from all of their fireballs threw Daniel clear over the barrier.

Finn took only a second to decide on her next course of action. Then she closed her eyes and kicked herself away from the wall.

Chapter Twenty-Seven

It was either a moment of stupidity or a moment of complete, blind trust. Finn would find out exactly which one it was that made her decide to plunge headfirst, down a seemingly bottomless cavern, after her friend, who could be unconscious at that moment. All without any definite way of saving themselves.

That was the gambler in her. She liked long odds. And if she was being honest with herself, the odds couldn't be much longer than they were. Then a fireball whizzed pass her.

'You have got to be vekting kidding me!'

She could hear the leathery wings of the Manticores beating and hear their roars as they chased their prey. There was nothing for it, she needed to get to Daniel fast. Luckily, she had an engineer as a step-father, so she knew all about aerodynamics and Finn took up a shape as non-resistant as she could, so she might cut through the air more efficiently.

Her assailants, however, had wings, so no matter how fast Finn was catching up to Daniel, the Manticores were closing in on her faster.

Even through the sound of the wind whistling in her ears, Finn could still hear the jaws of one of the creatures slamming shut over and over as it tried to take a bite out of her legs.

'Daniel! Can you hear me? Are you awake?' She could see that Daniel was still unmoving, his arms and legs loose, and the levels of the bank vaults continued to rush by, with no end in sight. They still had time, she didn't know how much, nor if it would be the bottom of the bank that would finish them or one of these blasted Manticores.

Finn could almost feel the beast at her back. But that was exactly what she wanted. She took one of her guns out and flipped over, hitting the creature hard in the head with the gun butt. The Manticore let out a cry and shook its head. Finn was half expecting to feel heat from its fiery mane but it seemed as though the flames were just for show as she wasn't burnt by it.

Finn's assault did little more than to anger the hybrid animal, unfortunately, and it folded its wings back and entered a dive. It ploughed into Finn's body, forcing the air out of her lungs. The two of them barged past Daniel which flipped and spun the young man, but ultimately helped him regain consciousness although he still felt partially numb from the poison tipped quills of the Manticores.

Daniel could see that he and Finn were in a dire situation. He remembered reaching down to grab Finn so they could be transported to what he hoped would be the correct vault. Then he remembered hearing the fireballs from the Chimaeras exploding behind him, but then nothing. And here he was again, plummeting to his imminent death (presumably, he still could see a bottom to the bank cavern). The difference between this fall and the one over Almedia city was that he had Nyriel there to catch him.

On the face of things, that could be a fundamental difference in deciding if he and Finn would survive this time.

He knew that the magical cloak that got him in to the trouble last time was in his satchel, but he also remembered that Finn's enchanted guns failed to work. He recalled what the gnome had said, that the bank was protected against unauthorised weapon and magic use; that ruled out the cloak and his own. If they were to get out of this alive it would be down to him, no magic, no enchantments and no Mortokai.

He sighted Finn and was initially taken aback by the fact that she was actually fighting the monstrous beast, hitting it repeated with her guns whilst it tried to bite her. The girl had no quit in her, he admired that.

With renewed determination, Daniel tried to guide himself towards the two of them. Since they were more focussed on fighting each other and not about wind resistance, it's wasn't long before Daniel was slamming into the winged creature. He bounced off of its muscular back and was rolling away when he reached out with his good arm and grabbed a handful of Manticore fur. With an almighty effort he pulled himself up and sat astride the beast.

Daniel smiled, happy with his achievements but he couldn't celebrate for too long as the other two hybrid creatures swooped past him, and was forced to duck. He crawled up the Manticore's back, evading the scorpion tail swipes of the other two as he went.

'Well, did you have a nice sleep?' Finn said when she saw Daniels head pop out over the Manticores shoulder. 'So nice of you to join me.'

'It looked like you were having so much fun,' replied Daniel. 'I wasn't sure if you wanted to leave or not.'

'Get me the vekt out of here,' she said as she continued to repeatedly strike and defend against her would be devourer.

Daniel reached out his arm just as the Manticore tipped forward. The action flipped Daniel head over heels off of its back, but the youngster had the wherewithal to grab hold of Finn's overalls. The extra weight of her friend jerked her down slightly in the creature's paw grasp. As small as it was the movement was enough so as to restrict his arms from swinging enough to defend against the mouth that was wide open above her head. She could feel the hot stench filled breath and spittle as the Manticore literally salivated at finally getting to eat its prey.

The creatures mouth slammed shut on nothing but air as Daniel and Finn vanished once more.

39469NH63763WT713. This had to be it, Daniel thought. He could already hear the Chimaera climbing down to their level and it wouldn't be long for the Manticores to home in on them either.

They helped each other to their feet, and like the walking wounded, Finn dragging her numb leg, leaning on each other, they hobbled towards bank vault 713 for the fourth time.

The pair reached the large round metal door just as they heard the snarls, growls and hisses of the Chimaeras that forever stalked them.

'You know we're vekted if this doesn't work, right?' Finn said as she looked deep into Daniel's yellow-coloured eyes. Even though she had seen him suffer from self-doubt a few times, that was only when he had time to think. But when push came to shove, he always did his best, did the right thing, gave it his all to help his friends, to help strangers, even to help his enemies. And now looking into his eyes Finn could see that he wasn't about to give up on her or himself. She never really knew if he loved her, she had never really asked him the question, and she wasn't even really sure of her own feelings, was she truly in love with him, or was it just infatuation. But in that singular moment of time, she knew one thing for sure, that Daniel would do anything to save her. She kissed him as if it would be the last time.

Daniel smiled back at Finn, pushed the key home and tried to turn it. But it wouldn't budge.

Both of their faces dropped as the realisation hit them. The Chimaera stalked them. It was over. The feline hybrid monsters readied themselves to pounce on their prey. Then Daniel noticed that there hadn't been any flash. No more beasts had been ported in, which could only mean one thing.

'It *is* the right door!' Daniel yelled.

He gripped the key again and with renewed determination and all the strength he could muster he tried to turn the key. He felt It move a little, not much but just enough to confirm it was finally the right vault door. Daniel turned it anti-clockwise and then forcibly clockwise. Over and over he did it and each time it turn just that little bit more.

By this time the three chimaeras were jostling for position to get to their live prey first. Finn had seen the progress Daniel was making and not being sure if he would get it open in time had taken up a position back to back ready to defend him if the beasts ever made an attack. She didn't have to wait long before the hierarchy had been established and they charged the two friends.

Finn loved a fight; anyone that knew her knew that, but she was starting to flag. Wrestling with that Manticore whilst falling had taken a lot out of her and the effects of its poisoned darts were still evident as she couldn't put any weight on her left leg. It may have been a hopeless cause facing off against the three Chimaera, but just as she knew Daniel would do anything to save her, so would she to save him. That was the foundation for any kind of solid relationship.

The first Chimaera leapt at them but Finn swatted it aside with the butts of both of her revolvers. The other two hybrids, seeing that there was still some fight left in this prey, were more cautious. They slowly walked forward, widening the gap between them, intending to flank her. Then they charged. Finn glanced at one then the other, trying to decide which one to defend against first. The one that would get to her first was the obvious answer but they were both coming at equal pace. But with a little patience she suddenly saw her opening. The Chimaera to her right had its mouth wide open, eager to get the first bite of this tasty morsel.

Finn jammed her gun into its mouth, forcing it to stay open, but as she turned to face the other Chimaera it pounced on her, she barely had enough time to bring her arms up in defence and grab its mane to hold it back from biting her head off. The situation was so dire now, Daniel couldn't leave his friend to fend for herself and longer. He directed several kicks at the Chimaeras head before it turned and attempted to bite his leg off then the snake headed tail took over as the lion head of the creature returned its attention back to Finn.

'Don't worry about me, just get that vekting door open!' Finn cried as the Chimaera clawed at her.

It was hard for Daniel to ignore the cries of pain from his friend. Several times he almost stopped to try and rescue her but each time he heard what she had said and went back to forcing the key.

The hopelessness he felt at not being able to help and the anger that welled up inside of him was exactly what Daniel needed and the key finally turned all the way.

The key melted into the lock and a golden glow shone out of the keyhole. A light appeared around the edge of the vault door and it grew larger and larger as the massive door slowly swung open. The Chimaera, its jaws inches away from Finn's face immediately stopped its attack and reluctantly cowered away, as did the one that had pounced first. The remaining one, with Finn's gun in its mouth, waited obediently for it to be taken out. Daniel gingerly reached into its maw to retrieve the obstruction. Once he had the creature joined the other two and one by one, they disappeared in a flash of light.

Daniel helped Finn to her feet and they hugged. They were both bloodied and dishevelled but also deeply grateful to be alive convinced that they had just escaped death. As they entered Daniel's bank vault neither one could believe their eyes, perhaps it had been all worth it after all.

The vault was a lot bigger than they had expected. To one side there were stacks of gold doubloons, silver ingots and copper geldings. It was more money than Daniel had ever seen, more money than Finn had seen.

'There must be thousands here, hundreds of thousands,' she exclaimed. 'The spoils of your dad's questing, I suppose. Just so you know, it's fifteen geldings to an ingot and five ingots to a doubloon.'

It wasn't just the coins that impressed them, there were gems and jewellery too. On the opposite wall we're more artefacts, weapons, and armour. Finn's jaw dropped as she recognised many of the items and called them off one by one; the ring of stamina, the lightning pole-arm, the dragon scale shield. She was like a kid in a candy store.

The first thing she picked up was a pair of goggles, much like the ones she already wore, Daniel thought, but these ones were completely black, even the lens. 'Do you know what these are?' Finn asked, giddy with excitement. However, she continued before Daniel could even answer. 'These are the goggles of night vision! Skelmin the giant used them in his underground lair with his huge Mephisto worms! I wish I could try them... Oh, Goddess!'

Another item from Eric Mondragon's adventuring days caught Finn's eye. A brown ridged spiral horn that looked perpetually wet, with little puffs of smoke coming out of it.

'The pirate queen, Captain Jane Wain's horn of fog! Blow this and it'll create a thick fog. Blow it again and the fog returns to the horn,' she said holding it in reverence. 'The Captain used it many a time to hide her dealings and her comings and goings. Your dad actually used the goggles to finally catch her.'

As Finn was about to put the horn back, Daniel reached over and took it from her. She watched him with wide eyes as he placed the horn in his satchel. 'You're taking it with you?'

Daniel was incredulous. 'Are you kidding? Of course I'm taking it! I wasn't expecting all of this cool stuff, besides, I'm kind of interested to see the affect.'

'Really? In that case...' Finn said as she saw an opportunity to try some other things and she grabbed them off the shelves 'Let's take the goggles, the pole-arm and these.' She held up two strips of purple cloth, each one had golden embroidery on them. 'These were given to Eric by Kay Haichi, master swordsman from Gorias.'

'The cloth and the goggles are fine,' Daniel said as Finn placed them in the bag, 'but I'm not sure about walking down the street with the spear.'

'This Ariest not Earth, so it's fine, but if you're a bit self-conscious about it, check this out.' Finn held the weapon out in front of her and gave it a short sharp jerk and it shrank down to the size of a pencil.

'Wow, that's pretty cool! Maybe I should get you to inventory all this stuff so I know exactly what they are and how they work,' said Daniel.

'Of course, I'll come to imperial City with you!'

'Huh?'

'You'll be going off to the academy soon and I'd need you to get into the bank. We could get the FTN from there and still work for Fungal!'

Inviting Finn to Imperial City wasn't what Daniel had in mind but the more he thought about it, the more he saw the benefits of it. He would be in a new city soon, so it would be good to have a couple friends with him in Trinity and Finn, as long as they could get along, that is, without fighting. 'Ok, sure! The Keep should have plenty of space.'

With the arrangement settled, Daniel turned his attention back to the principal reason they came to the bank in the first place. 'So, how much money do you think I should take out anyway?'

EXITING THE ALMEDIA Bank vaults was as simple as Niflek had told them; hold hands and think of the circle in his office. They were both aware that the injuries which had been inflicted upon them by the banks "security system" had been completely healed when they rematerialised In Almedia. The gnome mage had informed them that it was a small time-reversal spell, courtesy of the bank. It was a spell Daniel hoped to learn in his studies.

With their satchel of magical goodies and a few bags of gold and silver, Daniel and Finn made the short trip from the bank to Hyasda's Herb & Alchemy store. Daniel entered the shop first, his arrival signalled by the tinkling of the shop bell. He smiled as he gazed around the curio shop, happy at the chance to see something new and pleasant smelling in the city.

Daniel moved around the shop, investigating as many of the interesting contents as he could. He was so intrigued by the store that he hadn't noticed that Finn was barely in the shop, that she stayed at the entrance somewhat pensive and nervous, and that those feelings escalated when the store owner made her appearance.

They could both hear the rhythmic sound of the elderly woman's walking stick strike the stone floor and then her shuffling feet as she came out of the back to greet them.

'Ah, if it isn't the goddess, young Finn come to pay me a visit.' Hyasda had seen her first because she hadn't moved since arriving. The old woman thought the girl had come alone, but then she saw movement behind some shelves. 'and who might this be? A friend of yours?'

'This is - uhm - this is -' Finn uncharacteristically stammered.

'I'm Daniel. Daniel Welsh,' he said as he stepped out into the light.

'Ah, the consort! It was a shame that Tristan and myself were unable to see the crowning ceremony; we had important business to attend to.'

'He's also Eric Mondragon's son,' added Finn.

Hyasda peered closely at Daniel. Looked at him with a hint of recognition.

'Is something wrong?' Daniel asked, feeling a little uncomfortable with the elderly woman's stares.

'No,' replied Hyasda. 'You just remind me of someone I once knew from my youth. He was the one that set me on my path of discovery.' She fell silent as she reminisced about the days when she was Finn and Daniel's age. 'So, you're the one they're talking about?' Hyasda eventually continued. 'You're the one they're all scared of?'

Daniel shook his head. 'I don't know what you mean.'

'"The progeny of the champion shall bring death and destruction. The ghost of the dragon shall change Ariest forever. The Mortokai has come,"' Hyasda recited as she sat heavily into a nearby stool.

'What is that?'

'The words of our dear Queen. When she awoke from her deep dream sleep, she made this prophecy.'

'What's it supposed to mean?'

'Isn't it obvious? They believe the Mortokai will destroy the world as they know it.'

'And what do *you* know about the Mortokai?'

Hyasda scoffed. 'You do not get to live as long as I have without hearing a thing or two. Suffice to say that the Mortokai is a being of great power but more importantly, it is a faerie with a soul.'

Daniel looked distant as he weighed up what he was being told. The champion could be his dad. The ghost could be the name that he has been tormented with all his life, the dragon could mean Mondragon and Daniel had already been told that he was the Mortokai, he had experienced its power but he couldn't believe that he would cause death and destruction. 'You must be wrong! I'm not a killer. I refuse to believe that this is going to be my destiny!'

Hyasda held up her wrinkled hands. 'It's not my words, I'm just a messenger. But, on the other hand, how many faeries do you know of that have a soul?'

'I've heard that there are other children with faerie and human parents.'

'Yes, that is true, but how many of them can call their father hero or dragon?' Hyasda stated. 'Right or wrong, this whole thing was perpetrated by Queen Rhiannon and the other High Bourne of Imperial City, as well as Cernounos, the green man. Perhaps you could seek them out, plead your case, try and convince them that you are no danger.'

'Imperial City? I'll be there to attend the Mage Academy. Maybe I could ask Gydion to petition the Queen on my behalf.'

'Yes, that could work and, in the meantime, you could go to Cernounos yourself.'

'Is his home far?'

'The Druid Glade? No, it's not far, perhaps thirty miles.'

'Six or seven hours on horseback, less at a canter,' Finn added seeing Daniels exacerbated look when he heard the distance. She had kept quiet the whole time, for one simple reason, she wanted as little to do with Hyasda as possible. Finn had always thought of the little old lady as being just a bit odd, kept to herself, was amiable as much as she needed to be, getting faerie dust for Quinn, but after their encounter the other day, when she had ordered her to go with Daniel to Earth, Finn's opinion had changed. For the first time she had seen a different side to Hyasda. She didn't like the way she manipulated her, held her debt over her head.

'See, not far at all,' Hyasda said as she continued to try and convince Daniel. 'I'm sure you could obtain some horses from Murphy, the coachman.'

Daniel wasn't normally a proactive person. He tended to shy away and let things take their course. But that was the old him. That was the Daniel that suffered stares of curiosity on a daily basis. The Daniel that did anything so as not to bring attention to himself. This was his new life and he needed to leave that version of himself behind.

Both Finn and Hyasda could see that Daniel was slowly coming around to the idea. And the pair of them were pleased when he finally decided that he would make the journey to seek an audience with the Green Man.

'But what about Trinity?' Daniel asked. 'I was told that she had come here with Tristan; that you had sent them somewhere.'

'Yes, that's right. I asked Tristan to get me some Solecuss Root and Lunar Weed too.' Hyasda paused a moment to ponder. 'Come to think of it, the best area to harvest Lunar Weed is, coincidently, on the way to the Druid Glade, and it can only be gathered during a full moon. There hasn't been one yet, so perhaps you will find them camped nearby.'

'It sounds a good idea,' Daniel nodded. 'Are you coming, Finn?'

'You couldn't stop me,' she replied as she grabbed his arm and dragged him to the entrance. There, Finn, paused momentarily, before leaving quickly, when she heard the wizened old Hyasda call after her.

'Don't worry, Finn, I haven't forgotten your I.O.U. I will be calling to settle it soon enough.'

Chapter Twenty-Eight

'Isn't that your friend?' Finn asked. She knew that it was, he was hard to miss because of his size, but she wanted to deflect Daniel, get some reprieve, from his persistent questions about why she had acted so weird in the herb store. It was bad enough that she had used Hyasda's knowledge of magic to cheat during the Beltane Games but then to spy on Daniel and his family for the alchemist was a step too far. It was something that she would have to keep secret. He could never find out.

'Daniel Welsh, the Shade slayer!' Ch'tan brought his hand down on the boy's shoulder. Daniel's knees almost buckled under the weight of the heavily muscled arm. 'Greetings, my friend!'

'Hi, Ch'tan,' groaned Daniel as he tried to shrug the log like arm off of him. 'How are you? How's the Princess? It's a shame she isn't here; I brought her a book that I know she'd like.'

'Do not worry, I will give it to her on your behalf once I complete the King's bidding and I return to Murias.'

Ever since Ch'tan had first told him about this, in the back of Daniel's curious mind, he had wondered what could be so important that the King would order him to stay in Ariest, whilst the princess went back home without a guard.

He was just about to question the Undany royal bodyguard about it, when a group of people suddenly saw the Goddess and her Consort Shade slayer. Having to deal with fans and well-wishers was something that both Daniel and Finn were far from used to. Each of them had encountered disparaging attitudes towards them in the past for being different from the norm. Now, here they were, the social outcasts, sitting on top of the popularity tree.

Daniel had to admit that Finn was taking to it much easier than he was, simply because, in her mind she should have been getting this treatment already, even when she was raising hell. She regaled them with stories of their adventures home and away, of eating pizza and hamburgers, had them hanging on her every word as she told them about fighting three Shade in another realm alongside the legendary Mondragons.

The time eventually came for the people to go back to what they were doing before they had bumped into the Goddess and Consort. Daniel waved stiffly at them, glad to finally see the crowd disperse and move on so he could get back to questioning Ch'tan.

'Hold on!' Finn jumped in. 'Let's not stand out here when we can sit in The Dog and get some drinks at least.'

The other two nodded and they all entered the tavern. Finn signalled to Eveline who brought over three drinks with Daniel giving her enough coin to cover his accommodation also.

When the three of them were alone, and after Daniel had checked that no one was eavesdropping, he finally got to ask Ch'tan the questions he had wanted to. 'What is it that King Noi has gotten you to do? When we were in Murias he wouldn't allow the Princess to come to the surface without you. So, if he's telling you to stay here while she goes back unprotected, I know it must be pretty important.'

Ch'tan took a big gulp of his mead. 'For the King, it is,' he admitted. 'You know that Undany and surface dweller relations are strained, I have been sent to pay respects and parlay with the druids and The Green Man.' Daniel and Finn looked at each other as Ch'tan continued. 'The king is hoping that with the influence of Cernounos,

Queen Rhiannon might reverse her stance on my people and the alliance rekindled.'

'That would be a good thing, since you both live in this world,' Daniel said.

'Allies before can be allies again,' added Finn.

'Perhaps,' Ch'tan whispered his eyes glazed over as his thoughts momentarily went elsewhere.

'The funny thing, Ch'tan, is that me and Finn were preparing to make the same journey,' admitted Daniel.

'Really?'

'Quite a coincidence, to be honest,' mused Finn as she drained the last bit of her drink.

'Apparently there's a prophesy out there that people think is about me, that I'm a danger to Ariest. So, I'm on a similar errand, too. To show them that their thinking is wrong.'

The guard was about to comment but bit his tongue and changed his mind. 'Well, since we are on the same journey, it would be good to have company. But we will need to leave soon if we are to get there in good time.'

'Not a problem,' replied Daniel. 'Hopefully, we should find Tristan and a friend of ours on the way.'

'Friend of *ours*? Speak for yourself!' Finn downed Daniel's mug of golden honey mead in one. 'I'm ready to go whenever you guys are!'

LEARNING HOW TO RIDE a horse was now high on Daniel's list of necessary requirements for a life in Ariest. He didn't particularly need to become a master, just proficient enough so that he didn't need to be led by someone else.

One benefit of having someone else control the speed and direction of your steed was that it allowed you to take in and appreciate you surrounds more. Which was exactly what Daniel did. The sounds and smells of the nature put a smile on his face. He relished the chance to see more of Ariest. Just as Finn relished the chance to be away from Almedia.

The headstrong girl had always wanted to get out and see the rest of the world, she had come close to doing so on occasions, most notably with Crellis of the Tolgarr, but things always seemed to have a habit of bringing her back to the familiar surroundings of Almedia.

Not that that was a bad thing; finding out that Quinn was her stepfather and not just her uncle, made her wonder how that revelation would affect their current dynamic. She didn't think it would, but you never know. He might suddenly protest against her choices in life.

The convoy came to another clearing where they decided to rest for a while and stretch their legs. This was the second such break they had taken, the first coming an hour or two after they had started. Daniel thought that one might have been an ideal spot for Trinity and Tristan to have set up camp, but they found no such evidence.

Although there was a brook nearby the second site and they had found a patch of scorched earth, signifying use of a fire, Ch'tan determined that it was several weeks old at least.

It was always going to be a stab in the dark as to whether Trinity and Tristan had decided to gather the Lunar Weed before the Solecuss Root, or even if they had gone that way at all. With the lilac sun beginning to set and the light-blue sun already in twilight the pink sky of Ariest had become a deep fuchsia. Given the current situation there was only one course of action left to the threesome, proceed to the Druid Glade and hope to rendezvous with the others on the way back to Almedia.

CH'TAN HAD BEEN RIGHT to urge the party to pick up the pace. Even though they couldn't gallop at high speed, due to Daniel's lack of experience, at a canter they were still able to make it to the Glade before nightfall.

Glow worms illuminated the exit from the main path that led to the druid elves home. Other animals hooted, chirruped and scurried by unalarmed by the presence of the three strangers on horseback. The path led to a thick growth of trees, the sizes of which none of them had seen before. The walkway led into the home of the druids between two weeping willows whose drooping branches seemed to act as a curtain, hiding the beauty of the Druid Glade beyond.

Daniel, Finn and Ch'tan all dismounted. As they approached and were about to push aside the tree branches to enter, several of the animals transformed into elves. Some held staves, other's hands glowed with magical energy, all ready to attack. Finn, accustomed to getting caught being somewhere or doing something she wasn't supposed to be, put her hands up.

One of the elves spoke and although it sounded so beautiful and melodious the threatening intent that accompanied the speech wasn't lost on Daniel and the others.

'Point that stick elsewhere,' Ch'tan growled at them. 'I am on official Undany business on behalf of King Noi to speak with Cernounos.' Again, the elves responded angrily in their native tongue.

'It's because of me,' Daniel revealed. 'They won't let me enter. They keep calling me the bringer of destruction.'

'You can understand elvish?' Finn was astonished as were the elves themselves.

'I didn't know I could, it just kind of happens. It a similar thing happened before when I read the Book of Azul. That's written in Undany. Perhaps it's a mage thing,' he shrugged.

'If you speak our language or not matters little,' an elf responded in the common tongue. 'You are not welcome here. We all know of the prophesy. We all know of your part in it. You shall not set foot within the sacred Druid Glade and tarnish it with your presence, destroyer. Begone or we shall be forced to take action.'

'Action? Action is my middle name,' Finn said lowering her hands and placing them on her guns. 'If you're going to make threats, I hope you're ready to follow through on them.'

'The girl is right!' Ch'tan added. 'We come peacefully but if you want to bring the fight then a fight you shall have!'

Daniel didn't want this. Of course, he wanted to speak to the green man, but not this way. He wanted to convince Cernounos that he was not a threat. How could fighting their way into the druid home convince them that he was anything but?

The royal bodyguard had enough of the stalemate. 'I told the king, no matter the species, surface dwellers are all the same!' Ch'tan moved towards the glade entrance, determined to have an audience with the nature deity. Two elves crossed their staves, blocking his way. He pushed them aside.

Then all hell broke loose.

One of the elves swung their staff at the big man which Ch'tan caught in his two hands. Defending himself against the first elf left him wide open for the second one's attack. Sparks flew as he struck the Undany across the back with his enchanted staff. Finn jumped over the prone body of Ch'tan to tackle the elf who had put him there. Before Daniel could even act, the druids that had powered up their magic had called upon the roots and vines of the forest to tether and bind him.

Ch'tan had regained his feet and started to utilise his superior brute strength. He grabbed the staff of the elf that had first attacked him and swung her around, with the intention of using her as a battering ram to take out as many of the other elven druids as possible. But he wasn't counting on the remarkable elf agility as she somersaulted away.

'What is the meaning of this?' The voice was filled with authority and the elves immediately stopped and stood to attention in a line. Finn and Ch'tan remained cautiously on guard.

'We are sorry, Archdruid Tavisum,' the female elf said with a bow. 'The one known as Daniel is here. He tried to enter the Glade. We could not willingly stand by and allow the bringer of destruction access.'

'Daniel?' Trinity stepped out from behind the Archdruid. A mere wave of her hand and the vines and roots that bound him quickly retreated. The elves noted how easily nature responded to her. One or two wondered why their leader was so accommodating around this stranger, even going to far as to rush to her aid.

Once Daniel was freed, they wrapped their arms around each other tightly, both resisted the urge to kiss in the presence of Finn. 'What are you doing here?' Trinity was more than excited to see Daniel. The relationship between them was just getting started, in the early stages of budding, when he returned to Earth. But now that he was with her again, she hoped they could fully explore it.

'I came to speak to the Green Man and hopefully find you on the way,' smiled Daniel. 'I have so much to tell you.'

Trinity took his hand in hers and began to lead him toward the Druid Glade. 'You'll have to tell me how the family reunion went as well!'

'I cannot permit this to happen. These young elves may have been rash in their actions but never the less, they were correct. Daniel is not welcome here.'

'The prophesy is wrong,' Trinity said in desperation. 'My father knows it, that's why he has taken Daniel as a student.'

'Your father and I do not see eye to eye on a good many things,' Tavisum replied.

'And what of my father?' Daniel asked.

'Your father is a great man, an honourable man. But answer me this, Daniel Mondragon, are you or are you not the Mortokai?'

He was caught in a quandary. Daniel wanted so much to emulate his father, to be the honourable man just as the Archdruid said he was. But to be such a man he couldn't lie. And the truth would only further convince them that the prophecy is true. 'Yes, I am.'

'And so, it is.'

'That doesn't mean anything,' Trinity stated still fighting to convince them of Daniel's integrity. 'He has saved people from the Shade; strangers. If he were evil would he do that?'

'It is not a matter of being good or evil. It is a matter of protecting Ariest as we know it,' replied Tavisum.

'Oftentimes change can be a good thing,' Ch'tan added.

'Even if it is built on the blood, bones and destruction of those that were there before?' Tavisum countered. 'The decree stands, Daniel Welsh is banned and shall not be allowed to enter the Druid Glade.'

'You can't be serious!'

The stern look the Archdruid gave Trinity, let the youngster know that she was not one for levity. 'The rest of you are welcome within the Glade to recuperate, however.'

'And leave Daniel out here? That kind of hospitality I want nothing more to do with. Wait for me here, Daniel, and I'll be back after I get my things.'

A mischievous grin suddenly broke out on Finn's face. 'Don't be so hasty, princess. I haven't come all this way not to see this place. I've heard a lot about it and I intend to drink my fill of its experiences.'

'Whilst we leave Daniel out here alone? And you say you have feelings for him?'

'Put a sock in it!' Finn hugged Daniel and kissed his cheek before she whispered in his ear. 'It's a good thing we took those things from the vault because if you want to get in and see the Green Man, you're going to have to use them. Elves have night vision, so they won't be completely blinded, but they will be severely hampered, just be careful out there.'

'I'm not sure about this!' Daniel said as Finn walked off to join the others.

'Don't worry about a thing,' she called back with a wink. 'We'll be in and out before you know it!'

Chapter Twenty-Nine

Shadows around Gydion began to shake and then a Shade appeared, then another, then a third. With three quick frost bolts Gydion slowed them with ease. Just as he had done when they attacked Ariest, but this was their realm this was the home of the shade. Here their number was infinite.

Gydion looked all around; Shade were coming out of every shadow of the darken cavern. Hundreds upon hundreds of the creatures slowly made their way menacingly toward the arch mage.

'You should have taken the offer when it was there, husband,' chuckled Sayyidah, 'you could have saved yourself a lot of pain.'

'This is far from over, my dear,' replied Gydion before he clapped his hands together, which caused a ring of frost to rapidly radiate from the point of impact. Every Shade that was hit by it was destroyed but just as soon as they were eliminated another took its place.

The Shade, feared in Ariest, hungry devourers of essence, indiscriminate killers of the third Great War were being held in a stalemate with Gydion. He didn't want to show it but they were pushing him to the limit. There were so many of them that he had to use his spells at maximum affect. His dimensional energies were almost depleted and he couldn't see any way to end the battle. As long as he was able to keep them at range, unable to use their essence vampire abilities, it became a battle of attrition and then it would just be a matter of how long his essence would last before it was completely finished. Gydion decided that his plan B might have to be used after all.

Gydion had allowed the Shade to occupy his full attention and it almost cost him his head as the rock golem swung its huge fist and missed decapitating the Mage by mere inches.

'Your fight for survival has been very amusing, darling, but I grow weary of it. You have done well against the Shade thus far but what if the golem were to join the fray?' The golem attacked with more ferocity. Gydion dodged as best he could whilst blasting any Shade that came close, but he was still struck several times by the rock beast. 'Still you refuse to accept the inevitable? Fine. I shall finish you myself then.'

The course of the battle quickly changed. Gydion's offensive actions all but vanished as he desperately held off his attackers. But the end was near; he knew it was only a matter of time. All he could do now was to have faith in Trinity and Daniel. He believed they were destined to be the guardians of Ariest, no matter what the faerie queen saw in her dreams about the youngster. As long as they looked after his grimoire, everything would be fine.

Suddenly, out of the side of his vision, Gydion saw several rock spikes flying towards him. He managed to evade them just in time but in doing so he put himself into the path of the rock golem who delivered a devastating blow. He felt at least two of his ribs crack as the punch lifted him off the ground and before he had any time to recover the creature had lifted the Mage over his head and threw him like an unwanted toy.

Sayyidah had a maniacal grin on her face and her eyes widened with expectant glee as she watched the man she once loved near the end of his life. She had waited for this moment for so long, and now it was about to happen. She may only have been a duplicate of the true Sayyidah but she shared all the same personality traits, thoughts and feelings as the Egyptian, so even though she eventually considered him an obstacle to her ultimate machinations, she had married him, she had loved him but she was glad to finally be rid of him all the same. What affections she had left for him would be extinguished along with his life.

'This must be a hard spectacle for you to witness, beloved.'

'No more than it is for you, my Lord.' She turned to see Baelthorn watching her for any deceit. 'Well perhaps a little more. I have had three loves in my life; Gydion was third on that list.'

'And the first two?'

'My magic means more to me than anything, and the second love was the one that showed me that magic and what true power was, he set me on my quest to obtain more power.'

'I too know the lure of absolute power so to be second to that cherished phenomenon is acceptable.'

Sayyidah smiled at the dragon Lord. *He actually believed I spoke of him? I will show you how much I can love a so-called God in time, caliph.*

Gydion's sudden movement caught the attention of the couple as he struggled to his hands and knees; he coughed up blood as the shade closed in on their prey. It had been a long time since Gydion last found himself in such a condition; bruised, beaten and bloodied. He had neglected his own training during his search for Daniel, presiding over Trinity's development instead. Maybe this complacency had set in the day he became Archmage, after all what need is there for further training if you are already at the pinnacle of your class?

I should have studied more then I wouldn't be such a failure, he despaired. *I've failed at everything. I've failed everyone. Because of my failure I have doomed the people of Ariest.* He paused for a moment, his brow creased as he searched his memories, remembered moments of his life; he hadn't failed his life, his life was a success and it wasn't over yet!

The malaise that had descended on him lifted slightly. For the first time he heard a sound like wind rushing past his ears. With his head turned slightly to the side he saw the source, the mouth of a Shade open grotesquely wide. The blow from the rock golem had sent him into the shadows, the perfect hunting ground for the dark entities known as the Shade.

So, this is what it feels like to have them feeding on your Essence. And that sense of self-pity, like you want to give up, must be to stop the victim from fighting back, he thought. I've been getting these feelings on and off since I arrived here. Have they been feeding on me since then? Surely not. But it would explain why I felt weak against the Keeper and why my essence depleted so quickly, but if not the Shade maybe it is something in the atmosphere itself. And if that is the case no wonder the master made it a no-go area.

More and more Shade joined the feeding frenzy. Gydion could no longer discern where one ended and the next began. He could see his essence being drawn out of him in several different directions, like hyenas tearing at his soul. Time was running out for his escape, it was now or never, whilst he still had an ounce if Essence left.

She watched on with bated breath. She wished that hers was the last face Gydion would see but there were too many Shade on him now, all Sayyidah could see of her husband was some of his cloak and then that too was gone. Then, as the Shade began to disperse, she could see that it wasn't just the cloak that was gone, but he was, too!

'It is done.'

'What do you mean it is done? I wanted his body to parade before the council!'

'He is dead and his body has been taken by the Shade.'

'That's not good enough! To quash any thoughts of an uprising on Ariest they would need to see the corpse of their great hero, now they will still have faith that he will return! Hope that he will save them again!'

'But you know that will not happen.'

'Do I?'

'You doubt me?'

'I doubt Gydion will do the decent thing and stay dead and neither should you.'

'I do not fear ghosts.'

'As you wish,' Sayyidah replied with a curtsey and a strained smile. Bite her tongue and bide her time, that's all she had to do. Things were progressing nicely for her; Earth realm would be hers soon, then she would show Baelthorn what it means to underestimate. 'I think the time has come that I should return to Ariest and prepare the way for your arrival, my Lord.'

'That one over steps her boundaries. She needs to be reminded of her position.'

'As do you.' The voice rumbled throughout the cavern as if it came from everywhere. 'You approach god hood only because I allow it, do not forget that. The next time you try to siphon energy from me without my permission you will be severely punished.'

'That impudent mortal dared to challenge Baelthorn! Baelthorn would have crushed him, yet you almost made Baelthorn look a fool.'

An earthquake suddenly shook the cavern and just as sudden as it started, it stopped.

'Baelthorn begs forgiveness, mighty Salamida,' pleaded the dragon Lord as he fell to one knee.

'I could have destroyed you millennia ago when you entered my realm, but I chose not to because you opened the way out of the void I dwelled to your own burgeoning realm; fresh clean essence to feed upon. I spared you then do not make me regret that decision. We have a long journey ahead of us and you have a long recuperation after your imprisonment. Let your consort settle things for the time being, herald the word of your return, then you will have your revenge against the descendants of your siblings, and I shall venture further into this new world.'

Chapter Thirty

'You have got to be kidding me!' Trinity was fuming as she listened to Finn nonchalantly explain the plan, she had devised for Daniel to them. 'Are you crazy? What if Daniel gets caught sneaking in here?'

'Do you want to speak a bit louder, princess? I don't think they heard you in Gorias!'

'Would you both be quiet!' Tristan, though awake, was still feeling some of the effects of the poison he had been struck with by the Shadow Dancers, namely a headache worse than any hangover he had endured in his life. And having Trinity and Finn bickering wasn't helping the thumping in his head go away. 'Now, if we can all speak in a civilised manner, I actually think that this could work.'

'As do I,' Ch'tan agreed. 'I know of the Fog Horn and that magical fog it conjures up is thicker than anything you could imagine. With those goggles you mentioned, Daniel should be able to get in without issue, as long as he doesn't stand in front of anyone.'

Trinity rolled her eyes at Finn's smug look. 'And if he does get caught?'

Finn shrugged. 'Then were all vekted.'

'Excellent,' groaned Trinity. She slumped into her chair, worried out of her mind.

Ch'tan suddenly got up and made for the door.

'Where are you going?' Tristan asked.

'Well, I thought I'd go and see if I can get my audience with Cernounos Just in case things go wrong and we all get kicked out.'

'Sound idea,' stated Tristan.

Trinity's pleasure at seeing Daniel had been so short lived she didn't really have the chance to fully appreciate it. And now to think that at any moment he was about to attempt what she believed to be Finn's hair-brained plan troubled her. This time she really did need a distraction.

'I have got to say, this place is kind of special,' Finn said looking around the elevated treehouse they had been given for the length of their stay. 'You know when you hear stories about something and you're like "wow, that sounds great!" And when you finally get to see it, it doesn't live up to expectation? Well this place goes far beyond what I ever thought about it. How did you two get here though? Hyasda said that you were gathering herbs for her closer to Almedia.'

'We were attacked,' Tristan answered, 'in broad daylight by the Shadow Dancers. The druids rescued us and brought us here.'

'That's a bit weird,' Finn furrowed her brow in thought. Having dealings with the Thieves Guild made her privy to more of the shady goings on of Ariest. As much as the Shadow Dancers were a myste-rious organisation, it was almost common knowledge in the under-world that they excelled at stealth; striking when you least expected it. 'I wonder who their target was.'

'It seemed like it was both of us,' replied Tristan.

'Well I could understand them going after you,' said Finn rub-bing her chin thoughtfully. 'I'm sure there's a long list of husbands and boyfriends that'd like to see you buried.'

'And a list twice as long of wives and girlfriends,' added Trinity. Both girls broke out into laughter.

'Ha ha, laugh it up,' mocked Tristan. He didn't much like being the butt of jokes so he dropped a revelation that he thought the other two had overlooked, which stopped the laughter dead. 'The real question here is who wants you dead, Trinity?'

'He does have a point, princess.'

'Stop calling me that.'

'I will as soon as you stop acting like one.'

'I do not act like a princess.'

Finn was about to answer back when, out of the corner of her eye, she saw a thick fog rolling in through the Glade. 'Well, well, well,' she grinned, 'it only looks like Daniel's gone and blown the horn.'

Trinity and Tristan joined Finn at the window. They looked down and saw that the fog was, not only, moving quickly but it was raising. It was so thick that they could barely see any of the flaming torches that illuminated the thoroughfares and pathways.

'Great,' Trinity let out a worried sigh. 'Now what?'

'Now we just wait for Daniel to talk to the Green Man, get out of the Glade and blow the horn again to clear the fog and it'll be mission accomplished.'

'And if he can't find the Green Man?'

'Then we're vekted,' Finn shrugged, the smile not leaving her face. This was adventure to her and she was loving every minute of it.

IF THIS WAS ADVENTURE for Finn, then this was nothing short of dread for Daniel. He had waited, thought through Finn's plan thoroughly, weighed up the pros and cons of going ahead with it, and then put the horn to his lips, took a deep breath and blew it.

He needed to see the Green Man, and if sneaking into the Druid Glade was the only way that was going to be possible, then so be it. He didn't really want to do it this way and he hoped that Cernounos wouldn't hold it against him, but secretly he was anxious to try out the magical artefacts he had brought from the bank vault.

Daniel had made sure that he moved away from the elves when he used the horn; he wasn't sure what kind of sound it would make and thought it would be best to have some distance. Funnily enough, the horn made no sound at all. As Daniel blew, a thick fog noiselessly billowed out of the other end. He made sure to aim it at the glade and watched with fascination as the fog rolled towards the elf homestead, getting bigger and denser with each passing moment.

The magical fog was extraordinary; Daniel could barely see his hand in front of his face let alone any of the forest. He fumbled with his bag and replaced the Horn of Fog with the black-lensed, Goggles of Sight.

'Awesome!' Daniel breathed as he slipped the goggles over his head. Through the enchanted lenses he could see as if it were a normal, sunny day; his vision wasn't affected by the darkness of night nor the thick fog he had created.

He still had to be careful as he snuck pass the two guards and into the Druid Glade, so as not to make a sound and draw attention to his position. Through the amazing Goggles of Sight, Daniel was able to look in wonder and fully appreciate the aesthetic beauty elves are known for. He wished he could spend more time examining everything the Glade had to offer but he was on a mission. And that's when he came upon the one big flaw in Finn's plan; he had no idea where to find Cernounos.

He walked around half hoping to see some street sign directing the way, but there was nothing. Daniel could feel himself getting agitated and his head getting a little hot from the anxiety that was building in him. He was on the verge of calling the whole thing off and making his way back out of the Glade, when he heard an elf give a command in elvish.

Daniel's fortunes took a turn for the better. The elf was tasked with informing Cernounos of the mysterious fog that suddenly came upon the Glade. He set off with the assuredness of someone that knew his homestead like the back of his hand. Daniel had the luxury of being able the follow from a distance.

The elf continued towards the north to the far end of the Glade and finally came to a thick bush with an opening cut through it. More guards stood to attention here but these ones had more elaborate clothing than the guards at the Glade's entrance, this garb was almost ceremonial.

This must be the place, Daniel thought.

The druid he had been following entered the bushes through the archway, only to return shortly afterwards, and taking the two ceremony guards, headed back the way he had come.

Seeing that the coast was clear, Daniel headed through the archway himself, only to be almost knocked over by Ch'tan. He noticed that the Undany seemed to be a little preoccupied as he rushed pass, meaning Daniel had no chance to grab his attention without making a scene. The youngster decided that he'd talk to him later to see if he was okay, right now he had to finish what he had come here to do.

'YOU WON'T NEED THOSE here. Your fog has no effect on my sacred grove.'

As Daniel stepped through the archway, he pulled down his goggles. The voice was had been right. Although it was night-time this area seemed bright as if it were bathed in the light of a full moon even though there wasn't one in the sky.

The grove was almost circular in shape surrounding a lake which had an island at its centre. On the archipelago was a single tree but it had the widest trunk Daniel had ever seen. In its shadows he could just make out the silhouette of a figure with what seemed to be huge horns.

'I've come—,' Daniel tentatively began, 'I've come to speak with the Green Man.'

'I am the Green Man,' the shadowy figure replied. 'I am Cernounos. I am the spirt of nature. I am the one you seek. Cross the bridge and speak your mind.'

Daniel all of a sudden, became nervous. He was standing in the presence of a sacred entity and he didn't know what to say. His plan hadn't been developed that far. They had only devised how he would get here not what he would say when he arrived. 'Hi, I'm Daniel...'

'I know who you are, Daniel Welsh. I know why you are here and how you arrived within the Druid Glade. But you should know, the prophesy is not wrong.'

'Look, I'm sorry about that. I really am. It wasn't the way I wanted to see you but the Archdruid and the others wouldn't let me in and their reaction is directly the result of this prophecy. How can I be judged for something that may or may not be about me, for something that I may or may not do? I was told that you have the influence to change people's opinion, that I should petition you so that you can tell them the truth. That's why I decided to, why I had to, take these desperate measures to see you.'

'Yes, I am old, wise, well respected and yes, people do listen when I speak. Even the queen of all Ariest seeks my council from time to time. However, I cannot give you what you seek, for I believe the prophecy to be true.'

'But you're wrong! If I was this destroyer of Ariest why would Gydion take me as his student?'

'I cannot speak for the mind of Gydion. Not many can. Perhaps he hopes to guide you, to rewrite your destiny. Perhaps he believes it is best to keep the destroyer near to him. There are many reasons but only he can speak his mind.'

'I've done good. Saved people's lives. I'm the son of a hero for Christ's sake! How can people think I'm evil?'

'Good and evil are down to an individual's perception. All of our actions have consequences. You stop a child from stealing a loaf of bread today, but because of that action the child's starving sister dies of hunger tomorrow. What is the good and what is the bad?'

Daniel thought for a moment. It was a small crime but a crime none the less. Could he let another child die because of his intervention though? 'I would stop the child from stealing,' Daniel started, 'then I would buy two loaves for him and his sister.'

'Interesting,' Cernounos remarked. 'A simple outcome for a simple dilemma. What will you do when the stakes are much higher though? The progeny of the champion shall bring death and destruction. The ghost of the dragon shall change Ariest forever. The Mortokai has come. Do you deny that this pertains to you?'

'I accept that I am the Mortokai, but me bring death and destruction to Ariest? I love this place. I would never do anything to harm it.'

It began with a single leaf. Suddenly, it came loose from the tree canopy and fluttered down, landing on the ground between Daniel and Cernounos. It immediately turned black and crumbled to dust.

A whistling arrow was fired, out through the fog, high into the night air. Then another. And another, their sonic alert heard far and wide.

'The druids... are being... attacked! You have... already... taken your... steps down this... path of... the prophecy, Daniel Welsh,' said the Green Man, his speech became more laboured with each passing moment. A black tar-like substance erupted from his mouth and oozed from his eyes and nose. 'You... have... brought... death... to the Druid Glade.'

'What? No, I haven't done anything.'

The Green Man fell to his knees, which caused many more diseased leaves to fall to the ground. He fell onto Daniel as he tried to reach up for the young man's goggles. 'All... of our... actions... have... consequences,' Cernounos said with his last breath.

The dead body of the Green Man sprawled in Daniel's arms as the last ounce of energy left the nature spirits body. It was understandable that the youngster would be shellshocked, he had come seeking help and only found suspicion and now death.

His mind was a muddle. The last words of Cernounos resonated within him. You have brought death to the Druid Glade. Did he know he was going to die? Or did he mean someone else? All of our actions have consequences. Then Daniel remembered the fog he had conjured. That must be it! Someone was using the fog to attack the glade.

'Damn it!' Daniel fumbled in his bag until his hand found the shell. He pulled it out, blew it, and hoped that it wasn't too late.

'CAN YOU HEAR THAT NOISE?' Tristan asked Trinity and Finn as they all continued to look out of their window. 'That whistling sound? That's a distress arrow.'

'There's more than one,' Finn corrected. 'Something's going on out there.'

'Whoa, look at that!' Trinity suddenly saw the fog retreating like a blanket being pulled off of a bed.

'It's Daniel,' explained Finn. 'He's blown the shell again, but it's going the wrong way. He was supposed to do it when he was out of the Glade. The fog returns to the shell, the druids will know he's here!'

'I don't think they'll be too bothered about that right now,' stated Tristan as he tightened his grip on the hilt of his sword.

The receding fog uncovered a battle below between the druids and the Shadow Dancers. There were many dead on both sides of the conflict and yet it still continued unabated.

'We need to get down there!' Trinity said as she opened the window. 'I'll find Daniel, you two help the druids.'

'What about Ch'tan?' Tristan asked.

'He must be somewhere down there too,' replied Finn.

'Find him!' Trinity climbed onto the ledge and jumped out. As she was in free fall she transformed into a peregrine falcon and followed the direction the fog retreated to.

'I guess we're taking the long way down,' shrugged Finn.

Chapter Thirty-One

It wasn't possible to envisage a worse tableau than the one Daniel currently found himself in. Not only was he caught by archdruid Tavisum with the Horn of Fog at his lips, but he was also standing over the lifeless body of Cernounos, the Green Man, the physical embodiment of the spirit of nature.

'It was you that did this! You brought the Shadow Dancers here!'

'What? No, I didn't do anything.'

'So, it is just coincidence that those abominations used the fog that you created to attack the glade?'

Daniel had to admit that it was a damning coincidence, but it was coincidence all the same. He was about to tell the Archdruid so when she suddenly let out a scream of anguish.

'What have you done?' She looked up at the once strong and powerful tree that stood in the centre of the Green Man's sacred grove. Now blackened and withered with barely a leaf remaining intact. Daniel could see the eyes of the Archdruid glisten with tears as her gaze fell upon the lifeless form of Cernounos. 'You poisoned him!'

'It wasn't me. We were talking then the leaves began to fall and crumble before he took sick himself. It happened so quickly. I didn't know what was happening.'

'You killed him, that is what happened! Look at the black poison coursing through the veins of the tree!' Tavisum pointed at its trunk.

The only place the poison hadn't touched was an area the rough shape of a hand. 'The divine tree and Cernounos are linked; kill one and the other shall fall also.'

'I'm telling you, I didn't do this!' Daniel was desperate now. He could tell by the look on the Archdruid's face that discussions were over.

Tavisum stared at the boy with distrust and more than a hint of disgust. She hated the way that most other races of Ariest had a distinct disregard for nature. How they failed to realise that all life must coexist harmoniously. That contrary to what humanoids might think they were beholden to nature and not the other way around. Nature and its bounty should be respected and a swift death meted out for those whose acts are anathema to nature. And what bigger affront could there be than to bring unnatural death to the sacred grove and the warden of wilderness.

'I should have let the sproutlings finish you once I knew who you were. I could have saved the Druid Glade and the rest of Ariest from your atrocities, but with your sacrifice I can begin to atone.'

'What sacrifice?'

'Your life, of course. You have committed the most heinous of crimes against nature. You must be stopped.'

Tavisum began to weave a spell, green leaf shaped Essence surrounding her hands as she did so. Daniel didn't know what he should do. Fight back or accept his fate. By sneaking into the sacred grove maybe he did bring something with him from the outside. Maybe it was the fog itself, the shell did belong to a criminal after all, but surely Finn would have told him if it were poisonous.

Daniel braced himself for the end, but it never came. Before Tavisum could finish casting the spell that she intended to strike him down with, vines and roots suddenly burst out of the ground and wrapped themselves around her wrists pinning her arms to her sides. Try as she might, the Archdruid couldn't release herself.

A small bird then swooped down, transformed into Trinity and landed softly between Daniel and Tavisum. 'What do you think you're doing?' Trinity demanded.

'I could ask you the same thing,' replied Tavisum.

'I'm stopping you from making a grave mistake.'

'And still you defend him! Look to the tree behind you, does it not resemble the ones from your vision?'

'How did you know about that?' Trinity looked at the tree and she was stunned. Sure enough, Tavisum had been right.

'That was Cernounos you spoke with in your dream. You did not heed the warnings. Your friend has already begun his walk along the path of the prophesy and I intend to make sure he goes no further.'

'Your people are in a battle, that is what should be your priority right now.'

A look of concern momentarily crossed the Archdruid's face as she turned to the sacred grove entrance. 'It is a battle caused by the actions of Daniel Welsh! I have let his grievous act against the Green Man distract me from protecting the Glade with the other druids. Release me so that I might help my comrades. But rest assured,' she continued, as Trinity did as she was asked, 'I will be keeping a close eye on you Daniel and once your Shadow Dancers have been repelled, we will look into your crimes once more.' The spot where Cernounos had fallen was now covered in budding flowers and the Archdruid sent up a silent prayer before heading out of the Sacred Grove.

THE BATTLE HAD CONTINUED unabated in their absence. The druids changed into various animals to combat the Shadow Dancers who used their weapons of death with deadly efficiency. Casualties mounted on both sides and as soon as she could, Tavisum transformed into an armoured bear and charged into the fray.

'Come on,' Trinity said as she took Daniel by the hand and started to lead the way back to where she had left Finn and Tristan. 'Hopefully they would have found Ch'tan by now and we can all regroup and make our next plan.'

The pair had to fight their way through, taking down several Shadow Dancers as they did. They worked well as a team. Trinity restrained them while Daniel took them out with his frost magic. Other times it would be Daniel holding them and Trinity finishing them with her nature's wrath spell.

Daniel felt that he was becoming more and more proficient with the frost spells he had learnt. He still couldn't cast whilst on the move but he had more success than failures with his spells now. He put it down to the old adage; practice makes perfect. And he had been getting a lot of practice recently, at the bank, against the Shade on Earth and whilst fighting the Shadow Dancer that tried to steal the Book of Azul at Almedia Palace.

That's when he thought he saw her again, the same Shadow Dancer. He wasn't sure until he saw her suddenly move strangely, as if she were fighting herself. 'It is her!' Daniel shouted to Trinity over the sound of the combat. 'That's the elf that tried to steal the spellbook at the tavern and again from the palace. I think she's still under some sort of control.'

Trinity watched the female in question and was struck by how she held herself back at times. 'You might be right. If she is, who's to say that the others aren't as well, they just might not be as strong willed as her to try and fight against it. We have to find the Archdruid and tell her, she might be able to dispel it.'

They look around trying to spot Tavisum realising in their heart that it was almost like looking for a needle in a haystack since she could be in any animal form at that moment. 'I see her! She's over there! Not far from Finn.' The Archdruid was in a somewhat feral form, sharp claws and teeth but still recognisable as Tavisum.

Trinity began to lead the way through the crowds of fighting elves, pushing and shoving as she went. When all of a sudden, much to her surprise, the Shadow Dancers pulled back and retreated. The battle was over as quickly as it had begun.

The druid elves had captured many of the assassin elves but there had been many losses on both sides testament to the ferocity of the battle. 'Round up the prisoners,' Tavisum commanded, 'we will deal with them soon.'

'Wait!' Trinity called out. 'I think you might want to reconsider, Archdruid. It's possible that they might be under a spell or something. We saw one of them acting very strangely.' Trinity saw the elf amongst the prisoners and pointed her out. 'It was that one, in fact.'

'Bring her to me,' Tavisum said to the guards. She looked closely at the Shadow Dancer, barely able to hide her disdain for the other elf. Then she cast a spell which showed a green viscous substance coursing through the Shadow Dancer's veins. 'She has indeed been poisoned.'

Archdruid Tavisum took a dark brown pellet from her pouch and, not too gently, forced it down the throat of the Shadow Dancer. Within seconds she doubling over wracked in pain. She fell to her knees and retched up the green substance that the Druid spell had revealed. The poison was thick and seemed to melt the ground it rested upon. Tavisum cast a spell and the poison dissolved into nothing then she ordered the guards to give the rest of the prisoners antidotes.

'You were right, Daniel, she was fighting against something.' Trinity turned to congratulate him on his assumptions but her friend was nowhere to be seen.

'Is this another coincidence, Trinity?' Tavisum asked.

'No, of course not. He was right behind me when we came look-ing for you.'

'We couldn't find Ch'tan either,' Finn added.

Archdruid Tavisum had already made up her mind on what to do. To her Daniel Welsh was still the destroyer that he had proved himself to be by killing the Green Man. 'Find the boy and bring him to me. I don't care what condition, just bring him.' Four druid elves immediately despatched from the glade.

'You can't do this,' Trinity pleaded.

'I can and I am. You seem to forget that your friend has commit-ted the most heinous of crimes against nature. For that, he must pay.'

'You won't find him here,' the Shadow Dancer said. 'They've tak-en him to my lair. Release me and my comrades and I will take you there.'

Trinity anxiously turned to Tavisum. 'Well? What are you wait-ing for? We need her help.'

'I will not accept the help of a Krez. You are new to this realm Trinity. None of you know about the betrayal of the Krez elf clan. You would be wise not to trust them or their words.'

'I have no choice.'

'Then you should know who you are getting into bed with. You know that the war amongst the Tuatha created the realms and their spilt blood, the primal races: elves, dwarfs, gnomes, undines, sala-manders, sylphs and giants. There was a battle for supremacy in the early days of Ariest amongst these races. The giants were victors and enslaved the others. It was the High Bourne elves that knew that the only way to free themselves was for the other races to band together and overthrow their giant overlords. They did just that and the High Bourne elves were made supreme rulers of Ariest.

'Some elves dispersed from the High Bourne and settled their own clans, mountain elves, forest elves, artic elves, cave elves, ocean elves etc. The ocean elves went further afield to set up their colony on

Earth in your Atlantic Ocean. But seeing the path that humans were going down they decided to use the magic of the High Bourne and bring their Atlantis to Ariest.'

'Atlantis is real? And it's here?' Trinity was flabbergasted.

'It is an island off the northeast coast of Ariest. As I was saying, with most of the ordered minds of the High Bourne gone the more chaotic ones took control. Their reasoning was that elves had the right to rule and exert their dominance over others because they were the god's perfect creation. This led to a war among elves. The cave elves who had become the Krez clan, never openly declared their allegiance to either the High Bourne or the Dark Fae but they helped the dark elves remain in power and betrayed other elf clans to them, leading many to their deaths.

'Although the Krez shared the same "right to rule" belief as the Dark Fae, that commonality wasn't enough to keep the Krez loyalty when the Dark Days were brought about. The Krez were against diluting the perfect blood of elves in the pursuit of what they believed to be folly; life after death, an everlasting soul. So, in order to bring about a swift end to the dark days of Dark Fae, the Krez betrayed them and the High Bourne expelled them from Ariest.

'Even though the Krez had done the right thing in the end they were still made to pay for their initial betrayal. The High Bourne seers cursed their clan for all eternity, with something called the Rising. Those tattoos they have hold the psyche of all those they have killed. After a time, those spirits will rise up and attack the mind of the host, turning them mad, eventually killing them. The only way to suppress it is in a ceremony called the Quelling. The thing is, the Krez need to kill in order to live. To kill gives them vitality, sustenance, which is shared among the clan during the Quelling.'

Trinity looked at the female Krez elf taking particular note of the number of tattoos she had down her side. 'So, they must kill to live but in so doing they run the risk of being driven mad and dying?'

'Those that can survive are strong,' the elf said when she saw Trinity eyeing her. The other Krez elves that had regained their own minds repeated the mantra.

'What is your name?' Trinity asked her.

'I am Anjunel Lynsu'unara,' she replied. 'Many know me as Anju, the Mistress of Death.'

'Given what I have just heard, why should I trust you to take me to Daniel unscathed?'

'I must spend a lifetime atoning for the actions of ancestors long dead. Trust me or don't, it matters not to me but I shall deal out revenge against the one that would think to use me and my military chapter against our will.'

'Who was it that put you under a spell?'

'That is obscured from my mind, but once we had obtained what they wanted they were to come to my lair for it.'

'Daniel.'

'No, the book.'

'The Book of Azul? That's what you were after?' Finn asked. 'But you could have taken it numerous times. The palace for instance.'

'And I would have, had I not been controlled. I am the puppet of no one!'

'And what about in Almedia? It was you that rescued me against the Shade, wasn't it?'

'Yes. I was taken by your skill and warrior spirit. Those that can survive are strong.' Again, the other Krez repeated it.

Finn elbowed Tristan hard in the arm. 'I told you it wasn't a figment of my imagination,' she said with a satisfied smile on her face.

'We have to go and rescue Daniel,' Trinity said to Tavisum.

'We will do no such thing. You can do as you wish but the druids will not follow those traitors nor will we lift a finger to save the one that has murdered Cernounos.' A gasp went through the druids as many of them had no idea that the symbol of nature had been killed. 'Release the Shadow Dancers!'

'When I make it to Daniel, in one piece, maybe then you'll believe that people aren't locked into their destiny, that they can change and forge a new one. Maybe then you'll see how wrong this prophesy is.'

Trinity, Finn and Tristan gathered their things and soon they were headed northwest towards the lair of the Shadow Dancers. Even after what she had said to the Archdruid, Trinity still had a sense of trepidation as they travelled the unfamiliar route led by the Krez elves and she made sure that she remained on her guard.

Chapter Thirty-Two

Daniel could feel something cold and hard against his face. His head was pounding and he struggled to open his eyes. The only sounds he could hear were a constant drip drip drip from nearby and a raspy breathing that at first, he thought was his own but soon realised it came from the same direction as the dripping.

He finally got his eyes opened and he tried to focus his blurred vision on his surroundings. He was laying on a stone floor and as Daniel clamoured up to his feet, he discovered that his hands had been manacled and the chain attached was bolted to the rough wall.

He was in a cell. A cell roughly hewn out of solid rock, but a cell none the less.

Daniel moved closer to the bars of his cell, as far as the chain of his cuffs would allow. Wherever his cell was located it was a dark cold place, the only light source being a single flaming torch in a sconce down the corridor between the gaol cells.

In the opposite cell, Daniel could make out the shape of a figure in the darkness. 'Hello, are you awake?' He called out. The last thing he remembered was being at the Druid Glade and he wondered if it was Trinity in the other cell since he was with her when they were going to see the Archdruid. 'Trinity, is that you?'

Suddenly, the fire torch was lifted out of its holding and was carried down the dark passageway. Daniel struggled to see who was holding it, their face obscured within the shadows. 'No, Daniel, it is not,' the person said.

Daniel recognised the voice but couldn't believe his own ears. 'Ch'tan? Is that you? What's going on?' A thought flashed across Daniel's mind. 'Just who is in that cell?'

Ch'tan lowered the torch and Daniel could finally see the other prisoner. Nyriel lay on the ground in a poorly state. He couldn't tell if she was conscious or not but she was being barely kept alive by the drops of water coming from a contraption above her.

Anger and disgust grew in Daniel. 'You're supposed to be her bodyguard. You're supposed to protect her!'

'And I will... when I marry her,' Ch'tan replied. He watched Daniel begin to cast a spell. 'Don't bother. Those manacles are no ordinary restraints. They inhibit the flow of Essence. And as you know, no Essence, no magic.'

'Why are you doing this?'

'Why? Because my King, once strong against separation from the surface dwellers, was beginning to soften. How can he be so willing to bow the head and kiss the foot to re-establish a status quo with those that have repeatedly turned their back on us over and over again. We should be strengthening ties with the Atlantean elves, not the treacherous High Bourne. And there was someone willing to help strengthen my cause. All I needed to do was give them the Book of Azul. I couldn't think how I was going to get my hands on it, since only the king can release it. But then you came along as if Zephyrus himself was in my favour. I should really be thanking you.'

'The Book of Azul test back in Murias City had been your idea,' remembered Daniel.

'Exactly! The book was in the open all I needed was to steal it from you and that was where the Shadow Dancers came in. I would have simply hired them but my partner wanted no loose ends, so we have them mind-controlled to do our bidding.'

'So that fight outside the Dirty Dog?'

'Was all for show,' Ch'tan smiled. 'That would have been it, all done and dusted if it hadn't been for that Tristan interfering.'

'And what about Nyriel? Why are you doing this to her?'

'When we left you, before the Beltane, I told her my plans, everything. The marriage, dethroning her father, my allegiances and eventual war against the surface. She said I was crazy and knew that I would need her to marry me to give my claim to the throne legitimacy. She refused to give me her hand, so now she is going through re-education until she accepts my proposal of marriage.'

Seeing the depraved mind that Ch'tan had, Daniel suddenly made a realisation. 'It was you, wasn't it, that poisoned Cernounos.'

Not by choice. That was something my partner wanted done. Now if you would excuse me, these caves may be damp and dank but I still need to break from the fires they use down here.'

'WE HAVE ARRIVED,' ANJU stated. They had left their horses half a mile away and came the rest of the way on foot, so as not to attract attention. Just over 150 metres away was the entrance to Anju's lair. It was a large cavern entrance, at least 7 metres but because it was covered in brush and moss it blended in with its surrounds and the hill it was cut into. There were no paths to it and the terrain wasn't easy to negotiate, so to come across the cave accidentally would be very unlikely.

'I can see two guards,' whispered Tristan.

'And there will be two more that you cannot see,' Anju added. Something weighed heavily upon the elf assassin and she turned to her clan members. She looked each one of them in the face before she made her address. 'You should all know that we may be forced into having to kill our clan brethren because they don't know their own mind. I know they are friends. I know they are comrades we have eaten with. I want it to be clear that I will be taking full responsibility and the consequences for this matter.' The Shadow Dancers made to protest when they heard the words from their leader such was their respect for her, but Anju held up her hand stopping them. 'Those that can survive are strong,' she said and in unison that repeated it.

'What consequences are you talking about?' Trinity asked.

'The Krez have strict edicts that we abide by. The hierarchy may decide that my coming actions are in breach of those edicts but only time will tell. The best thing would be to avoid contact altogether.'

'Agreed.'

'That's why I should go in by myself.'

'I don't think that's a good idea,' Trinity shook her head. 'It's unlikely that Daniel will follow you without knowing that you're not controlled anymore. So, I'll be going with you. Finn and Tristan, you'll remain here with the other Shadow Dancers, just in case.'

Finn looked around uneasily at the group of assassins before turning to Tristan, 'Don't you vekting leave my side.'

'Okay, let's get started.'

Anju pointed at four of her troops and sent them off. Within moments they were in position and with a quick discrete signal from the angel of death the four guards were despatched.

With the way clear, they all moved to the mouth of the cavern. At that point Trinity changed herself into a fly and attached herself to the shoulder of Anjunel. Then the assassin entered her lair as an intruder, for the first time.

Moss had grown all around the cavern entrance, as if the earth had tried to reclaim it after it was abandoned, so many years ago, by its previous dwellers, the giants. They had been forced north of The Spine (or to give its full name The Spine of The Goddess) mountain range, after the Supremacy Wars. Few giants ventured south now, rarely spotted and never in communities. If giants were seen at all it was usually not far from their racial cousins, the ogres.

Anjunel continued down the wide spiral steps. The moonlight that had brightly illuminated the entrance diminished the deeper she descended. She reached the bottom and froze.

She heard footsteps coming their way.

Quickly, she-side stepped into a recess and almost vanished into the shadows. A Krez elf walked by down the passageway carrying stores. Anju slipped out behind him, he was going the same way she needed to, but instead of waiting, she followed him with her feather-like footsteps, her reared back to strike in case he turned around. he didn't and she eventually stepped off into another passage.

She had only taken a few steps when more footfalls were heard. With her keen hearing she could discern that there were three Shadow Dancers, one of which was female. Again, Anju found herself pressed up against the cave wall in a darkened corner. Two male Krez passed them and the third was indeed a female. Someone she knew intimately as she was Anju's second in command.

Her name was Tessara and once news of everything that had happened came out, she would likely replace Anjunel as the chapter head. She may even be sent to assassinate her. Anju hoped not because it would not go well for her student. Anju had taught Tessara everything that she knew, but not everything that Anju knew. If it came down to it sentimentality wouldn't interfere, Anju thought, even as she marvelled at Tessara's wavy tresses as the young elf walked disappeared down another passage. She was always taken by how they shone like a golden dawn even down in dark caverns.

Once it was all clear again, Anjunel Lynsu'unara continued her stealthy journey to the prison cells.

'NYRIEL! NYRIEL!' DANIEL was worried. He hadn't heard anything from his neighbour.

'I am here friend, Daniel,' she said weakly. 'I wish it were under different circumstances but it is still good to see you again.'

'I agree. I have a present to give you. It's a new, up-to-date encyclopaedia for your library.'

'Oh, Daniel,' she coughed. 'I look forward to seeing it.'

Daniel wondered how she was going to manage that. He knew she would never agree to marry Ch'tan. And he didn't know how else they could manage to escape. Of course, Trinity and Finn would search for him, but how would they find him. 'You know, I came back to Ariest with the intention of becoming a Mage but I've been questioning that decision lately, ever since I heard about the Mortokai and this prophesy really.'

'What prophesy is that?'

'The one that says I will bring death and destruction and change Ariest forever.'

'Change isn't always a bad thing. One person's revolutionary is another person's freedom fighter,' Nyriel replied in her laboured voice. 'And don't get me started on prophesies. I'm always being told about my destiny and I always tell them that I'll make my own.'

'Maybe you're right. But maybe it would be better if I didn't try to become a Mage then I wouldn't have the power to destroy anything. Like they say, "power corrupts, and absolute power corrupts absolutely."'

'But only if you let it,' she added. 'Your personality, your character, they wouldn't allow you to be any different than who you are. Unless you lose facets of your personality you will always strive to help people, Daniel Welsh, even if you don't realise it yet. You're fundamentally a good person.'

'I totally agree with her,' Trinity said as she flew from off Anju's shoulder and transformed back into her normal self. 'Leaders rise when they are most needed. Don't you remember what you did when you were in the Shade?'

Daniel couldn't believe his eyes. 'Trinity? Are you talking about when I ran?'

'And then you did the right thing and helped save those people, and gave the spirits of those that had passed a chance to say goodbye.'

'You helped my people, too,' Nyriel reminded him.

Daniel pondered over what they both said for a moment. 'This is Princess Nyriel, of the Undany, by the way. So, how did you find me?'

'You were right about the Shadow Dancer. Her name is Anjunel. She and the others have been mind-controlled all along. She knew that you would be brought here because this is her lair.'

'It was Ch'tan. He's behind it all. The kidnapping, the attempts to steal the spell book, mind-controlling the Shadow Dancers, even killing Cernounos. It was all Ch'tan and a partner.'

'Then I would like to have words with Ch'tan,' Anju said as she freed Daniel and Nyriel. Seeing the physical state of the princess caused concern for the elf and Trinity as they shared a look knowing that the weakened undine will hamper their escape. 'She's going to slow us down if we take her.'

'No, she won't,' Daniel jumped in. 'If I'm getting out so is she. All she needs is some water. Besides, Ch'tan has my satchel with both spell-books. We need to get it back.'

'Great,' Trinity rolled her eyes. 'So much for our plan to sneak in and sneak out.'

'There is a natural hot spring by my sanctum,' Anju said. 'Will that do?'

'Perfectly,' replied Nyriel.

With Daniel and Trinity helping the stricken princess, Anjunel took the lead and after checking that the coast was clear led them out of the prison cells.

She moved swiftly and silently like the predator that she was, using the shadows to hide her presence. They tip-toed past a room that had several Shadow Dancers sleeping. From there they took the first left into a passageway at the end of which steam could be seen.

'That was easier than I thought it would be,' Trinity admitted.

'That's only because they are still ensorcelled,' replied Anju. 'That doesn't mean that we should delay things though.'

Nyriel quietly stepped down into the hot spring and was instantly feeling better. Anju's sanctum lay behind the spring and they could hear a voice coming from within. With her extraordinary stealth Anju made her way to the place that was her personal quarters to investigate. Moments later she returned to the others with news.

'Ch'tan is in there, in some sort of trance, talking to somebody,' explained Anju. 'Your bag is there too, Daniel.'

He sighed with relief. 'Do you think you can get it?'

'Of course. As long as we get out before they find the empty cells. Once they do, the alarm is rung and everyone is alert and we have to fight our way out. Not ideal.'

'Okay, new plan. Anju, you retrieve the books and I'll lead these two out.'

'Are you sure you know your way back?'

'Of course! I'll just follow my scent back out,' Trinity replied as she transformed into a bloodhound. She was off, giving Daniel and Nyriel barely enough time to wish the Krez elf good luck.

The door was slightly ajar so it was no problem for Anju to ease it open and slide silently and unnoticed into her chambers. Ch'tan still kneeled with his back towards the door and she could hear him whisper his side of a conversation but couldn't quite make out what he was saying. But that wasn't what she was here for. The satchel lay on a table to the left. She silently inched her way towards it showing why the Shadow Dancers were top of the pile when it came to spy craft and assassination.

Unfortunately, a gong was suddenly struck repeatedly as the empty cells were discovered.

Chapter Thirty-Three

Finn let out another deep sigh. She hated all this waiting about; she wasn't a patient person at the best of times but this was torture. She would much rather have gone in guns blazing, raising hell like only she knew how. 'Can't we just have a little peek inside?'

'No,' Tristan replied. He was getting fed up with Finn's whining, even though he was as anxious as she was. Battle was in his blood as much as Finn craved adventure but he had a little more restraint, not much, but just a little. Finn on the other hand enjoyed letting everybody around her know her frustrations.

'You know, the only reason I'm taking that job offer from Fungal is so I don't have to do vekt like this,' Finn said to an exasperated Tristan. 'This is no fun. In fact, this is about as much fun as falling into the back of a giant's pants. A sweaty giant. A sweaty giant that had been exercising. A sweaty giant that had been exercising doing squats.'

'Vekt! Will you be quiet,' Tristan said angrily.

'What's that noise? How long has that been going off?' Finn asked.

'I don't know because of your incessant chatter,' replied Tristan.

'Well some people love my chatter.'

'Mores the fool.'

'Oi!'

'That sound is the alarm,' a Shadow Dancer revealed. 'They have been discovered.'

'Well, it seems like we will be seeing some action after all,' Tristan said drawing his sword.

'And about time too,' Finn agreed giving her guns a final check. 'Let's get going before it's all over.'

TRINITY WAS MAKING good headway. In her dog form she could almost see the scent she and Anju had left. She had to stop every now and again, not only to make sure that Daniel and Nyriel were keeping up but also to avoid any Krez elves she would hear ahead of them. She had to wait for them to move on because, unlike Anju, Trinity didn't know any other route out, she could only follow the scent they had left.

It was during one of those moments that they heard the gongs.

'That must be the alarm Anju was talking about,' Daniel said.

'I think you're right,' agreed Nyriel. 'What do we do now?'

Trinity changed back. 'There's no chance of sneaking out now, so instead of being a scalpel we can be a hammer. Climb up.'

Daniel and the princess looked at each other, not a clue as to what Trinity had in mind. Then she turned into a short-nosed bear and it became clear. They clambered onto Trinity's back and she charged into the growing number of Shadow Dancers filling the passages, sending them flying like skittles.

There was one problem with Trinity becoming the bear. Sure, she was strong and powerful like an unstoppable force, but she didn't have nearly the same sense of smell as the bloodhound, and she ended up blindly running this way and that, until she found herself at a dead end. Daniel and Nyriel climbed down as Trinity transformed back. Fighting their way out was now inevitable.

ANJU GRIPPED THE STRAP of the satchel as the alarm gong continued to ring out. The sounds had woken Ch'tan from his trance and he stood up to face Anju.

'Your duties are at an end, Shadow Dancer. You were meant to bring the book to me, now I have it, your services are no longer needed.'

'That is good,' Anju said as she stood up right and placed the strap over her head. 'The owner of this bag wishes to have it back. I intend to give it to him. There is something else that you should know. The Shadow Dancers never work for free. You never paid for our services. You made a very bad mistake in poisoning us into doing your bidding. Now your life is forfeit as payment for that slight.'

'Is that so? Well you should know that I won't be holding back this time, like I did in Almedia.'

'And now that my mind is not clouded by your poison, I shall be at my best.'

They circled each other. Each waiting for an opening to strike. He was the bodyguard of the Undany royal family. She was a chapter head of the Shadow Dancers. Though their training had been very different they were both experts in the art of fighting. Clear cut openings would be few and far between. In situations like this, you needed to make your own.

Ch'tan feigned a wild charge. Anju instinctively went for a low kick to the bigger man's leg but he hooked his arm under her knee, lifted her up and slammed her back against the wall before tossing her across the room.

'I've wrestled bigger and stronger animals than you, little one,' laughed Ch'tan.

'I am not surprised since big dumb animals tend to fight other big dumb animals,' smiled Anju.

The elf assassin was in no rush to get to her feet, intending to lure her assailant closer. And he duly complied. One, two steps then she kicked the door in his face before he could take a third. So much force was used in the attack that the door was left swinging on only one hinge, whilst Ch'tan was sent reeling back, clutching his face.

Anju pressed her attack and leapt to her feet. With lightning quickness, she sprung onto his shoulders and delivered several vicious elbow strikes to the bridge of his nose. Although Undany had denser flesh, to protect against the cold of the deep, so precise were each of her blows that the cumulative effect of her blows eventually broke his nose, splaying green blood across Ch'tan's face.

The bodyguard groaned in pain, his vision blurred and he held onto the pesky little elf and ran at the opposite wall. He slammed her into it, but she held on fast. Like an irritating gnat he tried to swat Anju away. He swung her into what was left of the door, freeing it from its last remaining hinge, then against the door frame, still the tenacious elf held on and continued to rain down blows on the head of the Undany.

Then Ch'tan had an idea. If he couldn't get her to release him, then he'd just drown her. He held onto Anju and jumped into the hot spring intent on letting his Undany physiology do what his brute strength couldn't, and kill the elf.

IT FELT GOOD TO BE fighting side by side with Trinity again, Daniel thought. Just as they had done, briefly, in the Druid Glade.

Nyriel couldn't be as involved as she really wanted to be since her Unzany magic needed water to start. But that didn't mean that she was completely ineffectual. She had been taught the ways of the sword from a youngster and, although she preferred not fight it didn't mean that she couldn't.

As the trio forced back the marauding Shadow Dancers and they finally came out of the dead end they'd been holed up in, the princess picked up a sword from one of the fallen elves. 'So which way is the way out?' Nyriel asked now that they had a little breathing room.

Trinity shrugged and shook her head as they found themselves at a crossroad. 'I really can't tell. One passage looks just as likely as another.'

'Maybe you should change to the dog again,' Daniel suggested.

'I could, but I'll have to boost my Essence a bit so I have enough for combat. I want to be able to help you out when I switch forms.' Trinity had been so preoccupied with keeping an eye on their surroundings that she hadn't noticed Daniel staring at her. 'What's wrong? What's with that goofy smile?' she simpered.

'Nothing,' Daniel replied as he stepped closer and kissed her lips before she had a chance to do anything. 'It's just that we haven't had a proper kiss since reuniting and now seemed as good a time as any, considering we might be lost down here forever,' he grinned.

'Ahem!' Even in a life and death situation Nyriel still held on to her princessly manners. 'Perhaps you two could continue that at a later date. We have company.'

More Krez elves were running towards them and Daniel instinctively grabbed Trinity's hand an action which wasn't lost on the young druid. He knew that she could handle herself and yet subconsciously he still wanted to protect her. 'This way looks as good as any,' Daniel called out to his two companions before setting off.

They made lefts and rights as they ran. A few times, Trinity, blocked the passage behind them with thorns. The three of them could have stood and fought but as discretion is the better part of valour, they had decided to conserve their strength and Essence for the times when they had no choice but to fight.

They took another right and Daniel immediately regretted it.

Trinity ran into him as he came to an abrupt stop. 'What is it, Daniel? Oh.'

'Well, I have to say that I wasn't expecting to be reacquainted with this place any time soon,' a deflated Nyriel added.

With all the twists and turns they had made; they had ended up right back where they had started. Ahead of them were the prison cells. And the guards that had sounded the alarm were still there.

'Just wait until I tell Eamon Wolff that I knocked off some Shadow Dancers,' Finn shouted at Tristan. She followed the Krez elves that had been freed from the mind control and fired off her guns taking down one assassin after another.

'I thought you said that you were leaving the Thieves Guild?' Tristan replied swinging his sword this way and that.

'I am! Weeding out the competition can be considered my parting gift to him. To sweeten the deal so to speak.'

Tristan laughed at his companion. He was enjoying the chance of exercising his sword arm in anger and not just practice. Watching the Shadow Dancers move, he could really see the difference between the ones who were still under control and those that weren't. It made him thing about the one he had stopped in Almedia and he realised that she wouldn't have been at her best then and yet she had still been a handful.

'Have seen any sign of the others yet?' Finn asked one of the Krez as a scout came back to regroup.

'Not of them,' he replied, 'but there were signs of a skirmish, thorns and ice.'

'Daniel and Trinity, it has to be,' Finn excitedly said. 'Let's go! Maybe we can catch them up.'

They carried on down another passage and soon they could hear fighting. As they rounded the corner, further down they could make out the figures of Anjunel Lynsu'unara and Ch'tan in vicious violent combat.

Finn and Tristan paused and wondered what was going. Ch'tan had been missing, and they all believed that he had been kidnapped along with Daniel, and here he was. But why was he fighting one of the people that had been sent to rescue them. Sure, he wouldn't have known that she was realised from the control, but surely Trinity would have told him. And where was she and Daniel?

The Krez elves had such thoughts going through their mind. One their own was being drowned and as they approached the hot spring, their distraction was enough. As Ch'tan looked up, in one fluid motion, Anju took hold of his right arm, grabbed his left shoulder with her left hand, forcing her arm under his chin. She then swung under him and placing her legs over his head, forced him onto his back and cinched in her arm-bar. He was strong, very strong, but when your elbow starts bending the wrong way, even the strongest are quick to fold.

She couldn't apply the hold for long since she was still under water, but it was more than long enough to be effective. He was quick to get away from the elf as she released him and Ch'tan almost leapt out of the spring, and grabbed the bag that had dropped, his right arm dangling uselessly beside him.

The Undany royal bodyguard barged his way past the Shadow Dancers, manipulating the water from the spring to slam them against the wall. Then he was confronted by Tristan.

'What's going on, Ch'tan? She's with us. She's no longer under the mind-control,' explained Tristan.

'Get away from me you, surfacer scum! You will all be bending the knee to me soon enough. With my ally at my side Murias City will no longer be dragged into the wars of the surface dwellers of Ariest and then tossed aside and abandoned! Murias City will be the capital of Ariest!'

'I don't much care what you say or do,' Finn stated, 'but I know that bag doesn't belong to you.'

'Then why don't you come take it,' Ch'tan replied with a snarl.

Finn levelled a gun at him. 'Why don't I just shot you and then take it?'

Ch'tan charged the cocky scoundrel before she could get a shot off. And they briefly wrestled before he tossed Finn aside and headed off down a passageway. She stood up and dusted herself off before picking up the spellbooks she had pickpocketed from the satchel.

'Impressive,' Anju nodded. 'I said that you had talent and I was right.'

Finn grinned at the compliment. She had no trouble accepting them, in fact she wished she had more. Something red and gold was caught in between the two books she recognised it to be the purple and gold hand wraps from Kay Haitch, the swordmaster.

'Well, well, well,' she said beaming. She was about to unleash a beating on anyone that happened to get in her way.

DANIEL, TRINITY AND Nyriel weren't too impressive with being back at the prison cells. And they were less than happy to have run into the party of guards that were there. Daniel could hear the Krez that were behind them catching up so they decided to leave by the only way left open to them. The north passageway brought them to a whole new area, somewhere they hadn't been to before and somewhere they couldn't really stay for too long, for Nyriel's sake.

The cavern that the passage led to was simply huge. It compared to nothing Daniel had seen in his travels of Ariest. It seemed as if it had been roughly carved out of the underground rock and Daniel couldn't help but wonder if giants like Skelmin with his Mephisto Worms, that Finn told him about, might have been responsible.

He felt like he was looking down into the core of the faerie world itself. The passage they entered from and two others from the west led into unsupported bridges. They ran around the cave, passed through the rock at intervals as they spiralled down to a large circular columned platform which rose out of the depths. There was an orange hue coming from the deeps but the bottom was so far down that Daniel couldn't tell if it was created by fire or lava, either way Nyriel was going to be feeling the effects soon enough.

'This place is unbelievable,' said Daniel as he looked around in awe.

'Totally,' agreed Trinity.

'This is more than unbelievable,' Nyriel said as she excitedly examined the rock. 'When I was first brought here, I deduced that it was once the habitat of gnomes or, more likely, dwarfs. But this is something else completely. Like most archaeology on Ariest, the deeper you go, the further back in history you go.'

'So, I imagine, judging by the depth of this cavern you're going back millennia?' Daniel asked.

'Oh, definitely!' She enthused. 'This is the work of giants, no doubt about it! Who knows how many more structures like this lay hidden beneath Ariest?'

'Sorry to interrupt the presentation,' Trinity said, 'but we better keep moving.'

'Perhaps we can go down and come up one of those other passages,' Daniel suggested.

'My thoughts exactly!' Trinity was already making her way down. The stairs and the bridges were a free-standing structure with nothing underneath and no safety barriers on either side. It would be a basophobe's nightmare, but then, anybody without a head for heights would suffer from a fear of falling if they stepped on this gravity defying structure.

That would have been Daniel once, but since his experiences with falling from great heights, in particular over Almedia when he took the cloak of flying off and again when he was falling down the seemingly endless cavern of vaults beneath the Imperial City bank, he had garnered a strength against. That didn't mean he wanted to flaunt it and take unnecessary risks, so he made sure that he stuck to the middle of the staircase, just to be on the safe side.

They made it down to the bridge, it was barely one and half metres in width, and as the three of them walked along, they saw a familiar person run out of one of the other passages, looking over his shoulder as he quickly descended the stairs.

Daniel squinted as he watched the person from distance. 'Isn't that...?'

'The traitor, Ch'tan,' finished Nyriel. The betrayal of her bodyguard was still a bitter pill for her to swallow. He had been a constant figure throughout her young life. She always knew that he hated her infatuation with surface dwellers and their history. But she never thought that he would take his separatist views to such extremes. It was like she never knew him at all. 'Well, now he gets to pay for what he has done to me.'

'Bad idea, princess,' Trinity drew their attention to their passageway and saw several Krez elves standing there. 'We wouldn't want to be caught between them and him, especially not on this bridge. Come on!' She was off.

They sprinted in the opposite direction to Ch'tan, who had spotted them. 'Get after them!' He yelled at the Shadow Dancers just as faerie-dust propelled bullets whistled past him.

Finn, Tristan, Anjunel and their Krez elves emerged from the same tunnel Ch'tan had. 'There's the little vekt!' Finn shouted. 'Hey! Look down there! It's Daniel and the others!'

'Good!' Anjunel said. 'They are headed down towards the platform. That will be our battleground where we will end this. Come, I have a short cut this way.'

Finn being Finn couldn't hide her exuberance at seeing Daniel again and she stood at the edge of the bridge. 'Daniel!' She shouted and waved when he looked up. 'Hey, Daniel! See you down there!' Then she followed Anjunel and the others.

A smile crept on Daniel's face. He was happy to see that Finn was ok. Which was more than could be said for Nyriel. The deeper they went to more she struggled with the rising heat.

'I'll be all right, Daniel. Don't worry about me.'

'Are you sure? Considering how long you were held captive; you weren't submerged for that long.'

'I'll... be fine,' she replied.

'I'll conjure up some rain once we get to the platform,' Trinity told her.

As she became weaker, Nyriel, became slower. Their pursuers were gaining. The knives they threw were getting closer to hitting home. Each time the trio passed a rock archway, Trinity would block it up with vines slowing down the Krez as they had to stop and hack their way through.

Eventually, they reached the bridge that led to the central column. They discovered that it was partially hollow and they climbed the internal staircase which became an external one as it reached the platform at the top.

There was very little protection atop the forty-metre diameter platform, as they found out when more knives began to rain down on them. Trinity daren't stand still to cast the spell.

Anju and the others came out of their hidden passageway, and directly into the platform's column. They rushed up to the top to be reunited with their friends. The thrown knives attack continued unabated.

Then a dog appeared at a passage entrance and ran towards the knife throwers. It changed into a bear and barged them off the bridge, sending them falling into the abyss. Then the bear jumped off of the bridge, transformed into a bird and glided to the platform where it changed once more into Archdruid Tavisum.

No longer under attack, Trinity took the opportunity to cast the spell of Healing Rain. The magical drops of water were not only effective for Nyriel but also for the others that had suffered any injury. 'You're the last person I expected to see,' she said to Tavisum.

'I'm only here because of you,' the Archdruid stated. 'If you were my child, Gydion would not let you do this alone.'

'Then you should know that you were wrong about Daniel. It wasn't him that killed Cernounos and the divine tree, or who brought the Shadow Dancers to the Druid Glade,' Trinity replied. 'Just as I told you,' she added.

'That honour is all mine,' Ch'tan said with an exuberant bow, as he and the rest of his mind-controlled assassin elves arrived atop the column.

'Perhaps I was too steadfast and unwilling to listen to any other possibility,' Tavisum admitted.

'No one is infallible,' Trinity said to her. 'But you can make amends if you can release the other Krez elves.'

'Unfortunately, I don't have enough pellets for of them.' Tavisum gave what she had to Anjunel. The forest elf and the cave elf looked at one another with tolerance and gratitude if not completely with respect.

Anjunel had already seen Tessera among the elves behind Ch'tan and she kept one pellet for her friend and gave the rest to her Shadow Dancers to use on their comrades.

The battle lines had been drawn. Friends had been reunited. Spellbooks returned. Swords drawn. Guns reloaded. Essence replenished. The final battle was about to begin.

Then the air between the opposing groups began to shimmer and a hole appeared in space and rapidly widened. An olive-toned leg, wearing white-leather Ptolemaic shoes stepped through. Sayyidah stood before them resplendent in her simple yet elegant, white diaphanous lace halter necked dress, as the goddess she purported to be.

Chapter Thirty-Four

The companions looked on as a bad situation became decidedly worse. Those that recognised her couldn't believe what they were seeing with their own eyes.

'You have got to be kidding me,' breathed Trinity.

'Who is that?' Asked Daniel.

Tavisum couldn't believe her eyes either. 'This cannot be real. It's not possible.'

'Who is that?' Daniel asked again.

'That is...' Trinity could barely believe that she was saying the words herself. 'That is Sayyidah. The woman that brought the Shade to Ariest. The architect of the second Great War. The wife of Gydion so - in effect - my mother.' The surprising reappearance of the Egyptian Mage had made Trinity overlook one important fact. Gydion had gone to Salamida to question her. So, if Sayyidah was here, where was her father?

Sayyidah had her back to Daniel and his friends. She had barely given them a backward glance since her arrival, such was her disdain for them. Besides she had more important things to attend to. 'Ch'tan, to me.' For all of his boasts of partnerships it was clear to Daniel and his friends that this was more of a 100/0 split arrangement as opposed to the 50/50 that he had led them to think it was. 'Give me the book,' she demanded.

This was the moment Ch'tan had been waiting for. The moment that their allegiance would be sealed. She would get the Book of Azul; he would get the Undany royal throne. However, the smug smile he had on his face vanished as he plunged his hand into Daniel's satchel and pulled out a book called History: From the Dawn of Civilisation to the Present Day.

'That's the book I got for you,' Daniel whispered to Nyriel.

The princess smiled back and thanked him enthusiastically. 'I can't wait to read it! I hope they don't damage it.'

'I don't understand. It was right here in the bag,' Ch'tan explained.

'You mean to tell me that you do not have it?'

'It was right here! I promise you!' He desperately looked around, as though he hoped it had fallen on the ground. Then he saw it. 'The boy - the boy has the book!'

'The boy has the book,' she repeated in exasperation. When she looked at Daniel, her face softened, ever so slightly, but it vanished as quickly as it appeared. 'You were supposed to bring me the book a long time ago. And could not because only the king can release it from its hiding place. I should have killed you then. But I thought, maybe having him on the Undany throne might be useful. But now I'm beginning to think not. Your slow actions forced me to get you extra assistance to obtain the book. So, I ensorcelled these Krez elves for you and still you could not get it done. Sending you to kill Cernounos was only a reprieve for you, even though his death will weaken the Alliance with no replacement readily prepared to succeed him.'

The anger in Sayyidah was growing. She had made a simple a plan, she believed, and yet, the people that she had entrusted to execute it had continued to fail her. Now she would show them what it meant to disappoint her.

'Now I shall have to get it myself, and as such, I no longer have need for any of you.' Sayyidah raised her hand and it began to glow at which point, the nearest Krez elf screamed out and clutched his head as it started to undulate. He fell to his knees still screaming in agony. Then another started to scream. And another.

Anjunel sprang into action. She was fast and from the corner of her eye she could see more of her comrades collapsing in death. The fatal edge growing ever closer to Tessera. Anju leapt through the air and tackled her friend, just as the Krez beside her begun to scream and convulse. She forced the Archdruid's pellet down the dark-haired elf's throat and hoped that she wasn't too late.

Tessera begun to scream. Her head undulated. Then, doubled over in pain, she threw up the green viscous poison that had been coursing through her body and allowed her to be controlled. 'Anju,' she said weakly, 'I always knew. I never stopped believing you would do something.'

'Those that can survive are strong,' Anju whispered to her friend as she helped her up.

'Those that can survive are strong,' Tessera repeated weakly. 'But never as strong as you.' She could see Anju look pass her. The beautiful face she knew was filled with rage and vengeance and she pitied the recipient of it.

'Interesting,' Sayyidah scoffed at the rescue of the elf. 'No matter. The chaff has been culled. And I am left with one.'

'Please no,' Ch'tan pleaded. 'I can still be useful.'

'I think not. You've outlived your usefulness. All I needed from you was the book. The book has now been released from its hiding place, one of only two useful things you have done, and with that, the end of your service to me.'

'You can't do this! You promised me! I did everything you asked of me. You couldn't do it without me!' The expression that immediately came over Ch'tan's face, showed that he regretted what he had just said.

'What? You think I needed you to do any of this?' Sayyidah laughed. 'I didn't need you for any of it! If I so pleased, I could have gone to your precious Murias City and ripped it apart until I had the book. I could have walked into the Druid Glade, right into their sacred grove and destroyed their divine tree and Cernounos.'

'Never!' Tavisum shouted. 'I would have stopped you!'

'Not on your best day, druid! Don't get it wrong, little Undany, I never needed you. I just used you, because I could and because I had bigger things to deal with. You were just a tool and nothing more. You are nothing but a guard. I could have manipulated any other separatist fool. You have nothing to offer me when I have armies of Frell, Firbolgs, Gnolls and Giants waiting for the return of their Harpy Queen. Soon they will know that their wait is over!

The pleading look that Ch'tan gave Nyriel was filled with sorrow. He realised how wrong he had been and the dire mistake he had made as he heard the words of magic leave Sayyidah's lips. 'I'm sorry, Nyriel. I only did what I thought was right for our people. I let it blind me into hurting you. I'm so—'

Ch'tan stopped short and clutched his chest. He let out a strangled groan as a bright orange glow shone out of his open mouth. Then smoke started to escape through his gritted teeth as his skin began to blister. His blood curdling cries reached a crescendo as watched in horror as Sayyidah burned Ch'tan alive from the inside out.

Nyriel buried her head into Daniel's shoulder, unable to watch the last excruciating moments of the person she once called friend. What he did to her was terrible, but she put it down to him losing his direction. It didn't erase all the fond memories she had of him. to meet your end in that manner was something she wouldn't wish upon her worse enemy... but then again, her worse enemy was standing before her.

'So,' Sayyidah sauntered over to the group to stand before Daniel, an imperious air surrounding her and continued as if the atrocities of moments ago had never happened. 'Now that I have dispensed with all the intermediaries, let us return to the business at hand. Daniel, will you give me the Book of Azul, please.'

It was that last word that threw Daniel. "Please." A simple word. Used to make a request polite. Yet, he had seen nothing from Sayyidah's actions to suggest that she knew the meaning of the word. She had just killed someone with as much ease and nonchalance that someone has when they breathe.

'I'm sorry,' he started, 'I can't do that.'

'Come on, Daniel,' the Egyptian pushed in ancient Hellenic, 'do the right thing. Hand me the book.'

'I don't understand what you said,' replied Daniel.

'You will, in time. Give me the book, Daniel,' she said again in common tongue.

'The way you talk to me... it's like you know me.'

'Because I do. I know the real you, not this mask you wear for everyone else. You used a different name, but it is you. You had a craving for knowledge, a desire to learn everything. It's there in your eyes.'

'Don't listen to her, Daniel. She's just reading it from your mind.' His friends all knew Daniel to be a seeker of knowledge. How else could she have known?

'Come, come, dear daughter. You know as well as I that reading an unwilling mind would cause tremendous pain for the participant.'

'Don't call me that! You're nothing to me.'

'I'm more to you than you know, Trinity.'

'Rubbish! I don't believe you!'

'That would have been a conversation for you and daddy dearest.'

'What do you mean, "would have"?'

'I mean that my dearly departed husband is no more.'

The world literally fell away from Trinity and she stumbled as she heard the news. 'I don't believe you,' She stammered.

'Being a person like Gydion,' Sayyidah continued, 'you are bound to attract enemies.'

'You...'

'No, not me, dear daughter, oh how I wish it had been, but that privilege fell to another of my puppets. Now, if you would be so kind, the book, Daniel.'

Again, he refused. 'I - I can't do that. I was supposed to deliver it to Gydion but if he is - if he is gone, as you say, then I suppose it should go back to Murias City.'

'I am beginning to lose my patience. I don't really want to hurt you, Daniel, I am who I am because of you, but I will have the book, and the others, and I won't let anyone stop me, not even you.'

'He's right,' Nyriel said defiantly, 'the book is not his to give. It was given to my people by our god. It does not belong to you.'

'It does now, as will they all. If your lizard does not approve, then let him stop me,' laughed Sayyidah as she reached for the book Daniel's hand.

'I said no!' The water Trinity had used to help rehydrate Nyriel had left the platform wet with surface water. Enough for the Undany princess to become an attacking force. She quickly manipulated the water into a bubble and sent it over Sayyidah's head, intent on weakening the powerful Mage by depriving her of air.

'About time!' Finn exclaimed. 'Was it just me that was getting fed up with all that yappity yapping? It wasn't, was it? Come on, own up.' Finn then saw another glimpse of the power they were about to face as Sayyidah simply phased through the water bubble. 'Uh - oh. I think you vekted up, she kind of looks mad.'

'Well, little princess, that was a bold move. Allow me to repay the compliment.' Sayyidah used her magic to will a ring of fire around the terrified Nyriel. The Undany had to continually douse herself to stay hydrated.

The Shadow Dancers were next to attack but they had barely taken a step when their feet became melded to the platform and anchored them in place.

'Is this all you have? Really?' Sayyidah mocked.

'We need to coordinate are attacks,' Tavisum said. 'If we don't, she will just pick us off one by one.'

'All together,' Daniel blurted out. 'We should go all together, wear her down.'

Trinity smiled at Daniel. 'I was thinking the same thing! Maybe someone will get a lucky strike, too.'

Tavisum nodded. 'Okay, all together.'

'Have you formulated a plan yet,' asked Sayyidah, 'or are you just going to surrender?'

As if in answer to the Egyptian's question, the group charged the mage. Anjunel, jumped at Sayyidah, two daggers in hand, but she was brought to a halt as her long blonde hair came to life and began to wrap around the Krez elf's neck and constrict tighter and tighter. Tessera, still regaining strength after her ordeal, ran to aid her long-time friend. Finn seized the opening to deliver a thunderous left hook, which was covered in the purple and gold hand-wrap.

The mage was sent crashing to the ground and the others ran in to press their advantage. Finn attempted to throw another punch but Sayyidah raised a hand and diverted the blow to knockout Tristan. Again, Finn attacked, as did Tavisum, who released a blast of fae magic. The bolt dispersed on Sayyidah's protective barrier and she evaded Finn's attack, touching the young woman's chest in the process. A green moss like substance grew from the spot and rapidly spread to cover Finn's entire body until she fell to the ground gasping for air.

With her Schiavona in hand, Trinity advanced on Sayyidah. Tavisum joined her. The Archdruid pulled out a dagger which extended to become a spear. Their opponent was unimpressed.

'You can't match my magic so you think to defeat me with the sword instead? I have been using swords since I was a child in the slums of ancient Alexandria,' she smiled as two golden swords appeared in her upturned palms. 'I don't fancy your chances.'

Tavisum attacked low, thrusting with her spear, whilst Trinity went high. Sayyidah jumped above the Archdruid's attack, blocking Trinity's at the same time. She landed lightly on the spear head, took a step and kicked Tavisum in the face. From there, in a fluid motion, the Egyptian somersaulted and slammed down on the auburn-haired druid with both swords. Trinity got her sword up but the strength of the attack forced her back.

Daniel had taken the chance to retrieve his bag, and with the Book of Azul placed back in it, he was now able to help. His fingers flashed as he sent volley after volley of frost bolts at Sayyidah. His aim was true and they all hit her. He was excited by the fact that he had her reeling, that Daniel, the novice that he was, lost concentration. He couldn't centre himself and his next attack failed to materialise.

Trinity, reluctant to relinquish her hold of Gydion's grimoire, continued to fight on with her Schiavona. She watched the others struggle against Sayyidah and felt that she would be more effective if she could use her own magic. Then the Harpy Queen unleashed a wave of energy which sent everybody flying back to the edge of the platform, scrambling to hold on. One of the Krez couldn't hold on and they fell off into the deep depths of the cavern.

This was the opportunity that Trinity had been waiting for, a break in the combat so that she could get to Daniel. 'How are you holding up?' She asked him while she rubbed his shoulder.

He had landed awkwardly on it and was grimacing. 'I'm ok. I don't think we're making any headway against her though. Even the Archdruid is having a hard time going toe to toe with her.' Trinity slipped Gydion's spellbook into Daniel's bag and was using a healing spell on his injured shoulder. 'What about Gydion's Book? Perhaps there's something in there that could help take her down.'

'I don't know. The most powerful spells would need rituals, possibly an altar. Somehow I don't think Sayyidah would allow us the time.'

'Well, what if we keep her occupied while you cast?'

She thought for a moment. 'It'll be dangerous...'

'But worth a shot,' Daniel added.

Trinity nodded. 'Okay. Tavisum, I'm going to need you to keep her busy.'

'With pleasure,' the Archdruid replied.

'Let's have a look at Grim, Daniel, and see if we can find something to finish this bitch.'

Daniel took Gydion's grimoire out of his bag and handed it to Trinity. But before she could take it, the book flew out of his hand, in mid-air the pages flipped back and forth until it landed on the right page. Everyone stopped fighting to see what was going on, even Sayyidah was intrigued. The words of the spell floated up into the air, merged together and when they separated a portal opened.

'Well, that's nice,' Gydion said as he stepped through the portal. 'I wasn't expecting a welcoming committee.'

Chapter Thirty-Five

'In the back of my mind, I think I always knew that you wouldn't stay dead. That would have been too considerate of you,' said Sayyidah upon seeing Gydion.

'I thought I might have left it a bit late, but here I am,' he replied.

'Exactly. Like a bad smell. Or a husband that just will not take the hint that the marriage is over.'

'I'll be more than happy to make the divorce final and permanent right now.' Gydion cast a dispel charm over Finn and Anjunel, releasing them from their magical restraints. And as they and the others recovered, he squared up to his wife.

It was a repeat of the last days of The War, when the alliance had finally overcome Sayyidah and her shadow forces. Back then, however, he still had feelings for her, still had hope that she could be rehabilitated. When he first saw her on Salamida, he thought that she had been but soon realised, the hard way, that wasn't the case and that, not only had it all been a ruse, but she had become more dangerous than ever.

The love that was once there was gone. This time he wouldn't banish her to another dimension. This time her would end her life.

'I will not be fooled by your duplication spell this time, Sayyidah.'

'I will not need to use it this time, Gydion. You should have joined me. The power of Salamida could have made us both gods; now I shall rule alone.'

'I have power enough!' Gydion yelled as he finished the last words of his Meteor Storm spell. Several fiery boulders came crashing down on Sayyidah. Each rock hit with a fiery explosion. Even behind Gydion Daniel could feel their heat and shockwaves.

The Egyptian held up her hands to bolster her magical shield, even so, such was the strength and ferocity of Gydion's attack that her protection didn't last long and the final meteor explosion sent her over the edge of the platform and into the abyss.

Daniel and his friends cheered, thinking the contest over, swiftly and decisively. Only Tavisum was reluctant to celebrate. Only she seemed to realise that the battle was far from over. They didn't really know what they were up against. Sayyidah was just as powerful as Gydion, some would argue more so. But couple that ability with the mind she had and that is what made her so dangerous.

'Was that all you could muster, dear husband?' Sayyidah's voice reverberated around the cavern. Everyone looked around, trying to find where she was, but they found nothing. It was like she was speaking to them from the other side. 'A spell such as that should have done more than just give me a tickle. Is it me that has gotten stronger, or is it you that has gotten weaker? I believe it is both.'

Gydion suddenly began to violently shake, then his blood began to literally be drawn out of his pores towards a shadow which Sayyidah slowly rose out of. The Mage had learnt to emulate the Shade.

'This is not good,' Tavisum said as she began to cast a spell. 'We must strengthen ourselves! We must go again! If we are to fall this day, then let it be known that we gave all of ourselves and held nothing back!'

The Archdruid released a Tempest spell around Sayyidah. The violent swirling winds and crackling lightning, disrupted the ancient Egyptian's Exsanguination spell, saving Gydion.

Sayyidah blindly fired off her own lightning attack from within the tempest. It struck Tristan and the electricity arced to Anjunel and jumped from person to person until they had all felt its effects. 'Now, I am starting to get annoyed,' she sighed heavily.

The battle remained at a stalemate which only made Sayyidah more and more frustrated. No matter how many spells she had in her repertoire, the Mage still didn't have unlimited reserves of Essence. She had expected to have this conflict over and done with easily. But she hadn't counted on the tenacity of Daniel, Trinity, Finn and the others. 'All you had to do, beloved, was give me the book!' She roared at Daniel with finality. 'Now you force me to take it from your dead, lifeless fingers.'

Sayyidah unleashed a continuous volley of mystic bolts at Daniel. He created an ice shield to defend against the attack. Gydion, for all his bravado was not fully recovered from his ordeal on Salamida and was all but spent, as was Tavisum. Finn helped Princess Nyriel who was struggling. Tristan and Anjunel, brushed, sweaty and bloodied, as they all were, charged the crazed Mage, but to no avail. She projected an arm of magical energy which caught the warrior's sword and shattered it as he swung it before it swatted both him and the assassin elf away.

The Harpy Queen's ferocious attack on Daniel continued. Each shield he projected collapsed quicker and quicker, able to sustain less damage each time as he became more tired and drained.

Then came the moment when he couldn't raise a shield at all.

A smile crept across the Sayyidah's face as she prepared to end the conflict. She cast a lethal spell, the one final killing blow delivered to Daniel that would allow her to retrieve the book unmolested and leave to plan her move on to her next target.

The ball of mystic energy flew true and straight at Daniel. He watched it coming, knowing that there was nothing he could do to prevent the inevitable. He wondered how much it was going to hurt and he closed his eyes, waiting for it to strike him down.

He heard several screams as Daniel was splayed out on the ground in a heap by what struck him. But it was a lot softer than he had imagined or expected. He opened his eyes and saw Trinity laid out across him; her chest smouldered from where Sayyidah's spell had hit her.

Daniel was in a state of panic. He didn't know what to do. His vision blurred with the tears that welled up in his eyes. He didn't need to see to know that Trinity had been fatally wounded. He could feel her warm blood flowing from her body unrestrained, her breathing had become wheezy and laboured.

'What were you thinking?' Daniel berated Trinity.

'The only thing I could. Isn't that what you're supposed to do, to protect those that you love?' she sighed as her last breath left her lips.

He shook her more and more vigorously as he called her name with ever more urgency.

Daniel finally relented. Finally accepted the fact that no matter how peaceful she looked; Trinity wasn't sleeping. She was gone.

Then Daniel heard a voice, a distant whisper. He couldn't understand the words at first but eventually they became clear. '...taken away from you. Embrace your loss. Someone must pay. Someone must feel your pain. Let your pain fuel your hatred. Let your hatred fuel your anger. Let your anger become chaos!'

Daniel screamed. A power was rising within him. A power like nothing he had felt before. A power that needed to be released. He could feel the malevolence raging through his body, feel the anger and fury corrupting his insides. He needed to get rid of it. He held up his hand and did just that. He unleashed it on Sayyidah. Both Gydion and Tavisum could feel something dread had been let loose.

The large dark red ball crackled with negative energy. It left a trail as it flew to its target. Smaller balls of mystical energy swirled around the main one like they were its astrological satellites.

Sayyidah nonchalantly raised her hand and conjured a shield to protect herself against the incoming missile. Against an ordinary magical blast, it would have been sufficient, but this was something different, something primal; A bolt of pure chaos.

It passed right through her shield as if it wasn't even there. When the chaos bolt struck her outstretched hand, it charred and withered it. Sayyidah screamed in agony. She clutched the blackened hand to her, then with one last look of pain mixed with fear she stared at Daniel before the Harpy Queen cast a teleport spell and vanished.

DANIEL AND THE OTHERS stepped out of Gydion's portal and into the Druid Glade. They may have prevented Sayyidah from completing her goal and obtaining the Book of Azul, but nobody felt like they had won anything, the price had come at too great a cost.

Archdruid Tavisum called over several druids and told them to take Trinity's body from Daniel and prepare it.

Seeing them take away Trinity's corpse was too much for Daniel to handle. It brought the shock of her death crashing back. He needed to get away. From everything. From everyone.

So, he ran. Something he *was* good at, unlike being a mage.

'Hey! Where're you going?' Finn yelled after Daniel. She was about to chase after him but Gydion stopped her.

'Let him go,' he told her.

'But...'

'He needs space, time. He'll be all right.'

Finn watched her friend disappear from view.

Daniel ran out of the Druid Glade and kept on running. He didn't stop until he could run no more and he collapsed. He lay there, panting heavily. He wanted to punish himself, seek penance for the guilt he felt.

'It should have been me, Trinity. Why did you do it? Why did you have to die?' Daniel despaired.

He took a deep, pained breath and closed his eyes. In his mind's eye, Daniel replayed what had happened and wished he could go back in time and change it. He heard her last words repeating over and over in his head. 'Isn't that what you're supposed to do to protect those that you love?'

'I love you, too,' he whispered.

Daniel sat up and took out the olive-green peridot crystal, the only cherished gift he had from their burgeoning relationship. He longed to touch her and kiss her one last time but took solace in the little memento.

It reminded him of better times. He had a smile that lit up his eyes as he remembered those first moments back in high school when they first connected and she gave him the gem. Remembered when her intervention changed the Council of Three's decision. Remembered that kiss. In time his eyes became glassy as they welled up with the tears of losing her. But he held them back.

'Come on, Daniel,' he told himself. 'You have to be strong. If not for you, for Trinity. For her memory. She won't want you to be like this. She'd want you to be the best version of yourself. She believed in you. Don't let her down.'

Daniel took another deep breath, a cleansing one this time, not strained with guilt like before. He let it out slowly, making peace with the universe. Willingly accepting all that had happened. A feeling of fatigue suddenly washed over him and Daniel lay down his head and instantly fell asleep.

Over a day had passed when Daniel eventually returned to the Druid Glade. Finn was waiting at the entrance, pacing up and down. Seeing her made Daniel realise that he had left her without so much as a word. He knew he was in for some trouble from her, but she couldn't hide her delight at seeing him return, unscathed. She still let him know that she was annoyed that he'd disappeared like that by punching him on the shoulder then she hugged her friend and tried her best to comfort him.

'I'm going to miss her,' Finn admitted. 'I know what you're thinking. That I hated her. Always teased her. That's not true. I liked her. We may have been rivals, but I still respected her.'

'If only I had been better,' Daniel said. 'Been more competent, known more magic. Things would have been different.'

'Maybe, maybe not,' shrugged Finn. 'Who's to say? This was Sayyidah we're talking about, not a Shade. With all of us together, she was still doing a pretty good job of kicking our behinds.'

'She's right,' agreed Tristan as he joined them. 'We shouldn't beat ourselves up over what's happened.'

Daniel watched the closeness between Anjunel and Tessera. He envied them. 'It's easy for you say that, Tristan, it wasn't Eveline that was taken from you! My relationship with Trinity was just beginning. Now it's been taken away. At least Gydion is here now. My training can begin properly so that the next time I see Sayyidah things will be very different.'

'Speaking of Sayyidah,' Finn interjected, 'What is it between you two?'

'It wasn't just me that noticed that then?' Tristan said. 'I have a little experience with women and there was definitely something there.'

'She called you "beloved" for vekt sake.'

'I honestly don't know what that was about. I've never seen her before. It did creep me out a bit though,' replied Daniel.

'Well, she definitely knows, because she's definitely seen *you* before,' Finn concluded.

'Just something else I need to talk to Gydion about, I guess.'

The Archmage, at that moment, was with the Archdruid, deep in discussion but in hushed tones, as they walked towards the Sacred Grove. What they talked about was not for everyone's ears.

'The princess agrees. Given that the Book of Azul was Sayyidah's target all along it would be best if I kept it at my sanctum. I'll be taking her back to Murias City after she's recovered a bit, and after the proceedings.'

Tavisum nodded. 'It's for the best.' The elf never one to shy away from speaking her mind to Gydion continued that trait as she brought up the tragic loss. 'I told you it was too early for her. Let her come to the druids at the appropriate time.'

'I disagree. She needed to learn important lessons. Lessons you and your druids would not have been able to teach.'

'Such as?'

'Love. Humanity. Things you know little about.'

True or not the words still stung the Archdruid. 'And what is your point, exactly?'

'I will tell you my point...exactly. The prophecy from Queen Rhiannon? All of you took it as verbatim. But prophecies can be all over the place. We all knew that her champion was Eric, so everyone assumed that the progeny was his child, and that he will bring death and destruction. But it says "bring". What if it meant, "bring into the world"? What if it is not Daniel?'

'But... his child?' It was a possibility, and as she thought more about it, reasons behind some of Gydion's actions began to reveal themselves. 'So, you were looking to the future. With him under your roof as your student you could keep a close eye on things. But what of his love life? How could you... by the goddess! You intended to manipulate that too? With Trinity? That's why you used her to find him in the first place. What did you do to her?'

'Nothing,' he replied but she pushed him further with a stern look. 'I did nothing to her, I assure you. I had planned to, but thought against it. I let love run its course.'

'You took a big risk. He is very close to Finn also. It could just as easily have been her that he chose.'

'It was a risk, I'll admit that, but a calculated one.'

'You cannot continue to use people's lives like chess pieces.'

'Sayyidah does and she's always several moves ahead.'

'So, you plan to match her to beat her? You and her are like two sides of the same coin don't lose yourself and end up on the same side.'

'If it saves Ariest, so be it. I have seen what is coming and we are far from prepared for it.'

'The dragon god, Baelthorn. He still lives; on the home world of the Shade and he intends to undo all of his brothers work.'

'You must be mistaken,' Tavisum couldn't believe what she was hearing.

'I wish I was,' Gydion replied disheartened. He knew the faerie world was ill-prepared for what was to come.

Just then, Tristan came up to the pair, seeing a lull in their conversation. 'Have you got a minute, Gydion?'

'No, I do not,' the Archmage replied sharply.

'Come on, it won't take long. I've wanted to speak to you for a long time.'

'Time is something I have very little of and cannot waste on trivialities.'

'I just wanted to ask you for the location of someone.'

'Begone, you imbecile! Matters of far more importance than your petty vendetta with Eric Mondragon are a foot!' Gydion let the stress of recent events get the better of him and he instantly regretted it as he glanced at Daniel.

'What's going on, Gydion?' Daniel asked in a panic. 'Has something happened to my dad? Did the Shade go back to Earth?'

'Your dad?' Tristan was incredulous. 'Eric Mondragon is your dad? All this time and I didn't know.'

'Yeah, he is. What do you want him for?' Daniel asked.

'Because I have vowed to kill him,' said Tristan matter-of-factly. 'He left me for dead in Cuthala. Left me with no honour. Because of him I can't return home. When I have his head, however...'

'He told me what happened. He regretted it deeply. That incident was what forced him to leave Ariest in the first place. If he had known you were his son—'

'What are you talking about?'

'That ring,' Daniel pointed at Tristan's left hand remembering the token of love that his dad had gifted. 'You got that ring from your mother, Aloena, and she was given it by our father, when they were together. You're my older brother.'

'Shut up!' Tristan lashed out almost hitting Daniel. 'He is not my father and I have no brother! If you get in my way and try to stop me, I'll kill you too!'

'It doesn't have to be like this,' Daniel pleaded. 'We could both go and see him together, as brothers.'

'Take your hand off of me,' said Tristan angrily. 'Tell you dad that I'm coming for him and know that I won't let you stop me.' Without so much as a backward glance, Tristan, headed to the entrance of the Druid Glade.

'Why didn't I see the ring before? I could have told him we were brothers the moment we met.'

'You really need to listen to some bards,' Finn admonished. 'If you had, then you'd know that he only wears it in battle. For luck apparently.'

'Forget about him, Daniel,' said Gydion.

'How can I? He's my brother,' Daniel replied.

'Yes, he is,' Tavisum said, looking at Gydion. 'Another son of Mondragon.'

The Archmage ignored Tavisum's comment and continued to try and get Daniel's mind away from estranged family members. 'Because we have bigger things to consider. The Book of Azul, we need to look more closely at it. If Sayyidah was willing to reveal herself it must be more important than we think.'

'More adventure? Sign me up,' Finn said as she excitedly rubbed her hands.

'That won't be necessary, young lady. In fact, I think you should go home. Daniel has no time anymore. After tonight's events are over, things are going to get serious.'

'What could be more serious than this?' Daniel asked.

'Mage Academy,' Gydion responded and strode off with Tavisum. 'Come on, Daniel!'

Daniel looked at Finn, then Gydion, then back to Finn. 'I need to go.'

'Yeah. you do.'

'Don't be like that, Finn.'

'How should I be? I feel like that's it. Like I'm never going to see you again.'

They were both silent for a moment.

'Here, take this.' Daniel pulled out the Horn of Fog, then the Goggles of Seeing and handed them to Finn.

'I don't want any gifts,' she said petulantly.

'You're going to want these ones,' Daniel insisted and pushed them into his friend's hands. Then he gave her a big hug and kissed her cheek before he ran off after Gydion.

Finn was left there with nothing but her memories to hold onto. The once happy group was fractured and all but disbanded. Daniel was being dragged off to the Mage Academy in Imperial City. Trinity had tragically passed away. Tristan had left under a cloud, intent on vengeance.

'It seems as if we are the ostracised,' Anjunel commented. 'The unwanted. The cast aside. Perhaps you would like to accompany us back to Darkenville, as you have been abandoned by your friends.'

Tessera was stunned. 'I don't think that's a good idea, Anju.'

'Why not? I am already in for a reprimand.'

'But there is no need to compound it.'

'Darkenville? What's that?' Finn asked.

'The home of the Krez,' replied Anjunel.

'Vekt yeah! Of course I want to go!'

'They won't be happy,' Anjunel added.

'And they will probably want to kill you,' said Tessera.

Finn listened to both elves then shrugged and said, 'meh! It wouldn't be the first time.' She started to adjust the goggles Daniel had given her so that the strap was hooked on her arm, and she heard something tinkle inside the horn. As she gave it a shake, a familiar looking key popped out. It was the key to the Mondragon estate. 'Seems like I haven't been abandoned at all! I knew you wouldn't back out on me, Daniel. I'll meet you there, buddy. Just don't take too long.'

Daniel smiled as he imagined Finn finding the key and note. He was looking forward to the next chapter of his life, his formal mage training, and although he had lost a love, he was glad that he had another important friend to share it with.

The forest elves sang a sombre melodic chant around the funeral pyre. Atop lay the still, peaceful body of Trinity Evergreen. The beauty of the elf song took Daniel's breath away. Then the moment came. The moment he had secretly been dreading; The lighting of the pyre. It was the finality of it he disliked. In his heart he was still hoping that Trinity would wake up from her sleep. He was willing her to.

Gydion was handed a flaming torch, and with it the honour and responsibility of being the first to light the kindling. The Mage, however, passed it to Daniel. He was reluctant at first but for the sake of his feelings for Trinity he faced the distinction with dignity.

Daniel set the torch to the pyre. The flames roared into life and enveloped the lifeless body. He stared into the fierce conflagration. Silently, he sent his last loving goodbye and vowed to become the Mage that she believed he could become.

Burning embers rose into the evening sky, mixed with the ashes of Trinity and rode the wisps of smoke through the air. Daniel watched them briefly in a reflective manner. He brought his attention back to the pyre, but if he could have followed the trail of the ashes and embers, he would have seen them do something very strange.

The matter drifted with purpose towards the Sacred Grove and there it descended to be absorbed by a sapling, which grew bigger and stronger with each passing moment that it consumed.

The new divine tree of the druids would be mightier than any that had come before...as would be the new spirit of nature that was growing within its trunk.

THE END

ACKNOWLEDGEMENTS

So, here we are, the second book in The Chronicles of Daniel Welsh. Yeah, I know. It's shocking to me too! I would like to take this opportunity to thank all those that helped me get this book out to you.

Thank you to my cover artist Maerel Hibadita and the awesome team at Polar Engine. I've always liked fantasy books of old that had original art on the covers. So, I was more than happy to be able to do that with this book! I would also like to thank my editor, Jadeediting and my amazing ARC team, The Pantheon.

Thank you to all my family, friends, and supporters and a final huge, big thank you to you, the reader.

A Call To Action

Thank you for taking the time to read this book from the mind of
D.G. Palmer!
If you enjoyed it, please take a moment to leave a review at Amazon, Bookbub or Goodreads to help spread the word, increase its visibility and help it reach more readers.
Leave a note even if you didn't, after all, one person's trash is another person's bestseller!
And finally, don't forget to sign up to <u>The World of D.G. Palmer</u> to stay up to date with new releases and get exclusive short stories and extra prologues and epilogues for the Daniel Welsh series!

About the Author

Currently residing in London, England, D.G. Palmer writes in the Spec Fiction genre, using his imagination to create vivid worlds and captivating characters.

An avid reader and player of video games, in the past, he was part of table top roleplaying groups where he nurtured his storytelling by penning several story arcs.

Feel free to follow him on Facebook[1], Goodreads[2], Bookbub[3] and Instagram[4]. If you wish to receive updates about his latest books, event dates and other exclusive news, sign up to The World of D.G. Palmer[5] and enter his mind. He warns it can be a mess sometimes, so make sure you wipe your feet on the way out – you never know what you might take with you.

---

1. https://www.facebook.com/DGPalmerAuthor/

2. http://www.goodreads.com/dgpalmerindieauthor

3. https://www.bookbub.com/authors/d-g-palmer

4. https://www.instagram.com/dgpcreativesolutions/

5. http://www.dgpalmer.com